The Heart's Strength

Book Two of the Briarcrest Chronicles

Anna Furtado

Yellow Rose Books

Nederland, Texas

ISBN 978-1-932300-93-2
1-932300-93-7

First Printing 2007

9 8 7 6 5 4 3 2 1

Cover design by Donna Pawlowski

Published by:

Regal Crest Enterprises, LLC
4700 Highway 365, Suite A, PMB 210
Port Arthur, Texas 77642

Find us on the World Wide Web at
http://www.regalcrest.biz

Printed in the United States of America

Acknowledgements:

A big *thank you* to my editors, Kathi and Brenda, for all the spit and polish. To the staff of Regal Crest Publishing, from Cathy LeNoir to Lori Lake and everyone involved, my utmost thanks and appreciation for everything you do for lesbian fiction—and to Donna for another fantastic cover.

Those grand ladies of the south, Elizabeth and Fonda, also deserve a great big thanks for beta reading—over and over again—and contributing many helpful suggestions and piles of encouragement, as did Earlene, from the time the first words were committed to the page until the manuscript was completed. Writing can be a solitary effort, but I've discovered it can also be the means to making new friends. That was so when Laney offered to take a look at *The Heart's Strength* with a professional eye. This, too, helped make *Book Two* a reality.

To my friends Robyn, Cheryl, Nancy and Joan, I would like to express my deepest appreciation for their love and support through this process. Their words of encouragement kept me going, even when I thought I couldn't write another word.

Finally, to those who gave of their time as the clock ticked down the final days to publication, reading and re-reading to help make sure this book would be the best quality possible—to Liz and Fonda, Earlene, Carol and Eve, Judy, and Michelle and Jacki—my utmost gratitude.

Most of all, to the love of my life, Earlene, for the love and encouragement she has provided all through the years. You're the best thing that's ever happened to me.

To Earlene — and to all women of great courage, past and present —
who inspire us all to a true strength of heart.

Prologue

Late Winter, 1481

THE CASTLE DOOR opened with barely a touch, swinging noiselessly inward. Striding purposefully the length of the Hall, he saw her near the hearth, dressed in splendor. Her auburn hair shone in the glow of the firelight. Her head was wreathed in flowers and ribbons. His heart beat faster as he approached, and she turned to him. Looking into her eyes, he felt taller, stronger...younger.

Soon, he would have her, touch her, take her to himself. He gazed into her striking gray-green eyes. A beautiful smile lit her face, sparking unaccustomed joy in his whole being. He broke into a run, closing the distance faster and faster, his only thought on his prize — her.

Almost within reach, he took a misstep, faltered, and plummeted out of control. He tumbled toward her, but he didn't care. Her loving arms would gather him to her breast — her lovely breast — that would finally comfort him. He had wanted her for so long.

Time slowed as he fell toward her; he thrust his arms out. She opened hers to receive him, and his heart fluttered. Incongruously, just as he reached her, she took one quick step to the side. He careened headlong toward the fire, his efforts to gain control of his movements futile. Stumbling into the hearth, he was quickly engulfed by the flames. The heat burned his face, his hands, his leaden legs. He cried out an elongated "No!" and opened his eyes with a start.

Cold darkness surrounded him. His eyes stung with a fierce pain as he wiped the sweat from his face. His chest heaved, not from the joy and anticipation of finally possessing the woman, but from fear and agony over the fate to which he had succumbed in his night terror. Not the first time this vision had visited him in his sleep, the memory haunted him. He could not stop shivering. Wrapping his arms around his chest, he heaved a great shuddering sigh.

Ever since he had gotten word that she was alive, that she had not perished as he had thought, this vision came to him when sleep would not let go of him. Night after night, he avoided slumber because of the dream, but when he could no longer stay awake, he fell into the same trap. He would reach her in great anticipation and utter joy that, finally, she would embrace him. But each time, his hopes were dashed as the dream ended with him perishing in the fire.

He struggled to find some meaning to it. Was it a message? Punishment from the Almighty for his thinking of her now, desiring her again, after all these years? How could a God he no longer believed in inflict punishment on him? He couldn't help his fascination for the woman. It was her fault. If only she hadn't been so willful all those years ago, perhaps they could have been together as he had desired. He would never have lost his temper and beaten her, leaving her for dead on the doorstep of St. Nicholas's convent.

In the darkness of his priory cell, he clutched his torso to protect himself against the recurring image of the fire. He breathed in the cold, damp winter air. His tremors finally quieted, but his obsessive thoughts did not.

He had to have her, but how? He would think of a way, he must.

Relief came in the form of the ringing morning bell, the call to prayer. Iago threw back the rough cover under which he had dreamed the terrible dream. When his feet hit the freezing floor, he winced and quickly stuffed them into his battered shoes. Almost as cold as the floor, the scarred leather did little to warm him. He threw his black robe over his head and let it slide down his arms and body. Over the robe, he pulled on the white scapula, protection of Our Lady, and let it fall over the first garment. The cowl came last, and he pulled it over his head before leaving his cell to join his brothers in the chapel. The deep hood would hide the sullen expression he wore.

Why he went to the chapel day after day when there was nothing there for him made him wonder. No doubt to appease Gaspar because he, as Father Superior, deigned it. He would not have understood that Iago had no belief in an Almighty Being, who granted blessings to His beloved people. If Iago wanted comforts, Gaspar was the one that he needed to concern himself with, not God. It was Gaspar's bidding that he was required to do. Iago's face contorted in contempt. He despised Gaspar's fawning over him. Still, he had no choice. He had to make some sacrifices, and that he clearly understood.

As he entered the chapel, still filling with the brethren for the start of Lauds, the woman materialized in his mind again—Lydia...those lovely, penetrating eyes...her milky skin...her fiery auburn hair. He had desired her for a long, long time.

When he had thought she was dead, he mourned and cursed his own reckless actions. As the years passed, he put the unpleasant thoughts behind him. He had almost forgotten, until a pilgrim on his way to visit the great churches of Spain had taken refuge in the little community of the brothers of St. Dominic, called La Madonna de las Colinas. Iago himself had taken refuge here twenty years ago when he arrived from the isle of England, battered and sick from his journey.

He wasn't called Iago then, but Father Gaspar had just lost one of the brothers from a case of putrid fever, and when Iago had presented himself at the monastery, bedraggled and devoid of spirit, Gaspar welcomed him and called him Iago, The Supplanter, the one who replaced the dead brother. When Gaspar took him in, Iago had not been certain he would stay, but Gaspar became enamored of him and made his life quite easy. The ease and the attention made it more difficult to leave. There were times, though, when he felt as if he were a prisoner at La Madonna de las Colinas, and he longed for the courage to leave the comforts that he had been given.

The new information that Lady Lydia Wellington had survived and was at Briarcrest Castle stayed with him and grew to a fevered longing. He fantasized about going back to England and taking her to himself. She would be happy to see him and would welcome him with open arms, having seen the error of her ways in rejecting him all those years ago. He would have her, if only he could figure out a way to get back to her.

Tomás de Torquemada proved to be his salvation. Iago could hardly believe his good fortune.

Father Gaspar had enlisted Iago to serve the priest a meal. Torquemada was the Father Superior's friend. Initially, Iago had resented being given the task of servant, but now...now, he was glad that he had been given the charge.

Torquemada, filled with enthusiasm, spoke freely of his views regarding heretics as Iago moved around him silently, placing steaming dishes before him and refilling his goblet. Torquemada wanted to rid his beloved Spain, even the world, of the lot of them.

At first, Iago only half listened as the man babbled on and on about himself and his aspirations in the Church. As he put course after course of delicacies in front of Gaspar's honored guest, Iago began to concentrate on what Torquemada was saying.

"So, my brother, we all have an obligation to Almighty God to rid the world of the infidels and heretics of every land. Do you know that these new printing presses are nothing but the scourge of Christ? Filth! Filth is coming off them. You should see it! All manner of worldly epistles and admonishments. A terrible thing. They must be controlled."

His words had made Iago think of Willowglen and the print shop there. Over the years, he had spoken to several visitors to the priory and had heard bits and pieces of news from the market town of Willowglen. In fact, he had heard Mistress Catherine Hawkins, the healer and herbalist, had left the town and her shop had been taken over by her assistant, a scrawny young wench named Sarah, who had taken up with a kitchen lad. But during another bit of gossip from another visitor some months later, Iago learned that the kitchen lad had progressed. He had become apprentice to Lord Pembroke, who had started the rumored print shop. Years later, he had heard that the apprentice had become Master and that he had become a well-respected member of the merchant class.

However, Iago never found anyone who knew about Briarcrest or Lydia's fate, until recently. He heard that Mistress Hawkins had close ties with Briarcrest, which caused him to wonder about Lydia. Still, until just a few days ago, he could find no one who could give him any more word of the woman for whom he carried such an obsession.

The pilgrim had come to the priory asking for a place to stay. Iago, having heard that the pilgrim had recently come from across the channel, was quick to offer to minister to the man. To his delight, the man had come through Willowglen from the north of England only weeks before. He had received the hospitality of someone from the little town right outside of Briarcrest, and during his stay he had learned that the Lady of Briarcrest was named Lady Lydia Wellington. The people who gave him shelter spoke of Lady Lydia's great generosity to the townspeople, much like her aunt before her. It had taken every shred of strength Iago had not to sneer at the praise expressed by the pilgrim, but the news that Lydia lived replaced his scorn with great joy.

Torquemada had given him the idea. This was not the first time the priest, who was close to the Pope, had visited his old friend Gaspar at the priory. Iago knew that Father Torquemada constantly badgered his old mentor to join his fight. "The Holy Father plans to institute a Holy Office of the Inquisition, Gaspar," Iago had heard him say once. And Gaspar had returned, "No doubt you will be the one appointed to head that Office."

If Iago could talk Gaspar into going off to England, to a town filled with what he would call wickedness and sin that could only be bolstered by the presence of a printing press, he might be able to accompany him and travel there. From Willowglen, perhaps it was a small matter to reach Lydia. A plan started to form for Iago.

"Father Torquemada," Iago ventured, "have you heard of a place called Willowglen in England?" Torquemada shoveled food into his mouth, barely acknowledging the question. Iago took a deep breath and plunged on. "This Willowglen has a printing press, and I have heard it is very evil."

"Oh?" Torquemada's head snapped up. He stared at Iago for a long while before waving the question away. "Why do you mention this, brother? My responsibility is here is Spain. I have no time to go to England to deal with a printer in some far-flung town."

"I mention it, Father Torquemada," Iago became more and more animated as he spoke, "because I know that you have long tried to get Father Gaspar involved in your ministry. It might be good for him to test this calling that Christ has given him through you, do you not think? He could go to this Willowglen and rid the town of this menace of a printing press. I would be happy to accompany him since I myself am from this same region."

"I have spoken to my brother about this many times. He does not feel that this is something he—"

"Let me speak to him, Father. I think he may be ready to change his mind. Perhaps, with your help, I can convince him. It would be one more place purged of the work of the devil."

"Yes." Torquemada stared at Iago, his eyes penetrating, calculating. "Why don't you talk to Gaspar, my friend? If you need any help from me, let me know."

Iago's eyes lit up. "Thank you, Father. I will speak to him." He poured the priest another goblet of wine and licked his lips as he thought of Lydia.

Early Spring, 1482

"SO, LITTLE BROTHER, you sail tomorrow." Torquemada sat, once again, before a sumptuous feast courtesy of his friend, Father Gaspar.

"Yes, Father Torquemada," Iago poured wine into the man's goblet. "It's true."

"Is Gaspar happy about this journey for Christ? I have not had the opportunity to see him yet."

"He is hearing confessions, Father. He will be here shortly." Iago knew Gaspar was not happy to be leaving the priory. He liked his creature comforts and did not like the unknown. Sailing to England was a great leap of faith for the man, and he had only come to it after much prodding and prompting from both Father Torquemada and Iago. In the end, he allowed Iago to talk him into it because he knew it was what Iago wanted.

"Brother Porter said that he has not been feeling very well lately. Is that true, brother?" The priest looked concerned.

"I think it is the excitement of the journey. He is eager." Iago did not look the man in the eye when he spoke.

"And you, my friend?" Torquemada tried to catch Iago's gaze, unsuccessfully. "How do you feel about the voyage?"

"I do not like to sail, Father," Iago admitted. "But I go willingly to do His work."

Torquemada smiled and raised his goblet to his lips.

From his position behind the priest, Iago's face contorted into a contemptuous smile.

Chapter
One

Spring, 1482

CATHERINE EMERGED FROM Briarcrest Hall into the crisp noon air, squinting as she looked up into the heavens. Winter was, perhaps, finally in its last throes. The warmth of the sun penetrated and warmed her cheeks as she stretched her arms above her head and lifted her knees toward her chest, one at a time. The chain mail that she wore *chinked* with her movement. As she bent from the waist to flex her back muscles, her grass-green leggings gave a little to the movement as her thigh muscles flexed. She touched the tops of her leather boots and raised herself up slowly. As she pulled on leather gloves, she saw Sir Hubert coming across the courtyard from the stable area. He, too, wore mail over his brown tunic, tied with a leather sash at his waist. The tunic covered his muscular thighs, ending just above the knee. His leather boots, similar to Catherine's, were scuffed from use. Catherine smiled, thinking of all the times she had suggested that he allow her to have a new pair made for him. Each time, he insisted that his old ones were still perfectly functional and they suited him just fine.

He carried two armored head coverings, the sun glinting from their highly polished surfaces. Both bore a finely worked metal crest of a silver, radiant sun with golden rays, the symbol of Briarcrest, surrounded by plumes of yellow and deep blue. Sheathed at his side, he carried two swords, each hanging from a thick leather belt fastened at his waist. As he reached Catherine, his smile widened revealing a mouth full of large, white teeth below a thick mustache.

Catherine held out her hand to take one of the helmets from him. "Good morning, Hubert. It's a fine morning to get some much-needed exercise, isn't it?"

He nodded in agreement and unfastened one of the swords from around his waist, handing it to Catherine once he freed it. "It's been a long, dreary winter, that's for sure. I'm eager to get my bones limbered up and moving again."

"As am I."

Catherine donned the armored head covering and held out her arms for Hubert to fasten the sword around her middle before putting his own helmet on. They moved to the center of the courtyard and drew their swords. Catherine heard Hubert's muffled voice from within the darkened slits of his helmet. "Ready, M'lady?"

From within her own protective head covering, Catherine smiled. "Be gentle, Sir Hubert. I've been too long away from these competitions."

"Have no fear, Lady Catherine. I would not risk the wrath of Lady Lydia by allowing you to injure yourself or to be injured by my hand." A chuckle emerged from both helmets.

They faced off, eyes locked on each other, each waiting for the other to make the first move. Catherine shifted slightly. The light chain mail, cinched at her waist, rattled softly. Tiny metal rings glinted in the afternoon sun. Leather boots covering muscular calves kicked up a small rock. It came to rest by Hubert's foot. In response, he flexed thick thigh muscles underneath tight leggings and grasped the handle of his sword tighter in his gloved hands. Catherine mimicked his gesture.

As if on cue, they both began circling slowly, never breaking eye contact. Hubert finally wielded his sword, swinging it in a wide arc above his head. He brought it down with a loud ring against the block of Catherine's blade. She, in turn, countered with a swift defense, hammering against his metal weapon. The two backed off and circled again, brandishing their swords threateningly. Catherine swung toward Hubert, grunting as their blades collided. He stepped back then quickly came forward again in a counterattack. Catherine sidestepped the strike with the skill of a seasoned warrior.

The two picked up the pace, charging and parrying, making contact and missing, then whirling to reposition themselves to attack again. The sound of metal striking against metal rang through the courtyard punctuated by the grunts and groans of the two opponents. Dust clouds rose around their legs as they evaded one another then rushed in to exact their blows. As they continued on, a messenger rode into the courtyard to be greeted by another of Briarcrest's staunch workers.

Finally, as Catherine's blows weakened with fatigue, Hubert saw his advantage and raised his sword over his head to strike again. As he did, she raised a gloved hand and backed away. He brought his sword to his side as she lifted her heavy metal helmet from a head soaked with sweat. Long brown hair streaked with gray cascaded down her back. Panting, Catherine said, "I'm sorry,

Hubert. I fear after a long winter without much physical activity, I cannot last as long as I once did at such pursuits. Forgive me. I must catch my breath."

Sir Hubert removed his helmet to reveal a furrowed brow etched deeply with concern. "Are you all right, Catherine?"

"Yes, yes, I'm fine." Catherine's chest heaved. "I just need a minute. I'm not as young as I used to be, I'm afraid."

The man, graying at the temples himself, grinned. "None of us is, ma'am. I'm a little winded myself."

Catherine knew it wasn't true. Lean and muscular, Hubert could fight alongside men half his age. She smiled at him. "You are very gracious to say that, Hubert."

"I think we've had enough for today, don't you?"

"Yes." Catherine gulped in air, still catching her breath. She handed Hubert her helmet and sword as she walked past him, the mail rattling against her body as she moved. When she reached the large, thick oak door that led to Briarcrest Hall, she turned and gave him a reassuring smile. "Anyway, I'm curious to find out what news the messenger from Willowglen has brought."

Hubert strode to the door and put the armor down before grabbing the large metal pull-ring worn smooth and shiny from countless hands. He tugged the door open saying, "You did well today, ma'am. We haven't had a chance to practice all winter, but you've not forgotten your moves."

Catherine smiled at Hubert's encouraging words. She enjoyed these matches. They gave her a chance to do something really physical. She and Hubert had begun them almost ten years ago when she first moved to Briarcrest with her beloved Lydia at the invitation of Lady Beatrice, Duchess of Briarcrest, and her companion, Lady Hilary Aylsham. Hilary used to spar with Sir Hubert's father, so Catherine had Hubert instruct her in swordsmanship and they began training regularly alongside the other pair. Catherine loved being able to wear leggings and a tunic for these activities. They were so comfortable. She could understand why Hilary had taken to wearing men's garb. The clothes were well suited to Hilary's duties as overseer of the stables and kennels. Hilary also served as forester and keeper of the lands of Briarcrest. These responsibilities kept her outside and on horseback a great deal of the time. So she often could be seen in the tunic, leggings and boots. But Hilary had been dead for several years now and she missed the quiet, soft-spoken woman.

Hubert interrupted her reverie. "Did you see that messenger's face, ma'am? When he told Tom that he had a message for you and Tom pointed you out, he nearly fainted at the sight of you wielding that sword. I think it was a great relief when Tom said he'd take the message for you. I've never seen anyone want to leave so quickly. He didn't even take the time to catch his breath or quench his thirst." He chuckled and shook his head.

Catherine joined in his laughter before stepping inside the cool, dim antechamber that led to the Great Hall of Briarcrest, anxious to find out what word had been sent from Willowglen.

IN SPITE OF the warm spring day, the huge stone masonry of the room had a chill to it. Many years before, Lady Beatrice had had the entire place refurbished. Rich paneling lined the walls of the hall, giving them a warm glow. Tapestries hung from the ceiling beams around the room's perimeter. However, the large windows that faced the inner courtyard, where all manner of beautiful plants and herbs grew in summer, made it difficult to heat the hall, even with the massive brick fireplace that burned brightly at the far end of the room. Catherine loved this old place in spite of the cold and the drafts. The Great Hall and service rooms, original to the house, served as the main part of the structure. In rooms above, added later, the private chambers and sleeping quarters lined a long hall extending from the top of the thick oak staircase.

Catherine walked the length of the hall and felt a wall of warmth as she approached the fireplace just to the right of the stairway. She unfastened her belt, unwrapped the mail jacket and laid it on a nearby bench. Glancing up toward the long stairway leading to the level above, she recalled her first visit to Briarcrest. She had arrived with Lydia on a warm spring day for the May celebration. The memory made her heart soar as she recalled the feelings of love and desire she had for Lydia during that visit. She had them for her still.

Looking up to the landing above her, she half expected to see Beatrice standing there, smiling down at her, or perhaps to see Hilary bounding down the steps with her endless vitality. She missed their kindness and their guidance.

Catherine bit her lip thinking about the day eight summers ago when Hilary had died in a hunting accident. They had all been devastated, but Beatrice, having lost the love of her life, never recovered. She followed Hilary the next winter, succumbing to an illness for which Catherine's herbs and potions could do nothing. Catherine realized with a heavy heart that no amount of skill as a healer could combat the loneliness and anguish that Beatrice felt from losing Hilary.

Catherine shook her head, trying to cast aside these memories. She looked for the message that had been delivered earlier and found it in a basket on a small wooden table near the stairway. She picked up the thick paper that had been folded in three with deliberate creases, tied with a dark blue ribbon and sealed with thick brown wax. Embedded in the wax, the ornately scrolled P told Catherine that the message was from Sarah Pritchard.

From years of experience with Sarah's handwriting, she could tell that her friend and former apprentice had penned it in haste. By the light of the fire coming from the big brickwork fireplace, she read:

Catherine,

> *There are things brewing in Willowglen that I fear will bring trouble to us all. A priest from Spain has arrived here with an assistant of a most curious and ominous nature. They are asking questions about the printing shop. On one occasion, they also asked about Briarcrest. Heed my warning. Do not come to Willowglen. It is too dangerous.*

Sarah

Catherine's heart pounded and she shuddered, imagining the implications of such a visit from representatives of the Spanish Church. Church power rivaled that of the Crown. Those who spoke against the Church often found themselves in dire trouble. It was best to avoid scrutiny, but sometimes it wasn't possible. The printing presses springing up since William Caxton established his in Westminster had drawn suspicion from a threatened Church. If the populace were given materials to read over which the Church had no control, it would lose its hold on its members — on the world.

Thanks to the press, Sarah and her husband, Will, were a rare success story. When they were first married, Will worked as an apprentice at the newly established printing shop started by Lord Pembroke. Catherine had spoken on Will's behalf to secure the position for him. As the years went on, Will became like a son to Pembroke and the print shop flourished. Upon Lord Pembroke's death, Will became the sole proprietor of the Willowglen print shop.

WHEN LYDIA ENTERED the room, she stopped, watching Catherine as she stood by the fire reading something, brow furrowed, lips pursed, cheeks flushed. Anyone else may have thought that she was perplexed but Lydia knew better. She recognized that the slight sag to her shoulders, coupled with her expression, meant that she was upset. "Catherine?" Catherine met Lydia's eyes, her own weary and pained. Lydia quickly closed the distance between them. "Catherine, what is it?"

She snapped the letter toward Lydia with a grunt. As Lydia read, her brow, too, formed into deep ridges. "What does it all mean, Catherine?"

"I'm not sure. But I do know that it can't be good." Catherine turned away and stared into the blazing fire as if hoping to find an answer in the flames.

"Sarah must be very worried about these men. What are they after, Lydia? Why come to Willowglen and scrutinize Will and Sarah? For that matter, what interest could they possibly have in Briarcrest?"

"I don't know. It's certain that Sarah and Will don't need such difficulties. They have enough turmoil with all that's happened with Cate."

Months earlier, Catherine had received word from Sarah that problems had arisen in their household when their daughter, Cate, as Catherine Lydia Pritchard was known, had been found to be with child.

"If only she hadn't been taken with that young troubadour. If she decided that she wanted to lay with him, then why did she not exercise caution? It was certainly not her ignorance that brought her to this. I taught her everything she needed to know about how to prevent conceiving a child in such a situation." Catherine's brow wrinkled in dismay. "Apparently I wasted my breath." The troubadour had left town as soon as he found out about Cate's condition.

Catherine's scowl softened to an affectionate smile at the thought of the strong-willed girl who was her godchild. Some said that her qualities of character were more like Catherine's than like those of either of her parents. "It is a shame, too, because Cate could have saved herself a great deal of strife."

"I know, darling, but what's done is done."

Sarah had written to Catherine and Lydia of Will's fury at the whisperings that moved through the town about their daughter's indiscretion. A sense of relief had washed over Catherine when, in another note from Sarah, she had been informed that, although it took a long time for Will's anger to subside, at last it had.

Catherine sighed. "I know that Will truly loves his daughter. No doubt, by now, people have lost interest in that particular bit of gossip—especially with the arrival of the clerics from Spain."

Lydia handed the note back to Catherine. "Why do you think these Churchmen have come to Willowglen?"

Lydia watched as Catherine's face reddened. The letter that she held in her hand trembled as she shook with anger. "I have no idea, Lydia. Why would they come to Willowglen, indeed? And who do they think they are that they could stop me from going to Willowglen for the birth of Cate's child?" She shook her head, trying to cast aside the tumult of emotions that she felt.

Talk of Churchmen gave rise to disturbing thoughts to Lydia, too. One in particular came to mind. She had not considered him in a long time — the priest Isadore. The notion made Lydia shiver. At least she could take some comfort in the idea that he must be dead by now.

Catherine watched her, concerned at what caused such a look of consternation. "What thoughts have you?"

"Many things. I don't know why this should come to me now, but I was thinking of how you tended me when I was ill — when Isadore..."

"Don't think of that now, Lydia. It is long past. It only troubles you so when you do."

"My thoughts are a jumble. My father. His angry demands the last time I saw him at Greencastle when he told me that I would go to France with him to marry — to think that he wouldn't even allow me the comfort of taking Marian with me. How much I miss her still. How much I missed you then. How I almost died."

"Oh, Lydia, do not concern yourself with these thoughts. It's been years. We've had twenty-three of them together in happiness, have we not?"

"Yes, it's true." Lydia stared into the flames. "But why are all these memories coming to me now?" she whispered. "And what of these Spanish priests? What business have they — Oh, gracious Mother, no! Do you think it's the..."

Catherine whirled to face her, eyes blazing like the fire. "I don't have a good feeling about this, Lydia. I'm afraid it might be — " She choked on the next word, unable to say it.

Lydia realized what Catherine would not — could not say. The word would bring it too close to them. Lydia's voice shook as she whispered, "Inquisition." It sounded strange, the expression of it an odd mix of fear and contempt.

Catherine's eyes grew larger, their brown color deepened to a muddy umber.

"Why would they ask about Briarcrest?"

Catherine let her head fall forward as she shook it. "I don't know."

Lydia knew that Catherine could be strong-willed; so could Lydia herself. Each had proved that on numerous occasions. It was a weakness both of them possessed. It was also their strength. A tremor of fear rushed through Lydia once again. Unable to keep the pleading from her eyes, Lydia said, "You will not go to Willowglen for the birth, then?" She hoped against hope that Catherine would give her the answer she wanted to hear.

Catherine looked into Lydia's eyes and fell into the gray-green pools that always left her breathless. She had been certain that she would go, in spite of Sarah's caution. Now, she faltered. Softly, she whispered, "I am not sure what I will do."

LYDIA STOOD LOOKING out into the garden from the main hall. "I wish you would reconsider making this journey, Catherine. If Sarah doesn't think it prudent for you to go to Willowglen, then perhaps you should listen to her. She only has your best interest at heart." She had been trying to talk Catherine out of making the full day's trip to Willowglen all morning, even though she knew that Catherine was determined.

"Lydia, we've been through all this. I told you, I don't know who these men are or what they think they're doing in Willowglen, but it is of no concern to me. I am merely going to be with my god-daughter for the birth of her own child and no ecclesiastical simpleton is going to keep me from them."

Relief swept over Lydia when she quickly glanced down the length of the room and saw that they were alone. Although the Inquisition had not come close to them in the past, it was wise not to be heard speaking against the Church under any circumstances. They both knew it, but Lydia knew that Catherine didn't think she should be made to check her convictions in her own home.

Both women turned toward scuffling sounds as one of the kitchen girls came into the room with some clean tableware and began to set the table for the mid-day meal. Plates and cups clattered against the thick table boards as the young woman went about her duty without regard for her mistresses at the other end of the room.

Catherine lowered her voice. "What gives these men the right to say what God ordains in matters that have nothing to do with the Church? They are always looking down on people with scorn who are just trying to make a living and be decent to their fellows. And what about their attitude toward us, I ask you? Women who know the art of healing with herbs, who have even nursed them when they have been ill? These men now insist that only men are fit to go to the centers of learning to acquire skills in healing. Having gone there, what do they do for those they treat? Cut them up with knives, I've heard. All the while their patients scream and beg to be killed rather than to endure any more of their treatment.

Barbarians! Yet it is these men that the Church says are true healers and women, people like us, Lydia, who have the knowledge and the ability to ward off ills with gentleness and herbs are called..." Catherine whispered the word, "witches?" Her tone conveyed her disgust.

"Catherine!" Lydia glanced back toward the young girl at the table before continuing. She returned an uncertain smiled before she retreated back into the kitchen.

Lydia watched her go before continuing. "This is an example of what I'm most concerned about. If you go to Willowglen, you must promise me that you'll stay out of the way of these men. And if you should chance to encounter them, say that you'll not put forth your opinions in this way. Promise me that you will be prudent, Catherine."

"I know. You're right. I shall try my best to hold my tongue." Catherine sighed. "But you know this enrages me so. Why do they presume to have authority to decide things that are outside the Church? Why scrutinize booksellers, for goodness sake? All Will does is print what other people write. He is not responsible for the ideas that come from other men's minds. He's only trying to feed his family."

"I'm not in disagreement with you, Catherine. You know that. I'm only concerned that you won't hold your tongue. That's why I'd rather that you forgo this journey. Wait a little while. Perhaps these clerics will grow weary of their stay in Willowglen and move on."

"No. I'm going, Lydia. That's all there is to it. I'm leaving for Willowglen in the morning."

Lydia sighed. It was fruitless to argue when Catherine got like this. The woman she loved was as stubborn as a ratter, and especially obstinate when she butted heads with the Church. The whole subject made Lydia feel as if a boulder rested on her chest. Ever since Catherine had shown her Sarah's letter, she'd felt that nothing good could come of Catherine's visit to Willowglen. Yet she could think of no way to keep her from going.

Feeling at a loss to do something, Lydia said, "Then you leave me no alternative but to go with you." Even as she said it, with as much firmness in her voice as she could gather, she knew it wouldn't work.

Catherine turned, red-faced and burning with anger. "It's too dangerous for me, yet you expect me to have you go with me? I think not. This is completely out of the question. I will go and see for myself exactly what the circumstances are in Willowglen. If it is nothing that we need to be concerned about, then, by all means, come to Willowglen to see Catie's new baby and visit our friends.

However, I don't want you to go until I know it's safe."

"And I, for my part, don't want you to go either. Clearly you think there is some danger, Catherine. Please, stay home."

Lydia recognized that Catherine's clenched jaw signaled that she would not discuss the matter any more. She hated it when they quarreled like this. Over the course of their years together, she could count on one hand the times that they had disagreed so strongly. But deep down inside, Lydia knew she had no chance of winning this argument and it perturbed her. She wanted to scream in frustration. Instead, she did nothing because she also wrestled with an underlying feeling of impending doom that frightened her even more.

LATER THAT NIGHT, as a sullen Lydia took the net cap from her hair to prepare for bed, Catherine watched the auburn tresses fall softly down Lydia's back. In the gentle glow of the candle that lit their bedchamber, she noted the silver streaks that now glistened through Lydia's hair. Once it had been highlighted with red. She recalled how very much she loved this woman. On a May Day long ago they had plaited each other's hair with ribbons. She felt an exquisite rush of desire course though her. Lydia could still evoke those feelings in her after all these years; however, that first May Day was truly a special memory that Catherine cherished in her heart.

That May Day, they had expressed their love for one another for the first time, after months of doubt and uncertainty. From then on, things were different. In spite of the hardships that continued to plague them, they knew they had no choice but to find a way to be together always.

They had triumphed. With Lydia's Aunt Beatrice's help, they found themselves living happily together without interference from anyone. It all seemed such a long time ago, yet when she saw Lydia like this, she felt as though time had stood still and they were back in those days, working side by side in Catherine's herb and spice shop in Willowglen.

Catherine's ill humor melted away. Her heart beat faster as she watched Lydia stroke her long hair with a comb. She came close and put her hand on Lydia's shoulder. Through the thin nightgown that Lydia wore, she felt the warmth of the noblewoman's skin. Lydia turned and found herself in a gentle embrace. Catherine rested her chin on Lydia's head. "I'm sorry I was so ill-tempered earlier," she whispered.

Lydia looked up into Catherine's eyes and kissed her gently on the lips. "I forgive you." With a twinkle in her eye, she added,

"Why don't you come to bed? I'll let you make it up to me."

Catherine raised her left eyebrow. "Oh, you will, will you? And what if I'm not quite as sorry as that?" Looking into Lydia's eyes, she saw reflected there all the love that she had for the woman with whom she had spent the past twenty-three years. Bending to return Lydia's kiss, she felt Lydia respond, opening her lips to find Catherine's tongue, inviting her in. Lydia's body trembled against Catherine's. Gently, Catherine guided her lover to the large carved oak bed and they nestled against each other under the thick deep blue and gold tapestry covers. Catherine searched for Lydia's mouth and kissed her passionately.

Gasping for air, Lydia teased, "I thought you weren't that sorry."

With a mischievous twinkle in her eye, Catherine replied, "I've changed my mind. I saw the error of my ways." She reached under Lydia's garment and heard Lydia's sharp intake of air as she cupped her breast in her hand. Catherine's own breath quickened when she discovered the nipple hard and erect.

Lydia's chest heaved in response to Catherine's caresses. "Good," Lydia managed to sigh in response to Catherine's statement. "I'm glad you're repentant." She moaned softly. Then she added, "It's about time."

With renewed energy, Lydia reached for the front laces of Catherine's sleeping tunic and yanked at them. Slipping the garment from Catherine's shoulders, she exposed her chest and then lowered her head, taking Catherine's breast into her mouth. As she sucked, Catherine drew a sharp breath from between clenched teeth and felt a familiar warm wetness between her legs in response.

Catherine cupped Lydia's chin in her large hand and drew her face upward. Her voice was hoarse when she spoke. "I thought I was to be the one to ask for forgiveness."

A smile lit Lydia's face, visible in the soft glow of the room. Catherine pulled Lydia's garment over her head and dove toward newly exposed breasts. Lydia's "Oooh," conveyed the pleasure Catherine had hoped to bring her. Continuing to stroke the dark, round aureola, she again found Lydia's mouth and thrust her tongue between her lips. Lydia opened to her without hesitation. Catherine caressed the length of her lover's torso, feeling the smooth skin glide beneath her palm. Her breathing reflected her own feelings of heightened passion. Desire grasped both women as they reached for one another urgently. Catherine had wanted to wait, wanted to make the moment last, but she found that she couldn't keep her hand from Lydia's soft mound. She knew that as soon as she touched the soft hair between Lydia's legs, she would want to be inside, feeling her lover's wetness in response to her touch.

She caressed the silkiness between Lydia's legs, feeling the hair against her hand. As Catherine pressed into her, Lydia moaned, her legs parting a little more in welcome. Catherine's own breathing quickened, knowing that Lydia was ready to receive her. She slid a finger between her folds and thrilled at the wetness that she had known would be there. Lydia cried out at Catherine's touch and she opened further. Catherine panted and she circled Lydia's wet, slippery womanhood, focusing on her round, hard center of pleasure. Lydia thrust toward Catherine's hand, begging for more. Catherine could feel her heat. With some effort, she asked in a husky voice, "Does my apology meet with M'lady's requirements?" Their eyes met, both pairs revealing the fire that burned within.

"I burn for you, my love," Lydia managed. "Very — " Lydia gasped, but she was unable to say anything more. She reached up and pulled Catherine's mouth toward hers. They drank each other in. In that moment, the raised voices and concerns of earlier that day melted away.

"Then let your fire blaze, dear one," Catherine responded.

Catherine felt Lydia tremble in response. Passion rose as Catherine continued to caress Lydia's wetness, until, finally, she cried out from the fullness of their lovemaking. She then relaxed into Catherine's embrace, breathing deeply, sated.

Catherine smiled and gently kissed her forehead. Then she moved to kiss her eyes, her cheeks, her mouth still swollen with desire. Lydia moaned with pleasure and wrapped her arms around Catherine, pulling her closer, their legs intertwined. Lydia's voice betrayed her sleepiness as she said, "I would pleasure you also, my lady."

"Not yet," Catherine whispered in Lydia's ear. "Just rest. Perhaps you will pleasure me tomorrow, my love."

Almost involuntarily, Lydia curled up in Catherine's arms. As she drifted off to sleep, however, Catherine knew that it would not be so. Tomorrow she would be on her way to Willowglen.

Chapter
Two

THE TWO ROBED figures stood at the entrance of the Willowglen print shop. Daylight framed them, black shadows punched out of the sun's brilliance behind them. Anger welled up in Will. His first thought was that they could bully him with their questions about the nature of his printed material, but they would not torment his family. Without turning his head, Will shifted his glance toward Cate as she worked at the press. He saw her concentrating on her work at the machine and knew that he would not be able to catch her eye. Conveying a good-natured manner he did not feel, Will pasted a smile on his face and approached the two men. "Good Fathers, you grace us with yet another visit. How may I help you today?"

The tall, lean Spaniard, Father Gaspar, looked down his nose at him and sniffed. Dark, beady eyes stared through him. Father Gaspar's Dominican habit hung on him as if he were a man with little flesh on his bones. He stood in stark contrast to the shorter, round monk who always accompanied him. Will thought it odd that the man did not possess the jovial demeanor usually thought to accompany someone of his stature. He looked threatening rather than good-humored. No one in Willowglen liked these men. They called the smaller one The Dark Monk, because he always seemed no more than a specter.

Father Gaspar's voice sounded almost melodious as he spoke. "We would only like to see what comes off your printing device today, Master Pritchard."

The smile faded from Will's face. He wasn't printing anything that these men should concern themselves about. It was a book of admonitions for women on running a household—a book that said things like, "always make sure that your husband's meal is warm and laid out for him after a hard day's labor" and "teach your children that their father is the head of the household and is to be honored daily and obeyed in all things." What difficulty might they have with statements such as those? He even remembered a passage about "praying at the holy sacrifice of the Mass and giving your tithe to the Church and alms to the poor." Surely they could not find fault in that.

Father Gaspar stepped into the shop and looked down his thin nose at the equipment beyond Will. Outside, Will heard the din of the busy street. People bustled back and forth on their way to and from the shops that lined Bookbinders Row. When Lord Pembroke had opened this shop years ago, there had been little more than a footpath here. Now, the street had grown to a thoroughfare with shops lining both sides of the newly cobbled street. A new tavern had opened only a few months ago. How Will longed to be there now, chugging back a flagon of ale, forgetting about the threats these men brought with them.

Dreams and phantasms Will thought. He had work to do. Best to get this over with, but he would not let them intimidate his daughter. He turned and eyed Cate, hoping she would understand that he wanted her out of the shop. He turned back and observed the curious monk who always accompanied the priest. In spite of his small stature, he still seemed menacing, perhaps because he always covered his head with his monk's cowl, and his face, buried so deeply within the blackness of his hood, could not be seen in the shadows. He'd never heard the monk utter a word. Perhaps he was mute. He couldn't help but think how much better it would be if all priests were silent. Yet this one for all his silence still gave a message that made Will cautious and concerned.

Will knew that arguing with the priests would be of little use. They would have their way. If he tried to deny them access to his work, they would only grow more suspicious of him. He bowed and motioned the men toward the printer that was poised to strike an imprint on another sheet of paper. Cate was nowhere in sight.

CATE PRITCHARD GRASPED the lever of the printing device and forced it from one side to the other. As she did, the heavy wooden screw turned, driving the platen that held the paper down onto the plate below. As she moved the handle back in the other direction, the paper lifted off the ink-laden letters, taking their black, glistening impressions with it.

Carefully removing the sheet from the apparatus, she hung it on one of the many lines of string spanning the length of the shop. The page joined the other printed pages hung to dry like a washerwoman's laundry.

She could do no more for now. Her father acted as beater in her brother Willy's place today. He would load the ink on two large balls of hide stuffed with wool tied on fat wooden handles with the thick, dark ink made by the Pewseys in their shop a few doors down. Using the ink balls was messy business and Cate needed to keep her hands clean to remove the pages from the machine once they were printed. The beater's job was dirty, inky. Usually, Willy had the pleasure of this job while her father pulled the pages from the machine, but since the beater's job was strenuous, her father had assigned her to the less arduous, although still difficult, task of puller.

Cate stretched her back by moving from side-to-side. She pushed a hand against her stiff side. Absently, she lifted her other hand to rub gentle circles on her large, protruding stomach. She felt a sharp pain and stifled a startled cry. She looked over at the two men talking to her father from the shop doorway. They didn't seem to notice her. *Easy little one*, she thought.

A wave of dizziness washed over her, and she carefully stepped to the back of the large room. The smell of the nutty linseed oil and pungent turpentine—elements of printing ink— hung in the air. These odors mixed with the mustiness of damp paper. Her stomach flipped as she stepped behind a screen and removed the delicate linen cover that protected her mint tea. The tiny beads that held the cover in place tapped against the side of the stylish cobalt pottery mug.

Raising the vessel to her lips, she took a sip, welcoming the soothing properties of the cool liquid. She hadn't felt well since she arose that morning, but she couldn't disappoint her father by telling him she was too ill to work in the shop with him. The tea settled her stomach a little. A smile graced her lips as she thought of working at the press today, as difficult as it was in her condition. Her father had not been on speaking terms with her for some time because of her pregnancy. Lately, though, he had softened and seemed to be more accepting of the imminent birth of his grandchild. This morning, he had asked her to come and help him in the shop since her brother, Willy, would be gone overnight for supplies. It was a huge step, and it had made Cate's heart happy. It gave her the strength to do the job her father had given her in spite of how poorly she felt.

The tall priest's words drifted toward her although she heard only the last part of what he said. "...see what comes off your printing device today, Master Pritchard."

She knew that her father wouldn't be pleased with this visit. The last time these men had come, she had not been working in the print shop, but later at home her father had made clear his displeasure over their visit. He had startled Cate that night when he had pounded his fist on the table and demanded, of no one in particular, to know who they thought they were to come to his shop and accuse him of sins against the Church. Hadn't he spent his whole adult life proving himself an upright, moral businessman? Didn't he go to Mass as prescribed? Didn't he fast during the penitential times? Why were these men tormenting him? Cate and the rest of her family had no answer, of course, for they didn't understand what these men were doing in Willowglen any better than he did.

Cate emerged from behind the screen in time to intercept the quick glance from her father. She understood the gesture. She should get out of the shop. He was protecting her from any attempt to question her. She wanted no part of these priests. Anyway, she needed some air. She retreated behind the screen, slipping out the back door, hoping they hadn't noticed her.

IN THE ALLEY behind the shop, Cate sat on an empty wooden crate and wiped the sweat from her brow with her apron. A welcome cool breeze blew across her face and neck as she sat trying to catch her breath after another bout of pain. The aching in her back seemed to worsen now that she sat down and she shifted, unsuccessfully trying to find a comfortable position. Distracted by her own discomfort, she didn't hear Isobel Pewsey approach from the back door of the ink and papermaking shop farther down the alley. If she had, she would have gotten up and headed for the busy street beyond them.

Isobel made Cate uneasy, and she much preferred the company of Isobel's younger sister, Winifred, who was quiet and polite while Isobel, in contrast, could be coarse and unpleasant. The older girl seemed to develop a fascination with every new young man who came to Willowglen, and the troubadour, Nathaniel Mistlewaite, had been no different. When he had arrived in town, he had seemed smitten with Cate, and had continually kept company with her. Isobel often lurked in the shadows whenever they were together in public. Cate thought that Isobel followed them because the handsome visitor had become the object of another of Isobel's fantasies. It didn't matter. Although Cate wasn't cursed with the vanity of some women, she knew that she was far more appealing than Isobel could ever be. This constant creeping about on Isobel's part had irked Cate to no end. She'd kept quiet about it, however, not wanting to provoke one of Isobel's fits of bad humor.

Cate glanced up to see Isobel staring at her stomach. Those tiny, black eyes chilled her every time she saw Isobel gaping at her. Cate studied the bulbous nose, now too close to her face for her liking. When the unpleasant woman smiled, revealing a black space where several teeth should have been, Cate turned her head away from the foul smell of Isobel's breath. A wave of nausea threatened to overwhelm her nonetheless.

Isobel pointed toward Cate's bulging belly and asked, "How is it today?" She looked away before Cate could answer, confirming that she didn't really care about the child. Cate wondered why she had bothered to come and speak to her at all. *She probably wants to know if I've heard anything of Nathaniel.* She knew that Nathaniel was the child's father. Everyone did. In spite of the fact that it was nobody's business, it seemed to be everybody's cause for gossip.

When her parents expressed concern over her involvement with the young man with no roots, Cate thought they just didn't recognize his good qualities. Then, he had been charming and funny. Cate had enjoyed his company — for a time.

Cate never really knew if she was smitten with Nathaniel or if she just liked his constant fawning over her. At first she merely enjoyed his attentions, but at Nathaniel's constant urging, Cate soon became his lover, an impetuous decision that caused her to have a tumult of mixed feelings. The troubadour kept up a constant course of flattery while in the presence of others, but when they were alone, he was petulant and uncontrollable. He had hit her several times, and then apologized immediately. Confused by his actions, Cate had surrendered to his demands for her more intimate favors. By then, she felt that there was no turning back.

Her father, on the other hand, couldn't understand why a man would want to wander through the land singing songs with no better reason than he liked to hear the sound of his own voice. He told his daughter that her attentions toward the young man were a waste. A troubadour would make a poor husband. He wanted no more to settle down than he wanted a secluded life. The more Will spoke in this way to his daughter, the more time she spent with the young minstrel.

One night, as Nathaniel sat mopping up yet another plate of stew with a fistful of bread from the Pritchard's table, he rambled on about his love for the open countryside and the advantages of having no real obligations in life. Cate saw her father's brow furrow in response. Will gave his wife a knowing glance. Sarah had returned a look of irritation. Cate feigned oblivion to her parents' reaction and tried to look as if she hung on the bard's every word. When Will tried, later, to tell Cate that Mistlewaite was the type of man who would just move on when his dinner invitations dwindled, Cate dug in her heels and refused to listen. She turned her back on her father and walked away. As she did, she heard him call after her, "Catherine Lydia Pritchard, you're as stubborn and unruly as the women for whom you are named." She had been accused of this ever since she could remember. She ignored her father's remark as she always had, glad to be more like the Ladies of Briarcrest than like her own parents.

Although Cate knew that her parents had tried their best to discourage Mistlewaite in his pursuit of her, she also knew that they would not forbid her from seeing the young man altogether, to avoid causing strife within the family. She realized now that they had hoped that she would come to see the troubadour for his true self, in her own good time. Too late, she had and she had no choice but to realize his true reason for bedding her was only to satisfy his own pleasure.

The first time Nathaniel brought Cate to the abandoned hut outside of town, she thought she could be strong against his coercion to lay with him, but once he touched her, kissed her, caressed her in places that no one else had ever touched before, she could no longer resist the thrill of it. Increasingly, though, Cate felt forced and threatened during their clandestine meetings, for Nathaniel had taken to telling her that it was his right to lay with her because she had enchanted him. By the time she realized that she no longer wanted Nathaniel Mistlewaite's attention, it was too late.

"CATE, MY SWEET Cate, you are all sweetness to me. I am so captivated by everything about you," Nathaniel had whispered the last time they met. But that was only after he had raised his hand to her when she first refused to lay with him.

The flash of angry fire in her eyes at the gesture had made him think better of it, and he quickly turned to allurement, which made Cate feel guilty and doubt her judgment, so she acquiesced.

Cate sat up and pulled her tunic back up on to her shoulders. She could still feel the wetness that Nathaniel had left between her legs, yet she felt empty, and frightened by what she must tell him. "I'm not so sure you'll say that you love me so much when I tell you my news."

Cate shivered as she thought of how he would react. She realized that he did not want to settle down, that he wanted no responsibilities. In addition, once she had spoken the words to Nathaniel, she would have to repeat the same message to her parents. Which of the two tellings Cate dreaded the most, she couldn't say.

"What is it that you have to tell me that puts such sadness into those stormy gray eyes?" Nathaniel ran his finger down her cheek.

Cate choked back her fear and pulled herself up straight, saying defiantly, "I have not had my woman-bleeding for two full moons. I am carrying your child, Nathaniel."

The blood drained from the troubadour's face and the smile faded from his lips. He said nothing. The next morning, Nathaniel Mistlewaite could not be found anywhere in Willowglen. He had vanished.

When Cate's father learned that his daughter was with child, it had distressed him greatly. When he discovered that the father was the cowardly singer and that he had left town, he raged on for days. At first, he'd refused to talk to Cate, but as time went on and her stomach grew bigger with his grandchild, his concern increased for her welfare and for that of the child. Gradually, he'd come to accept that he would soon have a grandson or granddaughter, and Cate suspected he was even starting to look forward to the baby's birth.

When Isobel Pewsey heard that Nathaniel had left Willowglen and the reason for his departure, she let her scorn for Cate be known. For months, whenever Cate passed the Pewsey's shop on Bookbinders Row, she often saw Isobel staring at her from the shop door. As she openly gaped at Cate with contempt, her sister Winifred would come and drag her away, back into the shop.

Then one day, the peculiar girl started talking to Cate again, following her around, asking if the pregnancy was going well, expressing implausible concern for her health, and asking if she could do anything to help. But it was always clear to Cate that Isobel didn't mean it. Cate would have preferred that Isobel not speak to her at all. Their conversations wore her down.

She flinched when a broad hand shook her shoulder.

"Mistress Cate, are you all right?"

It took Cate a moment to realize that Isobel was still there. She pulled herself back to the present and answered cautiously, "I'm fine, Isobel, just a little tired, but that's to be expected."

Isobel looked at her warily. "Yes, well, you should take care. You wouldn't want to jeopardize the child, would you, now?" The smile that followed Isobel's words sent a chill down Cate's spine.

"I have to go. My father has an errand for me," Cate lied. Putting a hand on the crate, she pushed herself up awkwardly and took a step forward only to find that Isobel's formidable girth blocked her path.

Staring down at Cate's protruding stomach, she demanded, "Have you heard anything from Nathaniel?"

"Nothing, Isobel." Cate responded sharply. "It's clear he is done with Willowglen and with *all* of us."

When their eyes met, the hair on the back of Cate's neck stood up. Why did this woman make her feel so agitated? Her backache steadily worsened and her stomach did not feel well either. She had difficulty catching her breath. She had to get out of the alley and away from Isobel's smothering presence.

"Let me pass, Isobel. I told you, my father needs me to get something for him."

Isobel squinted. Cate, sure that Isobel didn't believe her, decided that she didn't care. She tried to sidestep the massive bulk of a woman. Isobel matched her movement with surprising agility. Cate's temper flared. Her eyes grew threatening and she stared Isobel down. Isobel smiled a fiendish smile and resentfully moved out of Cate's way. Cate moved past her as quickly as she could.

As she stepped hastily into the street, she almost ran into the fishmonger's helper, a young lad named Jack. He carried a large carp in his arms as he rushed to make his delivery.

"Oh, please pardon me, Mistress Cate," he said nervously. "Are you all right, ma'am?"

Cate could see that he was trying desperately not to stare at her bulging stomach, but these days no one seemed able to see anything else. Grabbing his arm, she said, "Yes, yes, I'm fine. Walk with me, will you?"

"Uh, I have to make a delivery, mistress." He held his fish up a little higher to emphasize his mission.

The odor almost made Cate retch. She took a deep breath in an effort to calm her stomach. "Fine," she snapped, "then I'll go with you." She grasped his arm tightly and began dragging him down the street.

"Um, Mistress," Jack blurted, red faced, "could you ease up on me arm?" Then, shyly, he added, "I can't feel me fingers."

Cate eased her grip, but she refused to let go. "I'm sorry, Jack. Please forgive me." As she rubbed his arm, she glanced over her shoulder and saw Isobel standing at the edge of the alley with her hands on her wide hips. She didn't look happy.

Jack followed the direction of her gaze and saw Isobel, too. He seemed to understand Cate's urgency then. Brightening, he said, "It's nothing, Mistress. Don't concern yourself. You just hang on as much as you like. Come on. I'm going to Master Aldridge's house to deliver this fine fish."

In spite of Cate's aching back and the smell of the prized fish, she moved in closer to him. "Lead on, Master Jack. I shall walk with you." She wiped perspiration from her brow with her free hand as they started down the street, wondering if she would make it to the Aldridge's.

Chapter
Three

SARAH PRITCHARD MOVED from the heavy plank table to the kitchen fire, her apron laden with cut spring vegetables from her garden. She dumped them into the heavy black cooking pot that hung over the fire. They splashed and sizzled as the bubbling broth engulfed them. She stirred the contents of the pot, and wondered how her daughter and husband were getting along at the print shop. It was a big step for Will to ask Cate to join him. She knew that Cate was pleased at the invitation even though her daughter would find working at the press all day wearying in her condition. Her child should be born any time, they had reckoned, and Sarah smiled at the thought of Will being considerate enough to give Cate the job of puller. Sarah had worked the long lever that brought the paper down on the print surface herself and knew it wasn't an easy job, but the job of beater was even more strenuous.

Thunderous hammering at the front door made her jump. As she started toward it, the door burst open. There stood Jack, the fishmonger's helper. His eyes were wild with fright and his slight form bent with the weight of Cate as she hung on his shoulders. Sarah rushed to the door to meet them just as the young lad tried to heave Cate over the threshold. As Sarah took some of Cate's weight on her own shoulder, she noted the pallor of her daughter's face and the glistening perspiration on her forehead and upper lip.

"What's happened?" Sarah demanded.

"I...I don't know, Missus," Jack said, his own face rather ashen. "Mistress Cate and I went to the Aldridge house to deliver a fish—"

"What?" Sarah couldn't believe her ears. What was Cate doing delivering fish at the other end of the town? Jack's face contorted. He let go of Cate, letting Sarah take her full weight. He stood wringing his hands, muttering something that Sarah couldn't understand.

"Never mind, Jack, just tell me what happened."

His facial expression relaxed a little. "Nothing, Missus, I

swear. We were walking back to the printing shop and all of a sudden, Mistress Cate's legs gave out and she stumbled. I caught her, though," he added, proudly. "She said she couldn't walk. I tried to help her to the shop, but she said that she wanted to come here to you." His voice took on a whining tone as he continued, "We had a terrible time making our way, what with her legs giving out and her back hurting her so." The boy looked as if he might faint as he whispered, "I was just trying to help."

Sarah looked at her daughter's face, contorted with pain. Sarah understood. She reached for her, allowing Cate to lean heavily on her. "Come on. Let's get you over to the cot." Cate's skin felt warm and she perspired heavily. "Has your water broken?"

From behind them, Jack groaned, "Oh, no. Oh, no. You mean she…"

Sarah turned and glared at the boy. His face had taken on a green tinge. Afraid the boy might collapse, leaving her two people to attend, Sarah barked, "Jack, you'd better go."

The lad wasted no time. He turned and ran out the door, slamming it behind him as Sarah turned her attention back to Cate and repeated, "Your water, has it broken?"

"Yes." Cate stopped and grimaced before continuing. "In front of the print shop. I didn't want to tell Jack. He already looked — nnnnuhhhhh." She bent in pain as a contraction gripped her, ripping the air from her lungs. She moaned and stooped lower, holding her stomach trying to relieve some of the pressure. Her mother steadied her where she stood, knowing that she wouldn't be able to move until the pain subsided. When Cate finally relaxed a little and breathed a deep sigh, the redness in her face fading, Sarah whispered gently, "Let's get you to the cot, shall we?"

Cate leaned on her mother and shuffled to the bed at the far end of the room. No sooner had she gotten there than another contraction came on her.

"Just breathe easily, Catie. It's going to be all right." When the contraction ebbed, Sarah said, "I'm going to look and see if I can see the baby's head. You just try to keep calm and keep breathing deeply."

Cate gave her mother a weak, awkward smile.

Sarah lifted her daughter's legs and planted her feet flat onto the cot. When she raised the damp skirts and pushed aside the loose undergarment her daughter wore, she saw the top of a small head with black, wet hair.

Breathing in sharply at the realization that her daughter had barely made it home, she said, "Thank God you made it to the house, Cate. The baby's almost here."

In response, Cate lifted up her shoulders and grunted, then let out a piercing cry as another contraction pushed the child further from her.

THE SKY HAD begun to darken with the coming of night when Will stormed into the house and slammed the door behind him. He boomed, "I don't know which is worse, those infernal clerics who have come to town to make my life a living hell or a daughter who abandons her work."

As he looked down the length of the room, he saw his wife lift a bundle from their daughter's chest and place it at her side. When Sarah turned to him, Will saw tension in her face and blood on her arms.

"Don't just stand there, Will Pritchard, come and see your grandson." Sarah turned away then and walked over to a basin of water to wash away the garnet stains of childbirth.

His bluster forgotten, Will crept tentatively toward the cot. His emotions swirled within him like a thick pot of soup. There were only two other times in his life when he had felt like this, overwhelmed by a mixture of gratitude, awe and fear. The first was when his son was born, the second, when Cate herself had come into the world.

He stood over his daughter and recognized the signs of her labor — the hair in tangles, the perspiration-drenched skin. Cate lay under a blanket, her dress and undergarments thrown in a pile on the floor by the cot. With one bare arm, she cradled the baby. His little round face peeked out from his wrappings. He looked like a little old man, all wrinkled and red and angry at the world — perhaps at having left the warm protection of his mother. Realization followed that his own child had just birthed this tiny infant. *My grandchild*, he mused. In spite of himself, tears filled his eyes and he reached a tentative hand toward his daughter. Cate smiled weakly at her father and he caressed her damp cheek. "I guess I'll excuse you for leaving me with all the work today, Catie-duck," he said quietly.

Cate's tired grin widened, hearing the term of endearment from her father that he hadn't used in years. "Thank you, Poppa," she whispered through her weariness. Her eyelids fluttered, too heavy for her to hold them open any longer.

Sarah stepped to Will's side, bent down and picked up the child. "Rest, Catie," she said. "After you've recovered a bit, you'll suckle him some more." Cate gave in fully to her fatigue at her mother's encouragement. She closed her eyes and slept almost immediately.

As Sarah held the child in her arms, Will brushed his hand

gently across the child's head pulling the wrap that covered it down. A surprising shock of white hair protruded from one side of the boy's head. Will raised his eyebrows in question at his wife. She shrugged in bewilderment and sighed.

Chapter
Four

THE BIG SCOT gave his sister a look of concern and said, "You must come, Fiona. Father has talked about nothing but this journey for weeks now. He wants all of us to go. He has worked hard to make sure that everything is arranged. Our cousins will care for our animals and our lands in our absence, so there is no need for you to stay. It will mean a great deal to him to have the whole family by his side. What is there to keep you here, anyway?"

What, indeed? thought Fiona. When she first heard about their father's plans, she thought that she did not want to leave the peace and tranquility of her little house on the moors. She wasn't certain she wanted to make the arduous journey with her large family, which included several small children. It would not be an easy trip. Still, the family would be together and enjoying each other's company, even in the most challenging situations.

She knew her father wanted them all to go. He was proud of his family and what better way to show his father that he had been successful in life than to present his sons and their families and his beautiful daughter to their grandfather.

Fiona raised an eyebrow as she looked to Kynan. Maybe a diversion would do her good. Tessa had been gone for months. The house continued to feel empty. She still felt the loneliness of Tessa's absence. She closed her eyes in an effort to block out her thoughts of the woman she had loved and lost and shrugged off the dull ache. When the feeling dissipated, Fiona opened her eyes to find her brother looking at her with concern.

"It will do you good to have a change." He did not think it wise to mention that he knew the source of his sister's melancholy these past months.

"You're right. There is nothing to hold me here. Perhaps an adventure is just what I need. Let me think about it a little more. We have a while."

A twinkle appeared in Kynan's eyes. "Anyway, you might find a few more stories for your collection." He nodded toward the sheaf of papers that she had been reading when he knocked on her cottage door.

Fiona followed her brother's gaze and smiled. "Yes." A far-away look appeared in her azure eyes. "I suppose I could use the time to keep track of our family journey and write about everyone we meet. I've always thought that I'd like to meet Grandfather and Uncle John and I've often thought the town of Willowglen sounded interesting when father has spoken of it." Fiona tapped her index finger to her lips.

Kynan gave his sister a broad smile. "You don't have long to ponder."

"I know. Let me at least sleep on it. A good night's rest always makes things clearer for me."

DUNCAN SMITH WATCHED his children walking toward him over the heather-dappled hills in the distance. The morning mist rested just above the ground like clouds that had lost their way. Their feet cut a path through the gray swirls as they walked. Each person carried a travel bundle. Spouses walked beside their husbands. One woman cradled an infant in her arms. Three small children walked along in tow. Two belonged to Kynan; the third was Rodick's small son, as was the baby that his wife carried. Fiona and Kendrick walked along together, talking quietly. When Duncan saw them, his already broad grin widened to see that Fiona was among them.

He ducked as he turned to enter the sturdy stone house he had built for Adianna, his wife, years ago. "The children are coming." Trying not to betray his excitement, he added "And Fiona is among them."

"I'm glad," Adianna said, matching her husband's smile. She knew that the presence of their youngest child on this trip would make Duncan a very happy man.

"I'd better go ready the wagon," Duncan said. "We will want to start our journey soon, before the little ones get restless." He didn't want to admit to his own eagerness to begin this journey.

"Wait, Duncan, let me feed the children before we start out," Adianna protested. Although he tried not to show it, disappointment flashed across his face. Adianna quickly added, "They will travel better on full stomachs."

Her good-natured husband recovered quickly. He chuckled to himself as he thought, *I've been gone from Willowglen for thirty years. What are a few more hours?* His face brightened as he shrugged. "I guess you're right. I can't very well ask my children to come with us on such a long journey and starve them right from the start, can

I, then?" He glanced out the window and saw the troupe coming over the last hill, Fiona in the lead, carrying Rodick's little boy now. Watching intently, Duncan sighed, "Fioney," making his daughter's name sound more like a prayer than a proclamation.

"Whatever you do, Duncan Smith, do not call attention to your daughter. If you make a big affair of her coming, you know she'll not be happy with you."

"I know, I know, Mamma. I'll behave. I'm just so happy that she will be coming with us." His face beamed.

Adianna approached Duncan, wiping her hands on her apron. When she reached him, she touched the dark curls that had fallen into his eyes and drew them back up onto his forehead. His hair became more and more sprinkled with gray every day, it seemed. "I am glad, too, husband, but you know how your daughter is. Just leave her be. Act as though her coming is nothing to you, and we'll all be the better for it."

Duncan leaned down close to his wife's ear and whispered as if he were telling her a secret. "I didn't think that she would come at all."

The drumming of boots on the cobbled path outside Duncan and Adianna's home announced the arrival of their family. Duncan turned from Adianna and swung the heavy wooden door open wide, greeting his children with a toothy grin. "Welcome, welcome," he said to them as they passed through the entrance. The wives and children of various sizes all cleared the doorframe easily, but Duncan's sons, like their father, ducked so as not to hit their heads. Fiona, almost as tall as her brothers, did the same.

The sons slapped their father's back and hugged their mother. Children ran screeching their delight as they embraced their grandparents. Fiona hung back and placed her wriggling nephew on the floor and watched him toddle toward his grandfather, arms raised. She walked up to her father as he lifted the child. Everyone grew quiet. She cleared her throat and said in a deep, husky voice, "Kynan tells me that this journey is very important to you, Father. I thought that, since it is as momentous an occasion as he said, I should come along. After all, the whole family should be represented."

Duncan stood silent for a few seconds, his wife's warning still echoing in his ears. He didn't want to say the wrong thing to this woman standing before him, tall and lovely, with dark hair, strong frame and deep, penetrating eyes.

On her birthing day, they had thought her such a little thing that they thought she would be a delicate woman, so they named her thus. But she fooled them. Instead, she grew up to be as robust and sturdy as her brothers. She possessed as independent a spirit, as did her siblings, and her personality did not differ very much from that of her father. However, there was a depth to Fiona that even her family seldom saw.

One thing she had made clear as she came to adulthood. She wanted no one to find her a mate, announcing herself perfectly capable of finding one herself. When she expressed a desire to strike out on her own, her father gave her a small plot of land, and he and her brothers helped her to build her own house several hills over on the moors. Her father agreed to this arrangement because, secretly, he worried that his only daughter might want to follow in his own footsteps and embark on a quest that would take her far from home as he had done so many years ago. He couldn't bear the thought of his only daughter leaving him. Neither did he want to end up like his own father, whom Duncan had not seen since he left home at the age of nineteen.

It was difficult for Duncan and Adianna to come to grips with the fact that their daughter lived a solitary life, but they knew their Fiona. If she wanted something, she got it, and if she didn't want something, it was best left alone. Her parents took consolation that Fiona's brothers and their families were never far away, for they, too, lived on plots of land that their father had given them from his own holdings. Fiona could always call on them if she needed help, but it seldom happened that she needed to do so.

Duncan shifted the little boy in his arms. His red face betrayed the excitement that he felt. "I'm glad you will join us, Fiona" was all he said. From behind his daughter, Adianna smiled at her husband.

WITH A HEARTY Scottish breakfast under their belts, the group set out. Kynan, Duncan's eldest son drove their supply-laden wagon. It creaked and groaned as two large, thick-boned moor ponies pulled it along. Children sat atop the stacks of provisions, as did Kynan and Rodick's wives. Adianna held her youngest grandchild as she sat beside her daughters-in-law. Kynan's oldest boy rode with his Uncle Kendrick, the youngest of Duncan's three sons, on his mount. Rodick rode alongside the wagon joking with his brother as they went. Duncan led the band on his big dappled-gray horse, Hero. At his side, Fiona rode Brilliant, a tan colored mare with a flowing silver mane that had always been Fiona's favorite among her father's horses since childhood.

Surrounded by the verdant hills and warmed by the bright spring day, the group guided their horses southward toward the distant town of Willowglen. It would take several days to make the journey. Duncan had left his land and livestock in the hands of

Adianna's cousins, who were both capable and trustworthy and had long shared in the care of the territory that was the Smith land.

As they plodded along, Duncan said, "The weather will remain clear this day. We will make good time, I think."

Fiona made a noise that sounded like a grunt. Duncan understood that she agreed with him. Finally, she asked, "Do you think we will make the border by nightfall, father?"

"I'm hoping so. I'd hate to have to camp on the moors with the children. If we can make it to the Swan and Thistle, we'll have accommodations there that will please your brother's wives tremendously."

Fiona kept her gaze on the road ahead, but a twinkle appeared in her eyes. "They'll praise you for that, Father."

"I know," Duncan said. He winked at his daughter and she returned the gesture.

"Do they know we are coming?" Fiona asked. "Uncle John and Grandfather?"

"I hope they know by now. I sent a message weeks ago. I had thought to surprise them, but your mother convinced me that, since my father's condition is already deteriorating, the shock might not be a good idea for such an old man. Your mother is a sensible woman. I'm sure I wouldn't be where I am today but for her practical nature." He paused before he added, "You are a lot like her, you know."

Fiona smiled and raised an eyebrow. "And a great deal like my father, too, I think," she added in her low, smoky voice.

"Perhaps not so much to your credit." He met his daughter's gaze, his eyes sparkling, pleased that she saw him in herself.

BY THE THIRD day, the road leveled out and became easier to travel, although the children did not appreciate it very much. The older ones were restless and whining. The baby fussed and cried. Adianna, riding Kendrick's mount while he walked alongside the wagon, rode up beside Duncan. "We need to make camp and let the children run around. They are tired of being confined in the wagon. We'll never make it to Willowglen if we keep this up because your daughters-in-law will go crazy trying to keep the children from harming each other."

"But we'll lose a day, Adianna."

She looked at him sternly. "We need to stop, Duncan."

Fiona joined them just as her mother made this final pronouncement. "Remember, father," she chided, "this is the woman that you told me had the most sense in the family. Perhaps you should listen to her."

"And to you," Duncan sighed. He brought Hero to a halt and scanned the countryside, spying a sheltered ridge up ahead of them. He turned to the group behind him and shouted, "We stop early today. We'll make camp on that flat ridge over there." His grandchildren cheered.

AS THE ADULTS sat by the fire outside their tents later that evening, the children sleeping in their blankets exhausted after a full afternoon of play, Duncan watched Fiona. She sat near the fire, apart from the others, writing on her pages by the firelight. He wondered what she wrote but decided not to ask. Instead, he raised his tankard to his wife and daughter. "To practicality," he said with an admiring gleam in his eyes. Fiona stopped writing and looked at her father, meeting his eyes with a broad smile. Then Duncan added, "Tomorrow, we stay on the road until we meet the Old London Byway." A collective groan went up from the group. They would travel a long distance the next day.

Chapter
Five

THE CONSTABLE FROM Willowglen, Benjamin Godling, rode with his cohort of men. The group of four was bound for a wayside inn between Willowglen and London. The sheriff of Wiltshire had requested a meeting with them because of some trouble with bandits over the past several months. People had been robbed on the road that traversed the country from London to the western border, and the King had appointed the sheriff to put a stop to the thievery. Since Willowglen's booming market area often brought traders and noblemen to the town, the sheriff had thought it prudent to meet with the constable.

Godling wasn't sure how the visiting monk had gotten word of their journey and invited himself along, but he did. He was not pleased with the monk's presence, but then, at least only one of the Churchmen had been left back in Willowglen to wreak havoc among his people. There was something about these clerics he didn't like, aside from the fact that they just appeared one day and usurped the local priest's authority, bringing him under their own rule. He was pretty sure that they had no right to do what they had been doing, but he preferred to err on the side of caution before acting to control them. None of Godling's men cared for the monk and his companion, Father Gaspar, and they were not happy to find the monk accompanying them on this trip. Fortunately, he kept to himself for most of the journey.

Much to Godling's relief the monk had disappeared as soon as the band reached the inn. He didn't really want the sheriff to find out about him. It might cause too many questions about Godling's ability to command his people. Who knew what kind of trouble his presence might stir up? Benjamin Godling liked to have as little dealings with the sheriff as possible. Gerard du Prey had a reputation for being a hard man bent on getting his own way. No doubt his reputation got him this appointment to root out these highwaymen and put a stop to the robberies that had been happening over the past months, but Godling didn't understand

what role he himself might have to play in du Prey's plan. The chief
constable wanted to get the meeting over with and get back to
Willowglen, without incident he hoped. When he had made sure
that the monk understood that they would leave the inn to return to
Willowglen in three days, the Churchman had assured him that his
business would not take him far, nor keep him long.

THE MONK STEPPED out from the shadows at the edge of the
wood and crooked his finger ominously. Alfred hesitated, a ball of
fear forming in the pit of his stomach. He took a tentative step, then
another, wondering why he felt drawn to the man in spite of
himself. Coming within arm's length of the monk, he squinted,
trying to make out a face buried deep within the cowl drawn over
his head. The blackness revealed nothing of the man's features, and
Alfred wondered if he had a face at all. A shiver ran through his
small body. If he reached out and touched the robed figure before
him, would he dissolve away into a mist? Too frightened to make
such a move, the boy waited, gulping down large amounts of
spittle that formed in his mouth, trying not to lose his morning
meal.

When the monk finally spoke, Alfred thought that his voice
had a hissing quality to it. "Well, boy, did you succeed?"

Another shiver started between Alfred's shoulder blades and
ran rapidly down his back. "Y-yes, sir," he mewed.

Pointing to Briarcrest's shimmering shadow off in the distance,
the monk demanded, "You gained entry to the manor?"

"Yes, sir, I did." Having the right answer made him a little
braver now.

"And..."

"I got as far as the kitchen, sir. A maid who works with her
mother told me that the mistresses of the house were the names
that you said. One is Mistress Hawkins, but they call her Mistress
Catherine. The other is Lady Lydia Wellington."

The boy took a deep breath in an effort to still his trembling
body. When the monk didn't respond to his information, he
squinted again, trying to make out something, anything, in the
blackness of his hood. He saw nothing.

Finally, the man spoke again. "You've done well." Relief
washed over the boy and he brightened. "These ladies, were they
there?"

Not sure which answer would please the monk, the boy didn't
know if he should say what he knew. Finally, he decided he would
just tell the truth.

"The lady, Catherine, left on a journey only this morning, I heard, sir."

"Did anyone mention her destination?"

"No one said."

"And the other, Lady Lydia?" Alfred thought he heard something like a sharp intake of breath as the monk said the name. "Has she gone also?"

"No sir. She's still there, at Briarcrest."

The monk's shoulder's sagged a little at his answer, hoping she would have gone to Willowglen. After a few more minutes of uncomfortable silence, he spoke again. "That wasn't so difficult, now was it?"

"N—no, sir," the boy replied. He looked down at the ground and twisted a toe in the dirt. *Why does he have this interest in the ladies of Briarcrest?* Monk or not, Alfred decided that he did not seem a man to be trusted.

The boy scoffed inwardly thinking about how the monk had admonished him to find a way into Briarcrest and bring back the information he wanted. Alfred could have walked into the place any time he liked. As a matter of fact, he went there often with his father, but he hadn't told the monk that. The man really didn't want to hear what he had to say anyway, except to hear the information he demanded from the boy now.

Fine. Let him think that I've done something difficult and risked my neck to find out what I already know. What's it to me, then? But Alfred wondered if he had done the right thing. His grandfather had always told him that they were to help and protect the Ladies of Briarcrest, but he also had said to respect men of the Church. Something about the monk seemed menacing, however, and Alfred didn't like him one bit.

"Take yourself back to your own village now, boy," the monk said. He held up a stubby finger that would have been beside his nose had his face been visible. "And remember what I told you." A threatening tone marked his final words. "Tell no one about this. Do you understand?"

"Y—yes, sir." Alfred's knees knocked against one another. Another silence followed with Alfred uncertain if he should go or stay.

"What are you waiting for, boy? Didn't I tell you to go home?"

"Yes, sir, you did, only..."

"What is it, boy?" the daunting monk hissed.

Doubt and concern made Alfred bolder. He still wondered why this man spied on the decent folk of Briarcrest. Finally, he couldn't hold it in any longer. "The ladies are good people and are spoke highly of by them that works in the manor, sir. Why do you want to know about them?"

"Who are you to question me, boy?" the monk snapped. "My reasons are none of your affair." Taking a quick step toward Alfred, he raised his hand in a threatening gesture. "Go!"

Alfred flinched and took off running as fast as he could. As he retreated, he thought he could feel the monk's eyes on him, searing his back. After running some distance, and feeling bold again, he turned and looked over his shoulder. The monk had disappeared into the shadows just as he had emerged. The boy stopped in his tracks then took several steps back toward the spot where he had encountered the monk, wide-eyed.

Troubled by the whole incident, Alfred turned toward his village again and ran as fast as his spindly legs would carry him. He decided that he had to find his grandfather to tell him what had just happened. His grandfather would know what to do.

THE MONK HAD returned just as the sheriff rode off toward London. When Godling saw him, he breathed a sigh of relief that he had not come back a moment sooner. His men grumbled when they saw him, but they said nothing to him as the group set off back toward Willowglen.

Chapter
Six

THE SOUND OF the horses' hooves changed from the muffled beat on earthen road to the clatter on cobblestones as the riders from Briarcrest entered the walled market town and started down Market Street. Willowglen, the town in which Catherine had grown up, held a special place in her heart. As an adult, she had run her herb and spice shop and belonged to the guild there until she moved to Briarcrest with Lydia.

She still had many friends in Willowglen, Will and Sarah Pritchard among them. Her old herb and spice shop, just down the street from the Grouse and Pheasant Inn, had been taken over by a young couple who had moved from Salisbury to avoid a brief outbreak of the Black Death several years earlier. They had little knowledge of healing herbs, save what the average person knew, but she had heard that they were kindly folks and that they kept the shop well stocked.

When she and her companion, Sir Hubert of Middleton, reached the Market Square in the center of town, they would head down Bookbinders Row to the Pritchard house. Catherine could barely contain her excitement at the thought of seeing her old friend Sarah again and she wondered how Sarah's son Willy and his new wife were doing. The young couple had moved into a small house at the end of town only recently and it had been almost a year since Catherine had seen the Pritchards.

Of course, she couldn't wait to see Cate again and hoped that she would be able to help in the birth of her baby. Catherine's hand went to the medicinal bag that hung on her hip as she bit her bottom lip, restless and eager to reach her destination. She thought about urging her horse on, but Hubert rode in front of her and the street was so narrow that she dared not try to pass him. As if on cue, the horse in front of her slowed and came to a stop. Catherine's mount slowed to a stop behind Hubert's.

Hearing shuffling sounds, followed by the muffled tones of an argument, Catherine craned her neck and shifted her position to try to see what was happening. Hubert blocked her line of sight, so she decided to dismount. She pushed her way past Hubert and his horse to see a large man, dressed in the attire of the northern country, gesturing madly. She heard frustration in his voice. Then, she saw the wagon, with its left rear wheel badly damaged. The wagon had twisted as it came to a halt, blocking narrow Market Street almost entirely.

Hubert got off his horse and came up beside Catherine. The foreigner continued talking to someone Catherine couldn't see. She noticed his knee-length tunic with intricate embroidery around the hem showing from the opening in his cloak that wrapped around him in layers of folds. The man turned away and leaned his body into the back of the wagon; he muttered something, but with his heavy accent, Catherine couldn't understand what he had said. Apparently, he didn't get the response he wanted, because he repeated his order, speaking more deliberately this time.

"I said, you'll have to get out of the wagon. I don't want to risk anyone getting hurt. The wheel is broken. Your dad and uncles and I can lift it," he raised his voice and spoke with additional emphasis, "only you'll have to get out of the wagon."

Catherine heard a small giggle come from beneath a bundle.

"Come on," he said impatiently into the wooden boxes and bales stacked in the wagon. "There's someone behind us that wants to pass. You've got to get out of the wagon now."

Again Catherine heard a small titter. "Can Sir Hubert help?" she asked gesturing toward her companion.

The man looked Hubert over. "I doubt he will be of much help. He'll only scare him. My boys and I will handle it." As he spoke, three men equal in size but younger, came around the wagon. They were dressed in similar garb with tunics that came to their knees and large flowing cloaks wrapped around them.

One of them said, "Fiona is taking care of it. I don't know what got into the boy. I guess he's just tired from the long trip. He's got himself buried so far under all the stores that I couldn't even reach him. Fiona thought she could coax him out. The boy has a fondness for her."

"Aye. I see." The big man chuckled.

Soon a stream of women accompanied by children of various ages appeared at the rear of the wagon where the men stood. They were dressed in a longer version of both tunic and cloak. All were of similar style and color. They each also wore a head covering of un-dyed linen.

"My," Catherine said, feeling some of her irritation drain away, "you've got a full load."

"Precious cargo, ma'am." The man grinned as he said it,

sparking some old unnamed memory in Catherine. "This is my wife, Adianna."

A pleasant-looking woman with bright eyes and rosy cheeks nodded to Catherine.

"And these are my boys, Kynan, Rodick and Kendrick." The "boys" nodded. He pointed to each of the remaining women in turn and said, "That pretty thing over there is Kynan's wife." Kynan's wife nodded and blushed. "And that one is Rodick's." Rodick's wife cradled an infant in her arms. She nodded and smiled pleasantly. "My Kendrick, here," he pointed to a young man with smooth features and a slightly less robust build than his brothers, "fancies himself a ladies' man and hasn't settled down yet." The young man broke into a wide grin and shrugged.

"I'm pleased to meet your family, sir, but is it possible to get your wagon out of the way? I really must make my way to the other side of town, and I'm in a bit of a hurry."

The man raised his eyebrows at this woman's boldness. She reminded him of his Fiona. He explained that he needed to unload the wagon before they could do anything with it, but Catherine's growing frustration left her little patience. Hubert tried to intervene in an attempt to hurry things along, but everyone started talking at once, including the "boys" and their wives. From the outer edge of the chaos, a deep, booming voice called over the din, "Hold up everyone." They all stopped and turned in the direction of the command.

Fiona stood holding a child who looked to be about three years old. She lowered her voice. "The wagon is ready to be emptied. Then, we can move it."

Holding the child in her arms had pushed her cloak aside so that Catherine could see what she wore underneath. A soft yellow outer tunic, similar to those the others wore, with sleeves that hugged her arms and stopped just above her wrists, was belted at the waist with a red braided belt made of thick cord. From the larger neck opening of the tunic, Catherine could make out an unbleached under shirt that ended at Fiona's swan-like neckline.

The ends of her belt hung down her left side stopping mid-thigh. A small bag made of black and white goat hide with a tasseled drawstring at the top hung from the middle of the belt and a long sword was sheathed at her left side. A silver cup with detailed meticulous engraving was visible from the folds of her cloak. Her tunic was pulled up and bloused over her belt so that the red and gold embroidery-trimmed hem stopped just above her knees.

Her legs were covered to mid-calf with dark brown leather boots. Tightly laced long leather thongs held the boots firmly against her legs. Over the tops of the laces, each boot top turned down to reveal leather tooling similar to the metal work on her cup.

A black wool vest, embroidered with gold, silver and red threads, just peeked out from under the voluminous dark blue speckled cloak wrapped around her torso. The blue wrap was fixed in place with a large silver brooch and bodkin at her left shoulder. Catherine blinked. The woman was magnificent.

The brothers all looked at one another, somewhat baffled by their sister's announcement. The father scratched his head and muttered, "I knew you took after your mother, Fioney."

Fiona glared at her brothers and said impatiently, "Since his mum was busy with the baby, I thought I could coax him out of the wagon. While you were all out here arguing about how to get this little lad to come out, I just told him that he was holding us up and asked didn't he want to meet his great grandfather, and out he popped." The man's sons looked embarrassed. Kendrick scuffed his boot against a cobblestone.

The child, still in Fiona's arms, wore a smile from ear to ear. He stretched his arms and laughed. "See great gran!" he shouted. "Hurry." When Catherine smiled at him, he buried his face in his aunt's shoulder and giggled again.

Fiona fascinated Catherine. Her stature—taller than Catherine's considerable height, her uncovered hair—black as the night with a plaited cord tied around her forehead, and eyes as blue as the sky on a summer day, all gave her a striking look. She wore her tunic like a man and her appearance was formidable indeed. Yet the thought that she was as sinuous as a cat would not leave Catherine. Fiona kissed her nephew's head and handed him to one of her sisters-in-law.

Catherine approached her and put out her hand. "Thank you," she said. Then she lowered her voice so that only the young woman could hear and added, "Please don't take offense, but I don't think the men in your family would have been able to get themselves sorted out enough to get this wagon moved."

Fiona smiled as she took Catherine's hand and shook it firmly. Then she called to her brothers, "What are you waiting for? Are you going to unload the wagon or do I have to do that for you, too?" Then she winked and said, "It always takes a woman to do a man's job, doesn't it?"

Catherine smiled and nodded. She liked this young woman a great deal already.

"The name's Fiona. Have you met the rest of my family or have they been the louts that the Romans always said they were?"

"Oh, no. Your father—I presume he is your father—" Fiona nodded her assent. Catherine continued, "Your father introduced me to your mother and your brothers and their wives."

"I'm glad to hear it," Fiona said. Then turning her attention to her father, she said, "Shall we get on with it then?"

Duncan nodded and sent Kendrick to tend to the horses at the front of the wagon. He motioned Kynan and Rodick to his side and the three men started unloading bundles and boxes from the wagon. Hubert joined them, lending his hands to the work.

Catherine felt the tension leave her shoulders now that someone had taken charge of the situation. Her increased patience turned out to be a good thing, for their progress in getting the wagon emptied proved to be very slow. When Kynan climbed into it to start unloading it, the already damaged wheel gave way again and the load shifted. Kynan jumped over the side just in time to escape injury. They decided that they would have to unload very carefully while standing on the outside.

As they made a start, Catherine turned to the dark haired young woman. "Has your family come to Willowglen on business?"

"No, we've come to visit family. Our Uncle John has sent word that our grandfather is ailing, and father wanted to see him and have him meet his family before he left this earth."

Uncle John? There was only one John in Willowglen that Catherine knew. And John did have a brother who had been gone so long that he could have had grown children. A childhood memory washed over Catherine. A young boy, her friend, stood with her in the herb garden behind the herb and spice shop. *"I am a knight,"* he said. *"You shall be my lady in distress. I will rescue you."* To which young Catherine lifted her chin and replied, "Why would I need you to rescue me, Duncan Smith? I can take care of myself."

She had no idea that she had said the words aloud. The other women looked up from their huddled conversation. Duncan commanded the men to lower the crate they were lifting from the back of the cart. He turned to Catherine with a surprised look on his face, recognition dawning. "Catherine? Catherine Hawkins?"

"Duncan?"

He reached Catherine in two long strides and stared. "It's you! I recognize you now, lass." To Catherine's surprise, he picked her up in his big meaty arms and twirled her around. "Catherine Hawkins! What a joy, to have you be the first person I meet back in Willowglen." He beamed as he returned her to the cobblestone street and turned to his wife. "Adianna! This is Catherine, my childhood friend that I've told you about. Egad, we had some great times." Turning back to Catherine, he asked with a big grin, "Didn't we, Catherine?"

Catherine laughed. "Yes, yes, we did, Duncan. I can't believe it. You've come back, and this is your family. How wonderful."

Sir Hubert appeared from behind Duncan, his initial concern diminishing as he saw the broad smile on Catherine's face. "M'lady, it's going to be awhile before we can get this wagon moved. Do you think you should go into the Grouse and Pheasant and wait? At least you'd be sheltered there and you could perhaps get a bit to eat."

Duncan's eyebrows disappeared under the dark curls hanging on his forehead. "M'lady?" He glanced at the horses from which Catherine and Hubert had dismounted. They were fine animals, indeed, with beautiful trappings in Briarcrest's colors of deep blue and gold. "Catherine," Duncan said, "you've done well for yourself. Have you married well, then?"

A mischievous grin formed on Catherine's lips. "Only in a manner of speaking, Duncan."

He gave her a confused look, and then changed the subject. "Do you not live in Willowglen any longer?" he asked.

"No. I don't. As a matter of fact, I'm here on a visit myself. I've come to see friends on Bookbinders Row."

"Bookbinders Row? Where's that? I don't remember a Bookbinders Row."

"Oh, no, I guess you wouldn't. That part of Willowglen only came into being after you left. It's on the east side of the town square."

Kynan approached now and said, "May we give you a ride, then, on one of our horses, ma'am? You won't get your horses by our wagon for a while. One of us could escort you and bring the horse back. Your man, here, can take care of your horses when we get the wagon out of the way. That way, you can get to your destination before it gets too late."

"Thank you. Kynan is it? That's most kind. Actually, I am anxious to get to my friends' home. If you don't mind."

"I'll escort the lady," Fiona said.

Kynan turned and started to protest, but she stopped him. "You'd best stay here and keep unloading that wagon or we're going to have all manner of carts and conveyances backed up on this street."

"But..."

"I'll escort the lady." Fiona said it with such finality that he dared not object. Kynan gestured toward Hero waiting on the other side of the wagon. There was just room enough for a person to slip behind the wagon to the other side where the horses waited.

Catherine turned to Hubert. "Would you mind staying to help while I go on?"

"No, M'lady, not at all. When I'm finished here, I'll bed the horses at the blacksmith's stables. Shall I leave your horse or shall I take her back with me in the morning?"

"Leave her, please. I don't know if I'll have need of her while I'm here, but if I do, I'd like to have her at the ready. Thank you, Hubert."

Kynan helped Catherine up onto Hero while Fiona mounted Brilley. Settled onto the horse, Catherine smiled and nodded. Then she and Fiona started off down Market Street as the sun began to wane below the rooftops. Behind them, Catherine heard Duncan say, "Catherine Hawkins. What a surprise." Then, "All right boys, back to it. Let's get our shoulders into it this time. Kendrick, man the horses now. Keep the wagon steady while we lift this last box out."

AS THE TWO women rode their mounts down Market Street, Catherine asked, "Will you stay in Willowglen long, Fiona? I should like to have a chance to visit with your father and your family. It has been so many years and Duncan and I were such good friends."

Fiona looked surprised and asked Catherine how she could consider her father a friend when her remark back at the wagon sounded as if they had had disagreements. Catherine laughed, telling Fiona that she and Duncan had always had a warm relationship, in spite of their differences. She hoped that some of those arguments had helped Duncan see that women were not the fragile, incapable creatures he seemed to believe them to be. Fiona rode in silence for a few minutes before she spoke again. "Then I guess I have you to thank, M'lady. For my father has often encouraged me to lead my own life and follow my own heart."

Catherine lowered her head, hiding a smile of embarrassment, before looking Fiona in the eye. "Then I'm glad we had those differences all those years ago. It had the best effect it could have had on Duncan, knowing that he has a daughter who is allowed to make her own choices. But you must know that your father and I were truly the best of friends. We often talked about what we wanted from life. I felt privileged to be the one he told that he wanted to leave Willowglen and strike out on his own on his quest as a young man. He didn't make the decision lightly."

Fiona nodded. "My father spoke of his difficulty in making that decision. He was hesitant to leave his father and brother, but he didn't feel that he was made for the silversmithing trade as his father had expected. He knew that he was better suited to be out on the land. He managed to do quite well and gained both lands and animals, all of which he has shared generously with his children. The best thing that he's given us, though, is a sense of our own abilities to find what it is that we want to do with our lives."

"If I may be so bold," Catherine said, "how have you chosen to live yours, Fiona?"

Fiona smiled. "I want to follow in my father's footsteps. He's given me a place of my own from his holdings. I have a few animals and grow a great deal of my own food...and I have my writings."

"Writings? What do you write about?"

"I write about my experiences and about my thoughts and ideas as a woman. I have been thinking of printing a book. I have this idea that other women might find my views and my stories of interest."

"I'm sure many would. I have always been interested to read what other women have written. I'd certainly be interested in reading your writings, too. My friends, the ones I am on my way to visit, are in the printing trade themselves. They have had a printing shop for quite a number of years here in Willowglen."

"Then perhaps I should speak to them while I am here. I don't know the first thing about printing a book. I need to learn."

"I'm sure Will would be happy to give you some guidance."

Fiona's blue eyes deepened as she smiled. "I think it is remarkable that you happened upon us as we reached Willowglen, M'lady."

"Yes, it was, wasn't it?"

"Where did you say that you now live?"

"A place called Briarcrest, one day's journey from Willowglen. We have a great house there and some lands. It is a beautiful place."

"You have married well, then, as I heard my father say."

"No." Catherine continued to stare at the road ahead as they rode along. "I have never married."

"Ho, Brilley." Fiona stopped and let Hero continue on, waiting until Catherine realized that she had halted. After several more paces, Catherine pulled Hero to a halt. Still, she didn't look back at Fiona.

Fiona urged Brilley around Hero and faced Catherine. The women held each other's gaze.

Catherine didn't need to think too long to conclude that Fiona could be trusted. She just had a feeling that it was right to do so. "I live with the Lady Lydia Wellington. We are the stewards for all of Briarcrest's holdings...together."

Could it be? Fiona continued to search the deep brown eyes opposite her, wondering if her father's childhood friend found the companionship of women more comforting and fulfilling than that of men, as she herself did. She had only met one other with similar feelings. Tessa. But Tessa had succumbed to the urgings of her family to leave Fiona's house and marry.

"You and Lady Lydia are good...friends, then?"

"Yes." Catherine understood the meaning in Fiona's question. "We are very good...friends. Very close friends."

"Ah," Fiona whispered. "I had a friend like that once."

"You are no longer such good friends, then?"

"No. Unfortunately, her family succeeded in talking her into making a marriage with a man in a nearby town. She had not the will to resist them."

In the telling, Fiona had let her guard down just enough for Catherine to recognize the hurt in the young Scot's eyes. She thought about Lydia and the demands that her father had once made on her. Lydia, however, had no desire or intention of allowing herself to be commanded to marry against her will. Then, too, Lydia had the help of her beloved Aunt Beatrice, and her companion Lady Hilary. Catherine shivered at the thought of what life would have been like had she and Lydia not been able to be together all these years. She felt sorry for Fiona. "Perhaps you will be able to find another woman with whom you can form such a bond again. I will hope it for you, Fiona."

"Thank you. I hope it for myself, too."

They rode in a companionable silence until they reached the stone marker that indicated the middle of the town square.

"Which way, M'lady?"

In response, Catherine tugged at Hero's reins and trotted him toward Bookbinders Row, calling over her shoulder, "Over here."

Fiona kneed Brilley and followed. Three-quarters of the way down Bookbinders Row, Catherine halted Hero in front of a large house with a thick wooden door, flanked by two leaded-glass windows. The soft glow of candlelight lit the panes.

"This is it," Catherine announced. She threw a practiced leg over the horse and slid from Hero's back, her long skirts trailing behind her. She handed the reins to Fiona. "Would you like to come in? You might be able to meet Will and tell him about your writing."

"Maybe some other time. You will want to visit with your friends, and I'd better get back and make sure father and my brothers get the wagon moved properly."

"Indeed." Catherine smiled. "Please tell your father that I shall try to come to Edward's to pay my respects once I am settled. I would like very much to see your father and all of you again."

Fiona returned Catherine's smile. "I'm sure father would like that. I know I would. Until then, M'lady." She nodded at Catherine and turned Brilley. Hero fell into step alongside horse and rider.

"Thank you, Fiona," Catherine called.

"Do not trouble yourself." Fiona's voice echoed in the empty street. She called over her shoulder as she continued slowly down Bookbinders Row. "If you need anything else, just let me know. I'm at your service." Her face broke into a wide, charming grin that mimicked Duncan's, visible even in the fading light.

Catherine waved then turned to knock on the door of the Pritchard's house and almost ran into young Willy standing in the doorway. For a moment, he stood, blinking in surprise, speechless. Finally, he recognized her and threw his long arms around her.

"Aunt Catherine! How good to see you."

Before Catherine could reply, the door opened again and an arm reached around him and yanked Catherine inside the house. The door slammed shut, leaving Willy outside.

"Catherine, why are you here? Didn't you receive my message?" Sarah's face flushed with anxiety. "You shouldn't have come."

"I'm happy to see you, too, Sarah. What kind of a greeting is that?"

Sarah's expression changed from perplexed to embarrassed and apologetic. "I'm sorry, Catherine." She pulled Catherine into a long embrace. "But you weren't supposed to come. I sent a message."

"I received the message, but what's all this about priests and questions about Briarcrest? We have nothing to hide."

Sarah clamped her lips tight as she regarded Catherine. Her eyes were filled with worry and fear. She whispered, "I'm afraid we all have something to hide as far as these men are concerned, Catherine. I do wish you wouldn't have come. We have troubles enough without feeling that we've brought our difficulties on you."

"You'd better tell me what's going on, Sarah," Catherine said. She pulled the woman toward the table in the middle of the room. Sarah sat down opposite Catherine and shuddered a loud sigh before she began.

SARAH AND CATHERINE sat facing one another at the thick-planked table in front of the fire. Sarah had poured Catherine a cup of herb and spice tea, but she hadn't drunk any of it. As Sarah spoke, she tried desperately to keep her voice from trembling. "It was bad enough, when the priest and his fellow cleric, the Dark Monk, as he's known, bothered Will about the printing business. They harried him for weeks."

As the story unfolded, it was clear that something else had happened to turn their attention elsewhere. Someone had put it to them that Cate might be in league with the devil. They had called

Will only today to answer to the priest and his crony regarding their daughter's transgressions. It was the second time in a week that they had questioned Will about Cate. The more details that Sarah revealed, the higher the pitch her voice took as panic seized her. Catherine felt the same fear rising in her chest as she listened.

"Who has accused Cate?" Catherine demanded.

"We don't know. That's one of the things Will hoped to find out today. I expected him back by now. He's been with them for hours. I'm getting worried. That's why Willy just left. I told him to go and see what he could find out."

"So that's where he ran off in such a rush." Not wanting to alarm Sarah further, Catherine hid her concern about Willy having been sent to make an inquiry about his father. No matter how mature a young man he might be for his years, if the Churchmen were to question him about his sister, how could his parents be sure he would answer with discretion?

Catherine changed the subject. "The baby, has it come yet?"

Sarah nodded yes, tears welling up in her eyes. "He's a little over a week old; he's such a dear little one." She hesitated, mulling over her thoughts before saying more.

"Where are they?" Catherine looked around the room. She saw no sign of Cate or her son. "Are they all right?"

"They're both fine, but Will said that I mustn't tell anyone, Catherine. He said not even those considered friends must know. It would put Cate and the baby in jeopardy. I can't tell you."

"This is ridiculous, Sarah. Tell me where she is."

"I can't. You'll have to ask Will."

Catherine saw the fear in Sarah's eyes again. "Have they picked on Cate because she had a child without the blessing of the Church in marriage?"

"No," Sarah said. Then, almost in a whisper, she added, "I'm afraid it's worse than that."

Worse than that? What could be worse than that to these men? Never mind that Cate was probably seduced by a young man who could not control himself in the presence of one as beautiful as Catherine Lydia Pritchard. The Churchmen would never presume he would have been at fault. Never. Only the woman would bear the burden of responsibility for their sin. For all anyone knew, Cate may have been forced to lie with this young man who abandoned her as soon as he learned that she was with child. All of it would have been of no consequence to these men.

Catherine snorted at her own musing. Then with a look and a tone softened with concern, she said, "Tell me, Sarah. What is worse than that?"

Sarah buried her face in her hands and sobbed. When she could speak at last, she told Catherine everything.

AS SARAH WIPED her reddened eyes, she tried desperately to pull herself together. The door swung open and Will walked in. His shoulders were hunched. Dark circles outlined his eyes. He looked miserable. Sarah stared at her husband, unable to speak, fearing the worst. Silently, tears streamed down her face again.

"Will, what is it?" Catherine asked.

Will looked up. He didn't seem to recognize Catherine. When he finally realized who she was, he walked up to her and scooped her into a long embrace. "Catherine, you weren't supposed to come."

Catherine held up her hand to stop him. "I'm perfectly capable of making my own decisions, Will, and it looks as if I've made the right one this time. I can't let you and Sarah go through this alone. Sarah's just been telling me of these dealings of late. This is dreadful. Did Willy find you?"

Will nodded. "I sent him home to his wife." Pulling away from Catherine, he looked apologetically at his wife. "They want to see Cate and the baby."

Sarah's hand flew to her mouth in an attempt to stifle her cry.

"Someone told them about the child. They wouldn't tell me who, although I have my suspicions. They want to see him for themselves." He turned to Catherine and asked, "Has Sarah told you, then? Has she told you about the child?"

Catherine nodded and her heart went out to her friends. What could she say to console them? Sarah had told her about the baby, about his shock of white hair on the side of his head. They knew it would be considered a bad omen to less enlightened people. They had kept his head covered and not allowed anyone to see it. At least, they thought that's what they had done. Somehow, though, someone had found out about it and told the priests. Now these men wanted to see the mother and infant themselves.

Will sobbed, "They said that Catie is in league with the devil. They say..." Will broke down, unable to continue. A guttural sob burst from his throat. Catherine put her hand on his shoulder in an attempt to soothe him.

"Will, what do they say?" she asked softly. "Tell me. I want to help."

Will sniffed and gulped. "They say...they say that the child's hair turned white because..." He stopped short as he choked on his words. Catherine could barely hear his next words. "When the devil entered my Catie, his cold member turned the baby's hair the color of frost."

"Ridiculous!" Catherine bellowed. "What's wrong with these people? We've seen such things before. Babies are born with all manner of marks that disappear after a while." She clenched her fists at her sides as she spoke.

Her fury alarmed Will. He knew Catherine well enough to know that he might have to concern himself with her confronting these Churchmen, which would only make things worse. He couldn't let her good intentions get his family — or her — into more trouble. "Catherine, please, do not involve yourself with these men. They are looking to find themselves a — a witch. They will not rest until they do. I have taken care of it, for the time being anyway. We've sent Cate away. I told the priests that she was so frightened and distraught that she ran away and that I didn't know where she was. They weren't happy about it. The news left the old priest, Father Gaspar, rather befuddled, actually. I'm sure we haven't heard the last of those clerics, but I'm hoping this will buy us some time at least."

"I want to see Cate, Will."

"No," he said firmly. Then he softened and added, "Catherine, please. They may be watching us. If they follow you, they will find her. We can't risk it."

"You can't hide her forever, Will. There must be a way out of this."

"Don't you think I've tried to think of something? I have not been able to find an answer to any of this." He sat with a thud, his shoulders slumped, his head bent.

Catherine looked to her two friends. Their faces, drawn and tired, were full of pain. With desperation in her voice, she said, "There must be a way. We simply must find it."

Chapter
Seven

CATHERINE LEFT THE Grouse and Pheasant Inn and hurried along Market Street unaware of those she passed. She focused on her plan, going over details in her mind. She intended to distract Will so that she could get what she needed without his knowledge. Clear thought seemed to have eluded the man since the clerics from Spain had arrived in Willowglen. That and her concern for Cate and her child were driving her to this act of dishonesty.

It had taken Catherine days to get Sarah to divulge where Will had sent Cate and their grandchild. If Will knew that Sarah had finally given in to Catherine's pleas, she couldn't say how he would react, but she suspected that it wouldn't be favorable. No, she couldn't risk him finding out what she was up to. Therefore, Sarah would have to be kept in the dark about her actions as well.

At the market cross, Catherine turned and headed toward Bookbinders Row. In order to succeed, she might need the skill of the street children of London who could take things from within people's coats without their knowledge. She wondered if it would be possible, but shook the thought from her mind. She had to prevail; she had no choice.

The only other source for the materials she needed could be found at the papermaker's shop but she decided she couldn't risk going there. Sarah had voiced her suspicions about Isobel Pewsey. She and Will thought that she might be the one who had gone to the priests about the white hair on the baby's head, for Will had seen Isobel staring into the window of their home shortly after Andrew's birth. He had been on his way home from the printing shop for the noon meal. As he approached, Isobel saw him and fled.

At the moment, Catherine didn't want to have anything to do with Isobel or her family. Besides, she couldn't take the chance that the papermaker might be able to figure out what she was up to. As far as she was concerned, no one in the Pewsey family was to be trusted. She didn't even want to risk going to Cate herself. Success in carrying out her plan would have to rest in someone else's hands. She wondered if the person she had in mind would be willing to do it. She would find out once she had the materials she needed.

Walking right past the Pritchard house without so much as a sidelong glance, Catherine reached the printing shop and found Will and his son hard at work at his press. Will pushed the large lever from left to right and watched the platen holding a sheet of paper come down against the plate full of shiny black-inked letters. When he returned the lever to its original position, the plate lifted, taking the heavily inked print with it. As Will removed the paper from the plate, he noticed Catherine standing watching him. When his eyes met hers, she saw anguish in them. Anger welled up inside her against the Churchmen. *Why had they come? Why had they made the Pritchards the object of their persecution? Why now?* She had no answers. All she knew was that her plan must work.

"Catherine." Will's pronouncement of her name sounded like a weary sigh.

Young Willy smiled at her and put down his beaters, laden with viscous black ink, and wiped his hands on a rag. He walked over to a tray of letters and began cleaning them to use again.

Will recovered and brightened a little. "To what do I owe the pleasure of a visit today?"

A moment of anxiety ensued. She hadn't thought that Will would want to know what she was doing in his shop. She supposed that they would exchange some pleasantries and he would get back to work allowing her to wander the shop unobserved. What excuse would she use for coming? Then she thought of Fiona.

"I wanted to talk to you about meeting with the young woman I told you about the other day. The one that helped me get to your house when her family's wagon broke down in the middle of Market Street. Edward's granddaughter."

"Ah, the girl who fancies herself knowledgeable about writing."

She looked askance at him. She would forgive him his pompous remark because she knew constant worry overwhelmed him these days. "Yes, the *author*," Catherine replied, unwilling to let him think ill of Fiona.

Will stared at her for a long while before he responded. "Well, I am unable to take on any more work, right now. I have more than enough to keep me busy for a long time to come."

Catherine had to shake off a feeling of overwhelming sadness at Will's remark. "Will, that's not really the reason, is it?"

A thick silence hung in the air between them. He glanced over his shoulder at his son. The young man seemed engrossed in cleaning ink from the metal letters used for setting the pages of type. He turned back to Catherine and whispered, "I can't risk any more trouble with the Church. Don't ask me to do it, Catherine."

"Why would this trouble the Church? Tell me. Help me to understand. They are stories of her own personal experiences, according to what she tells me. They are truths, her truths."

"She is a woman, Catherine. I cannot do it."

"What?" Frustration welled up within Catherine. She didn't come to argue with Will. She only wanted to make light conversation, then think of a way to get what she needed from the shop and be gone. This wasn't turning out as she had imagined. Still, she found it hard not to point out to him that he used flawed logic. "Christine de Pisan, Will," she said, letting her irritation show. "The Church has nothing to say about her writings and they are many. Women write all the time these days and their work is printed. You told me last year that you had printed a book on how to keep a household, written by one of the ladies of Willowglen. What is so different about this young woman's writings?"

Will's shoulders slumped. "I just can't. Please, don't ask me to do this."

She knew she needed to leave this subject for now. Not only was it useless to pursue this topic but it also interfered with her real reason for being in the shop. However, it gave Catherine another idea.

"Fine, Will. I understand. In light of what you've just told me, you may not even want her in your shop. Would you let me watch you work, then? Perhaps you will allow me to ask you some questions so that I can pass on information to her. She will want to understand what goes on in the printing of books in order to decide how to proceed with her own work, no matter where it is printed. Surely you can't object to that."

He sighed in resignation. "It's the least I can do, Catherine. You have always been a good friend. I shall never forget that it is because of you that I am successful." He looked deeply into her chestnut brown eyes. "I am grateful."

"I know, Will. And I'm sorry that these difficulties have befallen you."

Another long silence ensued until Catherine broke it by saying, "I'll just look around a bit, then."

Will smiled weakly and walked back to his press. He placed another piece of paper on the machine and moved the handle back and forth. Then he removed the paper and hung it on the thin line. He turned to his son and said something to him. Willy walked over to the tray of set type in the press and tried to lift it out again. "It's stuck, father. I can't get it out." Will joined his son and the two started to push and pull on the bar holding the tray in place. They couldn't remove it.

Catherine turned from the pair and wandered around the shop, fingering a stack of finished tracts piled in one corner of a desk. As she strolled toward an open chest at the far side of the room, she turned to check on the other two. Still very focused on the problem with the machine, they weren't paying any attention to her. She moved quickly to the shelves, knowing that they held exactly what she wanted, for she had spied it as soon as she walked in the door. She bent down to the lower shelf and read the labels on the bottles. She found the one she wanted. Lamp Black, the label read. Extending her trembling hand, she plucked the bottle from its location with quick fingers. She rapidly concealed the container and glanced over at Will again. He and his son still had their heads together, struggling with the press.

It took a great deal of control not to hurry toward the door. She kept the pair in her line of sight. Neither man noticed her. When she reached the entrance, she put her free hand out and pulled opened the shop door. As she stepped out onto the street, she heard the thud as it closed behind her. She quickened her step and was halfway to the Market Square before something drew Will's attention from the tray full of metal letters and he looked up. Realizing that Catherine had left, he drew his eyebrows up and shrugged. Then he turned back to the press just as his son cried, "Success!" and he freed the tray from the machine.

SINCE ANY FINE smith work that needed to be done for Briarcrest usually brought John to them these days, Catherine hadn't seen Edward in a long time. It saddened Catherine to see how old and frail the elder silversmith looked, and she regretted having waited so long to visit the man who was, in part, responsible for her acceptance into the spice vendors guild many years ago.

After the death of her mother, her father left her with the nuns of Wooster Abbey outside Willowglen to continue her education while he wandered around the country under the guise of looking for new wares to sell in his shop. In fact, he had run away from Willowglen in an attempt to escape the pain of his grief over losing his wife. When he returned a year later, Catherine had made up her mind that she wasn't going to let him continue to live a lonely existence without her. She told him she was going to officially apprentice with him and become a member of the guild herself.

Once her training was complete, her father presented her to the guild, but they weren't happy to have her. They frowned at the thought of a young unmarried girl becoming the proprietor of

Hawkins and Hawkins' Herb and Spice Shop upon the death of her father. After all, it just wasn't done. She should get married and work with her husband if she wanted to, but to become the owner of her father's business? None of the members of the guild were sure that it was a good idea. Then Edward stepped forward and spoke for her. He had a soft place in his heart for her. He knew she had an independent spirit, but he also knew that she had a good heart and a gift for healing. She had saved his son John's life as a child. His oldest son, Duncan, thought very highly of her. Edward spoke eloquently on her behalf, and, as a result, she was accepted into the guild.

The old man brightened when he saw Catherine enter his living area. As cordial as ever, he expressed his gratitude for her visit in a thin, rasping voice. He reminded Catherine of a small bird on a nest, as he sat in a large chair by the fire, covered with blankets against a chill of early spring that no one else seemed to feel.

Earlier, in the shop, John had told Catherine that Duncan's visit had given his father new vitality, but she knew that the old man didn't have much life left in him. He looked worn out. Even his smile seemed to burden his face.

As Edward dozed by the fire, Catherine spent the afternoon visiting with Duncan, reliving old memories of childhood and taking pleasure in the company of his whole family. They were a bunch of rowdy, jovial Scots, to be sure. She enjoyed them immensely. Fiona joined in with her brothers and father, talking and laughing easily, but as the afternoon sun waned, Fiona went to her grandfather's side. She pulled out a sheaf of papers from a small sack and began to read him a story of her own composition until he nodded off. Catherine waited for an opportunity to speak with Fiona alone, to reveal the real reason for her visit, which had never left her thoughts. She had come to ask for Fiona's help.

With Edward asleep, and Fiona's family occupied in their own conversations, Catherine motioned Fiona out into the back garden and wrapped herself in her thick woolen shawl against the chill evening air. Fiona swung her heavy cloak over her shoulders. The sun dipped below the rooftops as the women spoke.

"You said you wanted my help, M'lady."

"Yes, Fiona, I do, but let's clear up one matter of importance, first. Please, you must call me Catherine."

A curious look appeared across Fiona's face. "My father has taught me to be respectful of my elders."

"You make me feel old." Catherine laughed. "I don't want to feel old."

"Oh, but you do not seem so. Far from it. Forgive me. I shall not refer to you that way again."

"Thank you," Catherine said. "A great lady once taught me that titles did not matter when people worked together for a common good. It's a lesson I've remembered and taken to heart for many years. I have always tried to value her lessons and follow her example."

"A wise lady, indeed. Then to honor both of you, I shall call you Catherine, as you wish." Fiona broke into a wide grin, reminding Catherine of a youthful Duncan. "And who might that great lady be?"

"The lady's name was Beatrice. She ruled the small Duchy at Briarcrest, about a day's ride from here. She was Lydia's aunt. Lydia and I live at Briarcrest Hall ourselves now."

"Yes, you spoke of it when I escorted you to your printer friends' house. I remember." Fiona's eyes seemed to deepen in color. She squinted just a little as she asked, "What you told me then...is it true? Two women rule at Briarcrest?"

"Yes," Catherine said matter-of-factly. "And two women ruled before us, the Duchess of Briarcrest and her companion, Lady Hilary."

"Amazing." Fiona bore into Catherine with her gaze for a long time before she said, "Perhaps I shall write a story about two women like them and like you and Lady Lydia one day." A whimsical smile appeared on her face. "Please, go on. I'd like to hear more."

"Well, this great lady of whom I speak was not only wise, she was resourceful as well. I learned a great deal from her over the years. Because of her, I believe there are always solutions to problems, if you are willing to think beyond the obvious answer. I have a problem, Fiona, or rather my friends, Will and Sarah, do. And I've been mulling over my thoughts trying to figure out how to resolve it. Last night, the solution finally came to me as I fell asleep, but I require the assistance of someone who is, as yet, uninvolved with my friends' troubles."

Intrigued, but wary, Fiona said nothing, her face a mask. Finally she said, "Perhaps you should first tell me about the difficulty."

Catherine debated whether or not Fiona could be trusted with the whole story or if she should only tell her what she needed to know to gain her help. She looked deeply into Fiona's eyes. There was a depth in the blueness of them. Catherine knew she could trust Fiona. Something strong and deep united them. In that moment, she knew for certain that Fiona's destiny now intertwined with her own. She decided to tell her everything.

"The problem lies with these men of the Church who have

come from Spain."

"I've heard of them. Grim business. I don't like it. I don't like it at all."

Catherine breathed a sigh of relief and felt the tightness in her shoulders lessen. "They have decided my friends' daughter is now the object of their...zeal."

Fiona's eyes widened. "No wonder you have a problem."

"I think I have a solution, but I need help. It may be that we are all being watched, those of us who are involved with the Pritchard household right now. I need someone to go to Cate to do something for me. Someone has to get to her unseen by these Churchmen or by anyone who is under their influence, in order to carry out my plan."

"What can I do to help?

"I need someone who is loyal, has a horse and can carry out my instructions. This will be a dangerous undertaking. You certainly deserve to know the whole story if you want to hear it." Catherine saw Fiona's eyes light up.

"Tell me," Fiona said with excitement.

Catherine launched into an explanation of what had transpired in the Pritchard house ever since the Spanish clerics came to Willowglen. When she came to the part about Cate's child's hair, Fiona expressed her irritation by using words Catherine had never heard a woman utter. Although the phrases Fiona used embarrassed Catherine, she knew she had made the right decision to tell Fiona everything, in part because of them.

"Perhaps you should accompany me," Fiona suggested after Catherine had explained the plan.

"As much as I long to see Cate and her child, I don't think that it is wise," Catherine said.

"What if I'm followed?" Fiona raised one eyebrow. "After all, if they're watching you, they've seen you come here."

Catherine admitted that it could be a possibility, so they hatched a diversionary plan. Both Catherine and Fiona would ride out together at the agreed upon time. When they got outside of town, Catherine would double back on the path that skirted Willowglen's river. Fiona would continue in the opposite direction toward her destination. If Catherine were being followed, the two hoped that a pursuer would continue to follow her and not Fiona.

Having heard the entire story, Fiona said, "You have my allegiance in this, Catherine. I have a horse. All I need now are your instructions for what must be done."

"Thank you," Catherine said softly. As their eyes met, another measure of relief washed over her. Cate and her son would come through this trouble. Yet something niggled at the back of Catherine's mind, telling her perhaps she was wrong.

Chapter
Eight

AT THE FIRST light of dawn, Catherine crept out of the Grouse and Pheasant and headed down the alley toward the stable. She wrapped her cloak around her to protect her from the cold, misty rain blanketing everything. When she entered the horse barn, Hero nickered his greeting as if they were old friends. A tall figure in a dark cloak turned. Even in the half-light, Catherine could see Fiona's eyes sparkling. She had fashioned her voluminous cloak so that it covered both shoulders and formed a hood that was thrown back to reveal part of her long black braid. The remainder of it disappeared under the dark blue garment.

"Good morning, M'lady." Foggy breath accompanied Fiona's words.

Catherine cocked her head disapprovingly before recognizing the young woman's jest, then smiled and said, "I'll prepare my horse."

"She's all ready," Fiona said. Catherine nodded appreciatively.

The women led the horses from their stalls, down the alley into Market Street. They mounted and raised their hoods over their heads to protect them from the drizzle.

Not wanting to call attention to themselves by racing out of town, they goaded the horses gently and started down the cobbled street at a leisurely pace. At the Market Square they turned toward the Governor's Hall. The few people stirring at this early hour paid little attention to them as they rode down Governor's Lane and out the Royal Gate. They stopped where the Old Roman Road bisected their path and, with nothing more than an exchange of glances, Catherine turned her mare to the west onto the path that would take her back toward Willowglen. Fiona turned east on the road and headed away from town. From Catherine's instructions, she knew that she would stay on this road only briefly. At the next crossroads, she would head south, and in that way, she would reach the miller's cottage. There, she hoped to find Cate Pritchard and carry out Catherine's plan.

PUFFY WHITE CLOUDS filled the morning sky now that the rain had stopped. The morning sun warmed Fiona in spite of a crispness in the air. When she reached the fork in the Old Roman Road, she stopped to remove her cloak and wrap it around and over one shoulder again. To ensure that she wasn't followed, she and Catherine planned that Fiona would take the long way around from Willowglen to her destination. She directed Brilley toward the southernmost path Catherine had informed her would guide her back toward the River Willow. She soon caught sight of the water and drove her horse to a trot along the compacted earthen road. Brilley's hooves beat in soft muted cadence until some buildings came into view across the river. Fiona slowed her to a walk to study the scene.

The road cut through a long expanse of meadow. To her right, delicate birches and flowing willows grew here and there along the banks of the river. The meadow grass, tall and bright green with the newness of the season, smelled sweetly aromatic as the scent rode on the light morning breeze. Fiona urged Brilley on, and horse and rider continued up the road. Soon the structures in the distance grew larger and took on more detail. Straining to see beyond the river, she could just make out the miller's cottage. Beside it, the big wheel of the mill turned, driven by the rushing of water from the river.

Armed with the knowledge of the area that Catherine had given her, Fiona knew that there would be no way to cross the wide, strong watercourse here. Instead, she pressed Brilley to pick up speed again. On the opposite side of the bank, the water crashed and sloshed as it turned the wheel, grinding millet for the townspeople back in Willowglen. She rode beyond the site of the miller's land, looking for a narrowing of the river and a small stone bridge that Catherine told her would allow her passage across the waterway.

Catherine had told her that the miller was widowed. He was an uncharacteristically educated man and had befriended Will as a young apprentice in the print shop. He had an interest in literature and, once Will had taken over the print shop on his own, the miller would visit when he came to town to discuss new books that came off the printing machine. Will always loaned him copies of new literature that he had available. The two men developed a fast friendship that extended to the whole Pritchard family over the years.

He follows some of the old religion, Catherine had said. Because of this, he stays out of the way of the Church and keeps to himself. His wife was a healer herself, although she didn't venture into the town very often. There was no need for her to do so because for many years, Catherine had been the one to tend to the ills of the people of Willowglen. By the time Catherine and Lydia made the decision to leave the town and take up residence at Briarcrest, the miller's wife had died. He was a good man, Catherine had insisted, but she had also warned that, in his fierce loyalty to Will and his family, Fiona could encounter difficulty getting through him to Cate and the baby.

She stiffened at the thought of some meager Englander trying to stand in the way of her promise to Catherine. More resolute than ever, she pushed out her chin and urged Brilley to pick up the pace as she continued down the road.

When the stone bridge came into view, Fiona brought Brilley to a halt. Turning in her saddle, she stretched to scan the landscape all around her. The only movement she saw was a small flock of sheep grazing in the distance. No shepherd accompanied them.

Pressing her muscular thighs firmly into Brilley's sides, she reined her horse toward the bridge with a grunt. She dismounted before crossing and put her foot on the bridge to test its soundness. It seemed well built enough. She dropped Brilley's reins and walked halfway across the bridge, examining the masonry as she went. Satisfied, she returned to the horse, mounted, and signaled for Brilley to move out. When they reached the other side, she turned Brilley onto a narrow walking path, back in the direction of Willowglen. Long before she would reach the town, the miller's cottage and the giant, powerful wheel would come back into view.

THE MAN WATCHED Fiona approach, his eyes hidden under the wide brim of a battered straw hat. He puffed on his clay pipe, the breeze pushing the smoke into a swirling pattern around his head. He sent the young woman who had been working in his garden into the house with her child.

As Fiona came up the path, she tried to read his expression to guess his thoughts, but his face was veiled. She pulled up outside the boundary of the miller's garden, noting that Brilley could easily step over the low wall surrounding the little plot of land.

"Good day to you, sir miller. I wonder if you could assist me. I'm looking for someone." He said nothing. She tried again. "I'm looking for a young woman. She has a son, a babe. One moon hasn't passed since his birth." She saw him eye the sword that hung at her side and ignored the look. "I've been sent to give her something." The man took one step toward her, staying on the other side of the wall of stacked stones, and held out his hand.

"I'll not give it to you, sir," she said indignantly. "I require Mistress Cate—Catherine Lydia Pritchard."

The man raised one eyebrow then a scowl appeared across his face. "Who sent you?" he demanded with a growl.

"Mistress Catherine Hawkins, who is young Cate's godmother."

The man took another step forward and stared up at Fiona, blinking. "Gad, you're a big one," he said, his eyes narrowing.

Fiona looked down at herself and frowned. Shrugging, she responded, "Maybe it's the horse."

"Your manner of dress isn't that of folks from this area. Where are you from?"

"From Scotland. From a borderland called Glenculley."

"How does a Scot know Mistress Hawkins, then?"

"My father is from Willowglen. He's been gone for many years, but he and our whole family have come to visit my grandfather."

The man contemplated her words. Then took one step back and picked up his haying fork from where it lay against the little wall. Holding it out threateningly before him, he said warily, "Mistress Hawkins doesn't live in Willowglen any more."

"I know." Fiona decided she'd better tell everything she knew. Maybe that would alleviate the man's fears about her and gain her access to Cate and the baby. "She lives at Briarcrest now, with the Lady Lydia, but she came to Willowglen several days ago to see Mistress Cate and her child. It distressed her to hear that her goddaughter had to flee from the scrutiny of prying Churchmen."

He cocked his head and asked gruffly, "What do you know about prying Church folks?"

"I know that sometimes they look for demons where there are none and that they should keep to their prayers instead of looking for ways to give other men difficulties."

The miller's expression changed to one of alarm. Almost involuntarily, he looked around as if someone might be listening. Turning back, he whispered, "Who are you?"

"My name is Fiona. I'm the daughter of the Laird of Glenculley, eldest son of Edward the silversmith of Willowglen."

Realization dawned slowly and he lowered his makeshift weapon. "Duncan has come back to Willowglen?"

Fiona smiled. A sense of relief washed through her. "Just for a visit," she said. "May I see Mistress Cate now?"

One eye squinting, he stared at Fiona. Finally, he motioned toward the cottage with his hayfork and grumbled, "Pass."

"Thank you," Fiona replied as she threw her leg over the horse and slid from Brilley's back.

FIONA STOOPED TO enter the little cottage and found the

young woman sitting by the fireplace stirring a pot of fish stew with one hand while cradling her child in the other arm. She didn't turn when the Scottish woman entered. Instead, she spoke into the fire.

"Who sent you?"

The fear in Cate's voice was palpable, reminding Fiona that she needed to let Cate know that she was a friend. "Mistress Catherine sent me. Mistress Catherine of Briarcrest, your godmother."

Cate stopped stirring the contents of the pot and turned on her stool. Fiona's breath caught in her chest. Catherine Lydia Pritchard's beauty disarmed her. The firelight cast a yellow radiance onto Cate's chestnut hair. Even in the dim light of the cottage, she could see alarm and concern in Cate's gray eyes. Fiona took a few steps into the room and saw gold flecks within the gray that seemed to dance in time with the flickering fire. Cate's skin looked white as milk, her russet hair spilled out in ringlets from around the cap that framed her face.

Fiona's cheeks reddened. She turned her gaze to the child in Cate's arms. The baby's wrap had fallen from his head, and Fiona noticed the shock of white hair at his left temple. Cate followed Fiona's gaze and quickly covered her child's head with the blanket.

"I come in friendship, Mistress Cate. Catherine has a plan. She asked me to come to you with it. If we can carry it off, you may be free to return home, you and your child." Looking into Cates's eyes, Fiona felt her heart pounding within her chest. She wondered if Cate could hear it, too. It was curious that Cate should shiver since she was sitting by the warmth of the fire. *Perhaps it is fear that makes her tremble,* Fiona thought. With her own knees weakening at the sight of the beauty before her, her voice failed when she tried to speak again. She found that she could only whisper the rest of her message. "I have given Catherine my oath of loyalty to see you out of harm's way. Please, let me help you."

Cate nodded and looked into a sea of deep blue. As she held Fiona's gaze, her own voice came out hoarse. "Tell me my godmother's plan, then."

THEY DECIDED THAT the miller had no need to know what they were up to. Since he hadn't returned to the house, Cate surmised that he had gone to the mill to check on the grain under the grinding wheel and that, having done so, he probably wouldn't return until supper.

Fiona brought out a thick glass container from a bag that she had carried slung across Brilley's rump. The label on the pot read Lamp Black. She also readied some cloths and had Cate fetch a bowl with a small amount of water in it.

Cate picked up the container and turned it thoughtfully in her hand. "This looks just like the lamp black from my father's shop."

Fiona's eyes crinkled, full of laughter, and her mouth twitched in amusement at the thought of Catherine, the thief.

Cate shuddered at Fiona's smile.

"It *is* from your father's shop, but he doesn't know it. I'm afraid that your godmother has become a robber for your sake."

Holding Fiona's gaze with intensity, Cate whispered, "If we get through this, I shall have to thank her for her dishonesty, and to my father, no less."

They both laughed aloud, breaking the strain of the moment. Fiona watched Cate's eyes soften. Then, the little boy in his mother's arms squirmed and started to cry. Without a word, Cate reached up and undid her top, exposing a breast. She offered it to her son to feed.

As the baby began to suckle, Fiona stared at Cate and caught her breath. *She is so beautiful in every way. Some day, I'd like to be the one caressing that breast.* It was Fiona's turn to shiver.

The child opened his newborn eyes and looked up at his mother. *Oh, that I could be gazing into those beautiful golden-gray eyes,* Fiona thought. Realizing that her chest heaved at her thoughts, Fiona took a deep breath to try to calm herself. It was of little use. She felt a warm stirring within her and wetness between her legs. The already tiny room seemed to close in on her as she thought about kissing Cate's lips, Cate's neck, Cate's bosom. Abruptly, she bolted for the door. Without looking back, she said in a husky voice, "I need some fresh air."

Cate sat nursing her son, blinking into the empty room.

When Fiona returned a few minutes later, after having dipped her head in the miller's rain tub, she felt a little more composed and in control. She had decided that when the child nursed again, she would leave the room as casually as possible.

"Are you ill?" Cate asked as Fiona entered the cottage.

"No, not ill. I just got...a little warm. Perhaps the fire..." Her voice came out an octave higher than normal. "I'm fine now."

A little concerned, Cate stared at Fiona. Finally, she offered, "Shall we continue, then? It won't be long before Uncle George returns for the evening."

"Uncle George?"

"The miller. He's always been called Uncle George by our family. He's been a friend of my father's for years. He's gruff around the edges, but he has a good heart. He's been good to Andrew and me."

"Yes, I see that he has. He was very protective of you. I

thought that he might not let me see you. I'm glad that he finally relented." Actually, she was grateful beyond fulfilling her promise to Catherine and the thought caused her face to flush as she looked into Cate's eyes.

Cate quickly looked down at the floor and added, "I'm glad he did, too." When she looked back up into Fiona's gleaming eyes, she said, "You know, Fiona, you should stay the night with us. We have plenty of stew, if you don't mind it. The only thing is..."

Fiona wondered what stipulation there would be.

"Uncle George is terribly concerned about impropriety. I must sleep in the mill house so as not to be found sleeping in the same quarters with him. I'm afraid that he will require that you sleep there, too."

"Sleep in the granary?" Fiona's temper flared. "How can he make such a young child and new mother sleep in a place like that? Surely a dust-filled place like that isn't good for you or your child."

"It's really no trouble. We sleep in the gear room below where the grinding takes place, so there isn't much grain dust. The walls of the mill house are thick and are warmed by the sun all day. Since we've not had too much rain, it's been quite warm in there at night. Besides, I have a good thick blanket to wrap up in. Uncle George makes pillows from grain hulls and I use one of those also. We have been quite comfortable."

"Are you certain?"

"Yes, I am quite certain." Cate glanced out the cottage window. The sun had gone behind a dark cloud. "It looks as though we might have a shower. Please, stay tonight," she pleaded. "That is, if you are willing to sleep in such rough quarters."

Fiona had no concern for her own comfort, but only for Cate and her son's health. In her grandfather's house, with so many of them visiting, all she had for sleeping was her own cloak to cover her and a sack of her belongings on which to rest her head, but she didn't mind. Even though the granary would be a far cry from her own comfortable cottage on the moors with a proper bed, she had always been able to sleep anywhere. Looking into Cate's intriguing eyes, she wondered how it was that this young woman could have captivated her so quickly. She already knew that she would do anything that Cate asked of her.

The air crackled with tension as Cate awaited Fiona's answer. At last, Fiona replied, "I'll stay." The Scot's reward, Cate's beaming smile, left her heart pounding against her chest once more.

"Shall we finish this, then?" Cate said as she placed the bottle of lamp black back on the table.

"Yes, "Fiona replied breathlessly. She tried to quiet her trembling fingers as she removed the stopper from the bottle.

The nutty aroma of the linseed oil based ink drifted through the air. Cate inhaled deeply and let out a tiny mewling sound that startled Fiona. "Does the odor bother you?

"No." Cate looked apologetic as she shook her head. "It just reminds me of my father's shop, that's all." Then she added shyly. "I miss my family."

This situation was intolerable, and Fiona's heart ached for Cate. No one should have to endure hiding their newborn infant this way, far from the comfort and care of their own family. Fiona had only heard about the Churchmen from Catherine and other people in Willowglen, but anger welled up inside of the young Scottish woman. Once again, she wondered why men of the Church inserted themselves into people's lives in such a manner.

Fiona took a deep breath, filling her lungs to calm herself, before she carefully dipped a twig, cut from the miller's garden, into the inkpot. When she pulled it out, a thick lump of black paste clung to it. Following Catherine's instructions, she dipped the dark viscous substance into the small amount of water in the bowl and swirled it around. The water quickly turned the color of midnight sky on a moonless night.

She looked up to find Cate watching her intently. When their eyes met, Fiona thought she would faint. Turning her concentration back to her task, she managed to ask, "Am I doing this properly? Catherine said that you would know, that you are familiar with mixing ink. She said to make the mixture thicker than normal, though."

Cate didn't answer. Fiona looked up.

"Yes," Cate said gazing into the deep blue pools that were Fiona's eyes, "you're doing it perfectly."

Cheeks tinged red, Fiona wiped the mixture from the twig onto of a piece of flaxen colored cloth and held the cloth near the baby's head. It looked like it would be a close match.

Catherine had instructed Fiona to use enough thickness of cloth when she applied the ink mixture to the baby's hair so that her own fingers would not stain. She wanted to take no chances. There could be no evidence pointing to anyone should the ruse be found out. She also warned her to make sure that she didn't stain the skin on the child's head so that it wouldn't be obvious that they had altered his hair color.

Fiona wadded up several thicknesses of fabric and tucked them under the tuft of white hair on the baby's head. She scooped up some of the ink from the bowl and swiped the dark liquid carefully onto the strands of the baby's thick hair. As she worked, she asked, "What did you say the child's name is?"

"I've called him Andrew."

Fiona's heart beat faster as she stopped and gazed into Cate's eyes again. "It's a fine name," she said huskily. Then tearing herself away, she looked down at the child again. "Well, Andrew, shall we rid you of the mark that's causing so much trouble for your mum?" Andrew gurgled as if he understood. Cate smiled and Fiona thought her heart would burst.

With some difficulty, she dabbed the thick liquid onto the baby's remaining exposed white hair using the twig to apply it, allowing the stain to soak into the strands as much as possible. After several applications, the white spot had almost completely disappeared.

"Catherine told me that we might have to do this more than once. It's a good thing that I've decided to stay. We can apply more tomorrow, if necessary."

The corners of Cate's mouth lifted again and she put her hand on her new friend's. An exquisite pain ran though Fiona's body at Catherine Lydia Pritchard's touch.

Cate looked directly into Fiona's eyes. "I'm grateful to you for doing this, Fiona. I know that you didn't need to involve yourself with my difficulties this way."

Looking away, Fiona grunted, "I don't mind." But in reality, she knew that now having met Cate, she could do no less for her.

THE TWO WOMEN had all the supplies stored and the bowl cleaned of its dark, sticky contents when the miller came in from the granary. Cate asked him if he would mind if Fiona stayed to share their evening meal and sleep in the mill house with her. Since the two women had talked about the possibility of Cate being able to return to Willowglen if their treatment of Andrew's hair was successful, Cate mentioned that she might return home with Fiona soon.

The miller protested saying that he didn't think it was wise for Cate and Andrew to leave. Fiona thought that he even looked a little disappointed.

Both women assured him that they didn't mean to return to Willowglen immediately and that they would do so only if they thought it was safe.

Finally, he mumbled that he didn't mind if Fiona stayed as long as the sleeping arrangements were to her satisfaction. Then he looked at Cate and added, gruffly, "It'll be good for you to have some company over there in the granary anyway."

It caused both Cate and Fiona to smile.

WITH BRILLEY HAPPILY bedded in the miller's paddock shelter, and the hearty fish stew under their belts, Cate and Fiona bid Uncle George goodnight and walked to the mill house using a small lantern to light their way. Cate led Fiona down a steep staircase to a small storage room inside the mill where stacks of grain sacks lined the rough-hewn walls. They passed the massive wooden gears in the gear room and knew that, although the enormous wheel still turned them, the grinding stones had been lifted apart on the floor above.

Several bags had been pulled down to the floor to use as a bed for Cate and the baby. At the edge of one lay the smaller bag of grain hulls that Cate had said she used for a pillow. A thick blanket lay neatly folded at one end on a stuffed grain sack.

Cate placed the small lamp on the floor next to the makeshift bedding and settled her sleeping baby into an indentation she made in one of the bags of grain. He opened his eyes for a brief time, and then slowly closed them again. His mouth moved as if suckling as he drifted back to sleep. Cate moved the blanket back from his head and stroked his hair. It was difficult to identify the area stained black by the ink applied earlier that day. No hint of the white patch was visible.

"I can hardly believe his hair hasn't always been completely black." Tears filled Cate's eyes. "Thank you. I'm very grateful for your help."

Fiona blushed. "You will need to thank your godmother. She's the one who thought of the idea."

"But you are the one who has put yourself at risk to come out here and act upon her plan. You may have saved my son's life." Cate briskly wiped the tears from her cheeks. "I'm sorry. I shouldn't weep so."

"Do not trouble yourself," Fiona said softly, putting a large hand on Cate's arm. She felt her tremble and tried to imagine what it would be like to have reason to fear those bastard priests, as she now thought of them, and to wonder if your own life, and worse, the life of your child, would be forfeited because of superstition and injustice. She knew there was no way she could comprehend what Cate felt about her situation. "You are right to be concerned. I shouldn't think I would feel any differently if I were in your place. You must be sure you want to go back. It might not yet be safe."

"I'm not sure." Cate's voice quivered. "I miss my family. Uncle George, well, he's...he's..."

Fiona thought she understood. The old man seemed stern and reserved, although he probably had the best of intentions and a good heart underneath his gruff exterior. Still, this was no place for Cate when she needed the love and support of the people who cared for her most.

"I can wait until you make a decision, Cate. Take your time. This isn't something you should rush."

A look of relief washed over Cate. "Thank you," she whispered. As the two women looked deeply into each other's eyes, Fiona felt her heart race and her thoughts blur under the influence of Cate's gaze. Cate's eyes turned almost golden in the lamplight. Fiona struggled to catch her breath, trying not to let Cate see her reaction. The baby fussed softly, and the moment ended.

Cate walked over to Andrew and lifted him from the grain sack. At this, Fiona assumed it was feeding time again. Uncomfortable with the effect the sight of Cate's exposed breast might have on her, Fiona headed for the door quickly.

"What's the matter? Where are you going?" Cate's brow wrinkled in concern and confusion.

"Out." Fiona plunged toward the stairs without turning. "For some air. I'll be back shortly. I want to check on Brilley." She didn't look back.

Cate gave Fiona's receding form a quizzical look. "But you just left her. She was fine."

"I know, but Brilley's special to me." Fiona didn't stop. "I just want to see that she's comfortable for the night."

"I see." She didn't really.

AS CATE UNWRAPPED Andrew from his blankets, she contemplated the young woman who had come at Catherine's bidding. Her strength of body and heart were obvious. It was also clear to Cate that she felt drawn to the Scot. She had to acknowledge that the pull was strong. A look from the woman caused her difficulty in catching her breath, and her palms had been sweating from the moment that she had looked into those deep blue eyes. She reeled for a moment thinking of Fiona. Her heart beat rapidly. And yet, a pleasurable feeling hummed beneath it all.

Cate shook her head, then untied the wrap from around Andrew's bottom and cleaned out the soiled straw that lined the fabric. She discarded it in a wooden pail in the corner of the room. Opening a bundle of clean straw, she removed two handfuls and deftly re-lined the fabric, tying it up at his waist again. "There," she told him. "You should feel nice and cozy again, my little man." Caressing Andrew, she added, "A clean bottom and a full belly is all it takes for you, eh? I wish my feelings were that easily understood."

Andrew stuck his tiny fist in his mouth, gurgled and pumped

his legs.

"Yes, I quite agree. Fiona is surely an interesting woman, isn't she? She makes your mum's heart skip a beat. Do you know that? I don't understand it. I never felt this way with your dad." She sighed at the thought of Nathaniel Mistlewaite. It seemed as if he had been gone for years instead of months. "What's happening to me, can you tell me that?"

Settled, Andrew grunted contentedly as Cate wrapped him into his blanket again.

"Well, I don't know, either, but one thing is for sure. I'm glad Fiona Smith is staying around for a while, aren't you? My heart hasn't been this happy in months and I know it's because of her. But she has her own life to live, so we mustn't get too attached to her, must we? You just remember that, now, will you?"

Andrew looked up at his mother with unfocused eyes and yawned.

WHEN FIONA RETURNED a while later, cheeks red from the cool night air, the baby was crying. Cate walked over to him, sat down on a low pile of grain sacks, and proceeded to feed him.

Fiona's brow knit into a tight collection of wrinkles as she turned away from Cate and started rearranging a grain bag for her sleeping pallet. As she worked, she mumbled, "I thought you fed the child already."

"No," Cate responded matter-of-factly, "I cleaned him up and now he wants feeding."

"Oh."

Using Brilley as a reason to leave wouldn't work again. Since she could think of no other excuse, Fiona busied herself by shuffling a sack of grain, trying one location, then moving to another area of the room under pretext of looking for just the right spot for her bed. When she finished, she picked up the leather pouch she had deposited on the floor earlier. She sat with her back to Cate and removed a stack of pages, tied with string, and something wrapped in a wad of leather. She set a small bottle of ink and a quill down on the grain sack and carefully removed the leather stopper from the ink. Methodically dipping the pen into the inkpot, she started writing on a blank page in the dim light.

Cate watched with interest as she nursed the baby. "You must be writing something very important to carry those things with you."

Fiona stopped, but didn't turn around. In fact, she blushed a little, because she was writing about Cate and her new feelings for the woman. Fiona shivered.

Cate noticed and said, "You're cold. Take my covering."

"I'm fine, really." Fiona turned now and looked into Cate's eyes. "I can't accept your only blanket. And to answer your question, I write about my experiences. It helps me to sort out my thoughts. Some of what I've written I think might be of interest to other people, other women." She thought of the intimate thoughts that she had just written and added, "Well, some of it anyway. I'm thinking about getting my writings published. I've been told many times that my stories would make interesting reading for other women." Tessa's face flashed across her mind and Fiona steeled herself against the pain that always accompanied such thoughts. She was stunned to find that she felt nothing.

"Oh, I'd like to read what you've written sometime."

Fiona blushed and shivered again, as her thoughts turned from Tessa to the words she had just penned. She couldn't let Cate read what she had been writing. She said nothing.

Noticing Fiona shiver again, Cate motioned to the blanket folded up beside her. "Please, take the blanket."

"No need. I have my brat—my cloak. It is excellent protection against the cold." She got up from her seat and unpinned the wrap. As she pulled it from around her, Cate's eyes widened at how large a piece of fabric it was. Fiona said, "You see, it's plenty big and it's very comfortable. You need your blanket to keep you and Andrew warm."

Cate smiled her appreciation. As Fiona met Cate's disarming expression, she sat back down with a thud. How was she going to resist Cate Pritchard's charms?

WHEN FIONA WOKE at first light, she didn't need to turn over to know that Andrew was feeding again. She could hear him suckling with contented little noises. She pretended to sleep, thinking, *Does that child ever leave his mother's paps alone?* She winced at the thought of Cate's lovely white breasts and the breath she drew caught in her throat. It wasn't as if she hadn't been in the room countless times as her sisters-in-law suckled her niece and nephews. She wondered why this was different. But, in fact, she knew the answer. Cate Pritchard was a beautiful woman. She allowed the fullness of her feelings to surface. They welled up within her, almost overpowering her. What was she to do? *Nothing*, she insisted as she pushed them back down. She jutted her chin out indignantly.

She would not, could not, act on these feelings. After all, Cate had lain with a man. In Fiona's mind, that made it clear that Cate Pritchard could never feel the same way about her as she felt about

Cate. It was out of the question. In addition, she had pledged loyalty and friendship to Catherine. She could not risk compromising that bond, so newly made, by acting unwisely. She would not yield to her desire to take Cate in her arms and kiss her. She shouldn't even be thinking such thoughts. How, she wondered, would she ever be able to keep her feelings in check? The sound that came from Fiona's throat as she wrestled with these thoughts sounded like a soft whimper.

"Fiona? Are you all right?"

Fiona stirred, but still didn't turn over. She tried to sound as if she had only now awakened. She yawned before she answered. "I'm sorry, did I disturb you? I must have been dreaming."

"No, you didn't disturb me. I was concerned for you, that's all. You seemed distressed."

"No, no. I'm just fine." Her answer sounded too enthusiastic, even to Fiona.

As she lay there with her back to Cate, she listened intently for signs that the mother still fed her child. Not hearing the telltale suckling, she decided to risk turning over. The baby was not feeding, true. Instead, he lay quietly in Cate's lap. Fiona's vantage point afforded her a marvelous view of Cate's half-exposed breasts, and her breathing quickened. She thought about turning over again, but decided that would only make her behavior seem even more odd. She closed her eyes and took a deep breath.

"Fiona?" Cate whispered.

When Fiona opened her eyes, she was just in time to see Cate tie the strings of her top. She breathed a sigh of relief and threw off her cloak.

Cate gave the Scot a curious look and mused that Fiona looked rather mysterious in her North Country garb. She wondered if all the women from that part of the country wore their tunics in such a manner, showing their legs — their fine, shapely legs. Cate gulped at the emotions that welled up inside and she pushed them aside. Cate thought that only men dressed that way, but she supposed now that she was wrong. When Fiona pulled herself up from her makeshift bed, Cate marveled at her height and her muscular body as she stood in her rumpled leine with her lower legs exposed. She easily towered over most men that Cate knew. It intrigued her that Fiona was so tall and robust, yet she seemed very much a woman, and a lovely woman at that. To her, Fiona's deep blue eyes and hair as shiny and black as ravens' feathers all contributed to her mystery and beauty. A shiver ran though Cate's body. She picked the baby up from her lap and nestled him against her shoulder.

"I usually make Uncle George's breakfast," she said.

"Will I impose if I join you?" Fiona asked.

"No, Uncle George won't mind. After all, if you're going to stay for a while, you have to eat."

"I could catch my own breakfast," Fiona replied, a twinkle in her eye.

"I don't doubt that you can. Say, why don't you catch us supper? We could use a bit of meat. Since I've been staying here, we've eaten nothing but the early spring vegetables from Uncle George's garden and the occasional fish that he catches from the river. Something different for tonight would be most welcome."

"Supper it is, then," Fiona replied. She felt a pleasant warmth surge through her body at the knowledge that Cate seemed to want her around.

Cate smiled and held out her hand to Fiona. Fiona's cheeks reddened as she grasped Cate's hand and pulled her from her seat. Fiona found that she couldn't take her eyes from Cate as she moved toward the stairs carrying Andrew. She turned back to Fiona. "Meet me at the miller's cottage then. Don't be too long. I'll make something quick this morning."

Fiona watched the swing of Cate's hips as she climbed the granary steps and disappeared from view out the door. Realizing she had been holding her breath, Fiona exhaled and licked her lips as Cate's image blazed within her memory. *Oh, Fiona,* she thought, trembling, *you're in deep trouble, lass.*

Chapter
Nine

LYDIA GOT UP from her seat at the large, ornate desk in her study. As soon as she saw the look on Tom's face, she knew that something was amiss.

"Good day, Lady Lydia," Tom said. His youngest son, Alfred, peeked out from behind him. Tom put his hand on his son's shoulder and drew him around in front of him. He prodded, "Tell the Lady what you told me earlier, Alfred."

Lydia knew the lad. He was usually full of confidence for his young age. She smiled at him and nodded, trying to convey to him that, whatever the difficulty, she would not be cross with him. She approached the pair.

Alfred's eyes bulged as he fidgeted. He looked from his father to Lydia and back again. He swallowed a few times before finally starting to speak. "There was this man..."

Tom interrupted, "A monk of some sort, M'lady, that's what the boy told me earlier. He talked to this monk days ago, but I just found out about it myself today. Actually, it was my father he told first and he's the one what just told me. I thought I'd better find out from the boy, here, exactly what went on and when I heard it, I brought him to you straightaway." He looked at Alfred and cocked his head toward Lydia. "Go on. Tell Lady Lydia, lad."

Alfred's chest heaved as he took a breath before starting again. "There was this...monk," he said. "He came up to me in the field behind the village. Asked me if I knew anything about the Lady of Briarcrest. Of course I did, but I didn't let on, truly." Lydia saw pleading in his eyes as he continued. "I said nothing about what I knew. He told me to see if I could find out who the mistress of the house was. Insisted that I try to get inside. Told me to find out who you were. Told me if I didn't do as he said and bring back the name he would cuff me on the ears and have me damned to hell with all my family going there, too." Absently, Alfred toyed with the cloth tie at his small waist.

Lydia watched his little chest heave up and down as he drew

and expelled his breath. His father gently nudged him in the back, prompting him to continue.

Alfred looked into Lydia's eyes, his own wide with fear. "I didn't want to go to hell, Lady. I don't want me mum and dad to go there either. Me granddad, he's old. I'd be afraid that if he died soon, he'd go to hell. I had to tell the monk." Tears welled up in Alfred's eyes and spilled down his rosy cheeks.

"It's all right, Alfred." Lydia put her hand on the boy's head. "Just tell me what happened."

"Yes'm. I waited until I saw him again. He was like a ghost of some sort, you know." He didn't wait for Lydia's acknowledgement. "He just appeared out of nowhere and you couldn't see his face. He kept it hidden in his monk's hood. If you looked into it, all you could see was black. That was the worse part. I never saw his face at all." The boy licked his lips and added, almost whispering, "I don't think he had a face, Lady." His whole body quivered.

Lydia's concern quickly changed to anxiety, her heart beating faster in her own chest. *What was this all about?* She had no idea, but she didn't like the sound of it. She masked her apprehension and encouraged the boy. "Go on, Alfred. Tell me everything that happened. Don't be afraid. When you're done, I'll get cook to give you a treat for being such a good boy." She knew Alfred. He couldn't resist a sweet from the kitchen. She saw his eyes brighten. She crouched down to his level and grasped both of his small hands in her own. "Tell me exactly what happened after you met this monk again."

Alfred took a deep breath before continuing. "He came out of Briarcrest Wood the next day again. At first, I wasn't going to talk to him, but I couldn't help meself. He bent his finger to me like this." Alfred lifted his hand from Lydia's and crooked his small finger. "And it was as if a rope was tied 'round me waist. I had to go to him. It was like he was using the rope to pull me to him."

Alfred placed his hand back in Lydia's. Gazing back into the boy's eyes she said softly, "Tell me exactly what he said to you."

"He wanted to know who the mistress of Briarcrest was. I told him there was two and that it was Lady Lydia and Mistress Catherine. Then he wanted to know if you—both of you—were at home. Mistress Catherine was leaving. I already knew because me dad said he had to get the horses ready for her and for Sir Hubert to make the journey. I helped him," he added, puffing out his chest. Lydia said nothing. The boy finally added, "He asked me if you were going, too."

Lydia tried not to let the boy or his father see her growing apprehension. She continued to speak quietly. "And did you tell him about Mistress Catherine's journey?"

"Yes, Lady, I told him. I didn't know what else to do. I couldn't let me Gran go to hell." The tears welled up again.

Lydia soothed, "It's all right, Alfred. You did nothing wrong. Your father teaches you to respect your elders, does he not?"

Alfred nodded with enthusiasm, causing a tear to spill over the rim of one eyelid again.

Lydia wiped it from his cheek with her thumb before continuing. "How are you to know if a man of the Church should not be given the information he requests? No, you did fine, Alfred. Finish the story now. Tell me the rest."

Alfred licked his dry lips and continued. "When he asked me, I told him that Mistress Catherine was going on a journey. He asked me where she was going, but I didn't know where at the time, so I told him so. Then he asked if you were going, too. I told him I didn't think you were."

The boy looked out the window of the study, wishing with all his heart that he could be out there playing in Briarcrest's courtyard as he had so many times as he waited to accompany his father home to the village outside of Briarcrest.

"Was there anything else, Alfred?" Lydia asked gently.

Alfred slowly moved his eyes from the window and he made contact with the gray-green of Lydia's. "Nothing, Lady, except..." He wasn't sure he should continue.

"Except what?" Lydia prodded.

"Except after I told him what he wanted to know, he threatened to box my ears anyway, so I ran off. That's when I decided I'd go tell Gran what happened. I didn't like that monk at all, so I thought I'd see what he had to say about it. He told me to tell Papa, but I was afraid and I didn't tell him right away. Gran forgets things sometimes, but he remembered just today and he told Papa about it himself. That's when Papa..." He looked up at Tom. Tom's smile was full of encouragement. "That's when Papa said we were to come here right away." Alfred looked down at his worn leather shoes and continued, "I didn't know that I did anything wrong. Please, believe me."

Lydia stood up and wrapped her arms around Alfred. "I believe you, Alfred. You did nothing wrong. Do not trouble yourself. Everything will be fine. You did well to tell Henry...and your father." She looked up at Tom and said, "And you did well to bring Alfred to me to let me know about this."

"Do you know what it's about?" Tom asked, his eyes almost as big and round as his son's. The next words tumbled from his mouth, uncharacteristically. "Should we be concerned for Mistress Catherine? Do you want me to tell Sir Hubert?"

Lydia held up her hand to stop him. "I'm not sure yet, Tom. Let me think about what Alfred has just told me. For now, take him to the cook and have her give him a honey cake. You like those, don't you Alfred?"

Alfred shook his head vigorously, smiling from ear to ear. Lydia smiled her reassurance back at him and walked to the study door. As the pair passed by her into the hallway, she put her hand on Alfred's head again. He looked up at her with eyes full of seriousness and innocence. "Thank you, Alfred," she said. He smiled sweetly in response.

She turned her attention to Tom and asked, "How is Henry doing?"

"As well as can be expected. He doesn't see very well any longer. It upsets him to be so dependent upon others. Sometimes, he gets discouraged. But Alfred is a great comfort to him." He looked down at his son and smiled. "He spends a lot of time with his Granddad — and it helps my dad a lot when he's around."

Alfred beamed at his father's words of praise.

"I'm glad to hear it," Lydia said. "Does he need anything?"

"No, M'lady. He's well cared for. He wants for nothing."

"Good," Lydia pronounced. "Please tell him I send my regards to him."

"Thank you, Lady. I shall."

As Lydia moved to close the study door, she saw Alfred grasp his father's hand and pull him in the direction of the kitchen.

LYDIA STARED OUT the window, wondering what the story that Alfred had told her meant. Who was this monk? Why did he want to know about Catherine and about her? What did he care where Catherine's journey took her or whether or not Lydia accompanied her? Her stomach churned with worry. Was Catherine in danger? She was in Willowglen, after all, with more Churchmen who were apparently stirring up trouble for the Pritchards. Were the two somehow related? She recalled that Sarah had said that someone had asked about Briarcrest in the note she had sent Catherine. Catherine had been gone for more than a week and there had been no word from her. Lydia needed to do something. But what? As she ruminated on these things, she watched through the study window as the last rays of sun faded below the tree line beyond Briarcrest.

The kitchen maid's knock at the door drew her attention back to the room. As the girl entered with a tray of cakes and a steaming hot herbal brew, she smiled pleasantly at Lydia.

Was it that time already? Lydia felt as though time had stood still since Tom's departure. She stared at the steaming teapot sitting on her desk, turned and said, "Call Sir Hubert. I need to see him immediately."

Lydia's stern face and tone told the girl not to dally. She gave a half-curtsey and moved quickly toward the door. Lydia heard the soft padding of her rapid footsteps as she hurried down the hall. A short time later, Hubert knocked on the study door and entered at Lydia's bidding.

THE NEXT DAY, Hubert walked briskly down the length of the Great Hall. Lydia got up from her seat by the fire and greeted him. Then she led him to her study where they could speak privately. Looking into his eyes, her own filled with concern, Lydia said, "Were you able to find out anything?" The day before, he had pledged that he would make sure that Catherine was safe.

"Nothing yet, M'lady, but I've sent someone to check on Catherine and to make careful inquiries around Willowglen to find out what is going on there. We are also checking the countryside to see if we can find out anything about this monk that Alfred encountered."

"Thank you, Hubert. I knew I could count on you."

"You can. You know that. My father was loyal to the ladies of this house for years, as I am now. Besides, Catherine is my friend."

"I know, Hubert. I know. It's just that these events are so unsettling."

"We will take care of her."

"I know," Lydia sighed. She hoped that it was true. Hubert's mention of his father made Lydia smile. Her memory of Sir Guy of Middleton was still strong, even though he had been dead for a number of years. It was the elder knight who had informed her of her father's death while she was in hiding. Those were difficult times. She had been severely injured by the treacherous cleric, Isadore. Only through Catherine's careful ministrations and the love and care of all of the women at Briarcrest did Lydia recover.

Hubert's voice broke through Lydia's reverie. "As soon as we find that it is safe in Willowglen, I'll prepare the horses and escort you there myself, but until then, you should stay here at Briarcrest." Earlier, he had tried to talk her out of going altogether, but she was determined.

After a little over a week without word from Catherine, wondering what was happening with the Pritchards, and, more recently, trying to figure out what this strange monk wanted with them, Lydia had had enough. She missed Catherine and wanted to be with her. She should never have let her go alone, but she had, and now she had to act. It was the only way she knew to finally quell her fear that Catherine was in danger. She had not even wanted to wait until Hubert had gotten an accounting back from his men, but he finally convinced her that it was the prudent thing to do.

"I shall be ready to go at a moment's notice. Just as soon as you know something, I want you to inform me."

He bowed and turned to leave the study. As he walked away, Lydia felt a surge of anxiety and impatience. How long could she wait before she would have to go to Willowglen, news or no news?

"I WISH FOR your sake that you would wait another day, Lydia," Hubert pleaded. "We need more information."

Another week had passed. Every time Lydia asked Hubert if he had had any news, he only had bits and pieces to report. He had found out the priests were indeed in Willowglen. It seemed that the monk that Alfred described was one of them. They harassed Will Pritchard often and there was a rumor that Cate was in some sort of trouble, but as far as they could tell, Catherine had no dealings with the Churchmen. Lydia wondered if Hubert was lying to protect her.

Every day since she had heard about the strange monk that little Alfred had encountered, she had a growing feeling of unease and fear. She knew that Hubert only had her best interests at heart, but the worry about what was going on with Catherine in Willowglen would not leave her. No matter how much Hubert tried to placate her, it did not work.

Finally, Lydia asked Hubert again if his men had reported anything new. He told Lydia that one of his men had returned only a few hours ago and that he said that Catherine was fine. About the other goings-on in Willowglen, he had little more to report.

Lydia said nothing but her look said it all. This was no longer a topic for discussion. Almost two weeks had passed and still there was no word from Catherine directly. The following morning, when she had arisen after another sleepless night of worry, she had packed a bag and called for Tom to ready the horses. Then she summoned Hubert to accompany her to Willowglen.

Hubert bit his lower lip and shook his head, knowing that arguing with Lydia would be fruitless. With a sigh he said, "I'll go and tell Tom that we need our horses."

"No need. I've already taken care of it."

Chapter
Ten

THE MORNING SUN had risen high in the sky when Fiona returned to the miller's cottage and held out the two hares to George for the evening meal. Before taking them, he rubbed the stubble on his chin with a thick, rough hand.

"Mistress Cate tells me you'll be staying for a time," he said, finally holding out his hand.

"Yes." She kept her eyes on him, waiting for him to protest.

The miller grunted. As far as Fiona could tell, it wasn't an objection. He nodded to her catch. "Since you'll make a contribution."

With that out of the way, Fiona decided to broach another matter. "While I was out looking for supper, I came across a small cottage up the river a little way. It looks as if it might be abandoned. Do you know who owns it?"

"Yes."

Fiona stared at him, waiting. When it seemed that he would not give her any more information, she asked, "Who?"

"Me."

Fiona broke into a broad grin.

"Would you allow Cate and me to use it until she's ready to go back to Willowglen?"

"It's for my son."

"Is he returning soon?"

"Can't say."

Fiona's grin faded from her face. What would it take, she wondered, to get this man to give her a direct answer? Then she had a thought.

Rummaging though her pouch, she found what she was looking for. She handed George two shiny silver groats. "Perhaps your son wouldn't mind if we hired his cottage for a short time. Cate misses her family and her home in Willowglen, yet she fears what may happen if she returns. Circumstances have changed for Cate, though, and she may well be able to go back to Willowglen soon. Still I can understand her hesitancy. It may just take some time for her to decide. In the meantime, your son's cottage has a nice little fireplace to ward off the coolness of the evenings that we still experience. That little house is better suited to Cate and her son than sleeping in your granary, don't you think?"

It wasn't really a question. She hoped the miller didn't take it as one. The cottage would take some cleaning. It looked as though it had been empty for a long time, but it would make a better temporary home than the storeroom in the mill.

George stared at the coins in his hand. It was tempting. Yet he didn't want Cate to go too far away. He looked up at Fiona. "I like it when she makes me breakfast. Haven't had that since my wife died," he said.

Fiona understood. If Cate left to live at the cottage, he might lose the fine meals that she cooked for him each morning. "I'm sure Cate would still make your morning meal. It's just a short walk to your cottage from your son's. Why don't we ask her?"

He stared at the coins in his still outstretched hand. Then he handed them back to Fiona. "You keep 'em," he said. "She might decide to go back to Willowglen today."

"I don't think so. Besides, whether we go or not, I'd like you to have these for your hospitality to Cate, and to me."

He rubbed his chin again. Fiona held out her hand ready to drop the coins in his.

"Guess it wouldn't harm. I could use it to fix up the lean-to. It's getting kind of battered."

"Yes, you do that. I'll go talk to Cate."

"I like her cooking my breakfast," he called to Fiona's back as she walked to the cottage door.

"I know," she said without turning to face him. "I'll see what I can do."

CATE WAS THRILLED at the prospect of going to the cottage. The two women spent the day cleaning the place. Simply furnished, it didn't take much to get it in order. The cottage was a sturdy little house with a small stone fireplace. Fiona gathered and cut wood for the fire they would have that night, and for some reason, looked forward to the evening more than she had in a long time. The place had no bed, so Fiona set to work hauling several bags from the granary for them to sleep on.

After Fiona set the last bag of grain in place beside the fireplace, she stood and wiped her brow. She had removed her brat and the dark wool vest and wore her tunic unbelted so that it came to her ankles. Cate admired the outline of Fiona's strong shoulders and back and felt a rush of warmth as she stared. When she sighed, Fiona turned and raised one eyebrow. "Is something wrong, Cate?"

"No. Nothing is wrong whatsoever. As a matter of fact, this is better than it's been for weeks. To have some privacy and a nice warm fire is more than I could have imagined I'd have during my stay here. Thank you for thinking of it."

Fiona blushed.

LATER THAT EVENING, after they'd eaten and Fiona had banked the fire for the night, she contemplated what Cate had said about having privacy. Although she didn't want to leave Cate and her son alone in the secluded cottage, she thought it might be what Cate wanted. She donned her woven belt and tied it around her waist following it with her black woolen vest. When she was done, she wrapped her brat around her body in one practiced motion and secured it with the pin that resembled a small dagger.

Fiona cleared her throat. "I'll be going, then."

Cate, used to Fiona needing fresh air at what sometimes seemed odd times, thought she meant that she was going out to check on Brilley, and she said as much.

"I'll check on her on my way to the granary," Fiona responded.

"Why are you going to the granary? Did you forget something there?"

"No. I just thought I'd sleep there."

Cate tried not to show the disappointment that surged through her at the thought of Fiona leaving. "God's wounds! Why would you want to do that? You said it would be so much more cozy here than at the granary."

"For you and Andrew," Fiona said.

"For you, too."

"But you want your privacy."

Cate sighed. "Fiona."

Fiona held up her hand to stop Cate's words, but Cate wouldn't be stopped.

"Fiona. When I said privacy would be nice, I meant that living in a one-room cottage with Uncle George all day and sleeping in the open granary all night, where he could enter at any time, was burdensome. Uncle is used to living his own way, and he doesn't think about whether or not he is intruding on my privacy. It will be nice to be away from him." Then she added shyly, "Not you. I...I like your company. Put your things down. Stay."

Fiona's dark eyebrows disappeared under the hair on her

forehead. "You're sure?"

"Very sure."

Cate's smile enchanted Fiona. Her knees trembled and she wondered if she'd be able to hold herself upright.

"Please," Cate reiterated, "I'd like you to stay. Besides, you hauled that extra sack of grain all the way over here. I think you should use it. Don't you?"

Unable to speak, Fiona nodded once and dropped her brat on the floor. Then she strode over to an empty stool and sat down before her knees buckled.

AS THEY SETTLED in for the night on the large bags of grain, Cate and Fiona took the outside bags and Cate put Andrew between them on the middle one. Fiona drifted off to sleep that evening feeling more warmth and happiness than she had felt in a long time. She knew that she felt that way because of Cate Pritchard.

THE NEXT MORNING, Cate got up to feed Andrew, then made the brief walk to George's house to make him his morning meal. By the time she returned at mid-morning, Fiona had gathered more wood and stacked it in the little room in the cottage. Late in the afternoon, Cate returned to the miller's to stir the pot with his dinner in it and make sure that everything was in order for him for the night.

Several days later, the miller informed Cate that she would not need to come to make his breakfast the next day. He had finished grinding the grain, he said, and he would take it into Willowglen at dawn the next morning.

"Will you stop to see my father and mother?" Cate asked. "I'd like them to know that Andrew and I are well."

"Do you think it wise?" George took a step back, as if to distance himself, a look of concern in his eyes.

"You always stop to see my father in his shop when you go to Willowglen, do you not?"

After a brief pause, he nodded his agreement.

"Then why would you do otherwise this time?"

An uncharacteristic smile appeared across his face. Cate was glad to see it.

"Yes, I suppose you're correct," the old man said. "I'll call on Will and Sarah as is my usual custom. While I'm there, I'll let your father know that all is well." As an afterthought, he added, "And don't worry. I'll keep my own counsel about my affairs to everyone else in Willowglen. I'll make sure that there is no reason for those Churchmen to have any cause to interfere around here."

Cate felt a great relief at his reassuring words.

FIONA HAD GATHERED a handful of herbs from the miller's garden and put a pot of water on to boil while Cate and Andrew still slept. When Andrew began to fuss a little, Fiona took him from his sleeping mother's arms and rocked him as she walked around preparing the tea. He nodded off back to sleep, and Fiona felt pleased that she could give Cate some rest from caring for her child. The two women had been in the miller's son's cottage for almost a week. Cate's skin no longer looked sallow and Fiona noticed the color had begun to return to her cheeks. The dark smudges under Cate's eyes had all but disappeared.

When Fiona finished brewing the tea, she wrapped Andrew in her brat for extra protection against the early morning chill, and stepped outside the cottage holding the baby in one arm and a thick pottery mug in the other hand. Steam rose from the hot beverage as Fiona watched the sun rise over the distant treetops and color the sky with a breathtaking swirl of red and gold. As the sun rose higher, warm air replaced the cool morning breeze. The day promised to bring unseasonable warmth, so she removed the cloak from around the baby. The smell of fresh green plants mixed with rich moist earth already hung in the morning air. From her vantage point outside the cottage, she watched the River Willow run swiftly toward the miller's wheel. It held Fiona in a peaceful trance for a long time.

When Cate touched her arm to take Andrew, she didn't start. Instead, she just turned and smiled at Cate.

"Thank you for taking him," Cate said. "It was nice to be able to just sleep a little longer and not worry about him." She looked down at the sleeping baby and added, "You're good with him."

Fiona smiled. "I've got brothers with families of their own. I've had lots of practice with their children."

"Well, I am most grateful. It was very good of you."

Fiona's smile broadened.

"How many children do your brothers have?"

"Kynan and his wife have two boys. Bran is five and Eadan is three. My brother Rodick has two children, too. The boy, Dwyn, is four and his daughter was born only this past winter."

For a magical moment, the two women locked onto each

other's eyes and nothing else existed. Time suspended. The cadence of the flowing river filled the spaces around them. They were lost in one another's gaze. Finally, Andrew made a baby grunt, and Cate looked down at him, ending the moment.

"I'll make breakfast this morning," Fiona said. "Today is your day to rest. I see how hard you work for your uncle. He's good to you and Andrew, but he also doesn't stop you from working the way you do. Sometimes you work too hard."

"He's all by himself. He hasn't had any help since his wife died."

"Where's his son? The one who should be living here?"

"I don't know. I don't even remember him, so I guess he's been gone a long time. I suppose that Uncle George can't admit to himself that his son may not be coming back. It makes me feel sad."

Fiona pressed her lips together tightly until they formed a thin line, at a loss to respond to Cate's observation. Finally, she said, "What would you like to do today?"

Cate thought for a few minutes, then she looked longingly at the river and said, "I'd like to bathe. I haven't been able to clean myself up much between taking care of Andrew and Uncle. If you could come down to the river with me and hold Andrew, that's what I'd like to do."

Fiona's heart pounded as she gazed into the gray eyes. The golden flecks within them sparkled in the sunlight as Cate looked up. Fiona's eyes darkened deeply in response. "I'd be happy to take care of the little lad," she said. Cate rewarded her with a beaming response that warmed Fiona down to her toes.

LATER THAT AFTERNOON, Fiona sat on a rock in a small stand of birches cradling Andrew in her arms as he slept contentedly. She could barely make out Cate's form farther down the river, as she hid in a small, rocky outcropping in the riverbed to wash. When Andrew started to fuss, she knew that he probably needed to eat, but she hated to hurry Cate. As if summoned, though, Cate soon appeared, walking toward them with only her smock hanging loosely about her, the rest of her clothes in her hand. The deep red highlights of her long, chestnut hair glistened with moisture in the sun. Fiona tried, unsuccessfully, to suppress a wide grin as Cate came toward her. Her hair hung freely around her shoulders. She wore no shoes and seemed delighted to be walking barefoot in the soft, tender spring grasses that grew by the river. As she came closer, Fiona could see her cheeks flushed pink from the cold river water. She looked contented and happy. Fiona hoped that she was.

"Oh, that felt so good," Cate said as she dropped down on the rock beside Fiona. Andrew fussed again on hearing his mother's voice and she held out her arms to take him. As she cradled him, she untied the tie at the neck of her smock and lifted him to her breast.

Fiona, already having difficulty looking at the beautiful Cate Pritchard, now found herself hardly able to breathe. "You look so...uh, refreshed. I think I'll do the same," Fiona said, and she fairly ran down the length of the river in long strides to the spot where Cate had just bathed.

The cool water soothed the burning in her heart as well as the fire between her legs. She waded out farther into the water than Cate had done and stood neck-high letting the power of the river wash all around her. When she felt that she was in control again and could no longer bear the cold, she dunked her head under the water several times before swimming back to the outcropping.

As she stood up among the rocks, waist high in water now, she looked up to find Cate watching her from her rocky perch. Fiona turned a bright shade of red and plunged back down into the river to her neck again. Cate giggled like a small child. Fiona shivered and shouted, "Cate Pritchard, I left you alone while you bathed. You could at least give me the same consideration. Where are your manners, lass?"

Cate laughed a hearty laugh and called back, "I just wanted to give you the drying cloth." Cradling Andrew in one arm, she waved the cloth with her free hand as if it were a banner. Then she added, a teasing tone in her voice, "Come on. Don't dally. Come out of there."

"Just drop it on the rocks," Fiona shouted. "I'm not coming out until you leave."

"If you insist." Even from a distance, Fiona could see Cate's eyes sparkling with mischief. "But I'll need something of yours to make sure I get Uncle's drying cloth back."

Fiona lifted an eyebrow as she watched Cate bend over and start to rummage though her clothes. When it finally dawned on her what Cate was up to, she growled her warning. "Ca-a-a-te!"

Holding on to Andrew with one arm, Cate ransacked Fiona's clothing with her free hand. As she did, Fiona pushed through the water, no longer giving any thought to her nakedness. Before Fiona could reach the shore, Cate found what she was looking for. With Fiona's leine and vest in hand, she jumped down from the rock and scuttled toward the cottage.

The sound of Cate's laughter lingered in the air all around

Fiona as she climbed out of the water and tried not to think of the tingling sensation that sound elicited from her body. A fat lot of good the cold river water had done. One word from Cate set her heart pounding and her blood rushing. It would take another dip to quell the heat that burned in her breast and between her legs, but she didn't have time for that now.

She dried off quickly and donned her thin undergarment. It came down to the middle of her thighs. In her anxiousness to get to Cate, she didn't tie the tie at the neck, but left the shirt open down to the middle of her chest. She scooped up her boots and belt in one hand and the drying cloth in the other as she stormed off toward the cottage.

Fiona pushed open the door to the little house and found Cate poking at the dying embers in the fireplace. Andrew lay asleep securely in an indentation on a sack of grain, her black vest wrapped around him. Fiona tried to sound masterful, demanding, "Give me back my leine, woman."

Cate turned around to face her. She had put her outer tunic back on over her smock, but it looked oddly deformed. Fiona realized that Cate had stuffed her leine down the front of the smock. Cate batted her eyes and tried to look as innocent as she could. Then she quickly turned away from Fiona. "I have no idea what you're talking about, Fiona Smith."

"Ca-a-a-te..." Fiona warned again.

"What?" Cate said, trying to suppress a smile. "I can't help it if you can't keep track of your clothes." She turned to Fiona, now and looked directly into the azure eyes. They held each other there for a long moment until Cate glanced at Fiona's torso and realized that her under shirt wasn't covering her sufficiently. The round globes of her breasts were clearly visible on either side of the opening in the garment and her nipples protruded through the thin fabric. Cate felt her breathing quicken as she stared.

Fiona focused on the bulge in Cate's dress and tried not to think of her staring at her half-naked body. Her voice was hoarse when she spoke again. "We both know perfectly well where my shirt is. Give it back, you rascal!"

"Call me names all you want. I don't know where you left your clothes. You should take better ca—"

Fiona lunged at Cate without warning, dropping everything. When she reached Cate, she shoved her hand down into her smock. As she did, she touched Cate's full, fleshy breast. Lingering there for an instant, Fiona moaned with the unexpected pleasure. Then, as if stung by a poisonous spider, she pulled her hand out and stared at Cate. Cate's cheeks were still flushed. Her chest heaved.

Fiona's breathing matched Cate's. She swept Cate into her arms
and kissed her roughly on the mouth.

Cate didn't pull away. Instead, she kissed back. As she did, she
reached a hand inside of Fiona's linen garment and placed a warm,
smooth palm over Fiona's breast, pressing into it firmly.

A whimper came from deep within Fiona at the pleasure Cate's
touch brought. Then, she pushed her away and stood, blinking at
Cate, panting, desperate to gain control over her own passions.
Finally, she cried, "Cate, I'm sorry. I shouldn't have —"

Cate held up her hand. Her chest heaved as she pulled Fiona's
shirt from her smock slowly. Holding it out at arm's length, she
said softly, "I shouldn't have taken it." Embarrassed, she stared at
the floor.

Fiona said nothing but took the leine. Turning her back to Cate,
she removed her damp under shirt, letting it drop to the floor.
Drying herself quickly with the retrieved cloth, she put on the light
yellow top and belted it. She turned in time to see Cate pick up
Andrew. She handed Fiona her vest as she walked past and headed
out the door.

FIONA FOUND CATE walking by the river. She stopped a
short distance from her and watched as she picked up a small,
round rock and flung it across the water. Fiona wasn't sure she
knew what to say, but she knew that they had to talk about what
had just happened. Taking several long strides, Fiona stood beside
Cate and looked down into brooding eyes.

"Cate, I'm sorry. I don't know what came over me."

Cate wondered whether she felt sorry or not and concluded
that she did not. But since Fiona apparently felt some remorse for
what had happened, she thought it better not to tell her that.
Instead, she asked, "Why?

"Why?" Fiona repeated. "What do you mean?"

"Why are you sorry?"

"Because I shouldn't have...I...you... Well, I just shouldn't
have."

"That doesn't answer my question, Fiona. Tell me why you're
sorry."

Turning away, Fiona looked out over the water. "I don't know.
I guess because I don't want to force you to do anything you don't
want to, because you probably find such advances from a woman
repulsive. After all, you've lain with a man."

"Yes, I've lain with a man. I can't deny that, can I? But I can tell
you that I found being with a man left me empty and unfulfilled. I

liked Nathaniel Mistlewaite's attentions, but I didn't like what he demanded in return for his interest. I could say that I was sorry I had ever lain with him, but then, I wouldn't have Andrew. Of late, I've come to realize that my son is the only reason I am not sorry for my actions with Nathaniel."

"But," Cate stepped in front of Fiona, "about what happened just now, I am not sorry." Cate turned away and hurried back toward the cottage before Fiona could respond.

Stunned for a moment, Fiona had to run to catch up with her. "Cate, you have enough on your mind right now. I can't add to your problems. I won't. I've promised Catherine that I would help you and Andrew and see you safely back in Willowglen if that's what you want. Once you're there, though, you may still have to deal with those Churchmen and make them see that they have no cause to think you are anything other than an upright woman who made a mistake."

"I did not make a mistake, Fiona." Cate's eyes darkened. "Nathaniel left me little choice. He lied to me, telling me he wanted to marry me and that it would be good to lay together. I'll never forgive him for that lie, but it doesn't matter, because even before I knew I was with child, I knew I didn't want anything more to do with him. He just made it so difficult for me to tell him so. He could be very persuasive. If I had any idea that my predicament would have brought such trouble to my family, I would have..." Tears welled up in Cate's eyes. "I would have used the herbal concoction Catherine taught me about and...and...gotten rid of him."

Silence hung between them as Cate's admission filled the open space around them. Finally, she spoke again. "But I didn't know, and now that I have Andrew, I love him and I want nothing to happen to him. I just want to be left in peace. I haven't done anything wrong. Nathaniel Mistlewaite is just as responsible as I am."

"But no one sees it that way," Fiona sighed. "I know. And I want to help, Cate. But if I act on my feelings for you, it will only complicate the situation. I don't want to be another Nathaniel Mistlewaite. I could never do that to you. All I want to do is help you and Andrew and see you both safe."

Cate sighed in resignation and looked down at the sleeping baby in her arms. "I know," she whispered. "I want to go home, but I'm still afraid. These past days since you came and we've been staying in this cottage have been wonderful. But they can't last. I know that. I just wish this time didn't have to end. I wish we could be here in this place, just the three of us, forever."

Fiona thought it best not to add that she was of the same mind. "Perhaps I should go back to Willowglen to see what's happening there," Fiona said. "If we know what's going on, it might help you to make a decision about when to return. I think you need your family, Cate. Besides, I left my own family thinking that I might only be gone a day or two. I should tell them that there is no need for any concern."

"Yes," Cate whispered. "That might be good to do and I'm sure your family will feel better if they know you have come to no harm. Only, I ask one thing."

"Anything," Fiona said as she gazed into the golden-gray eyes.

"When you go, come back before nightfall."

"Yes. I shall."

The two women stood outside the cottage door for a long time before they decided to enter as they basked in a new understanding of their feelings for one another. That night, as they lay by the fire waiting for sleep to overtake them, both women found themselves still immersed in these same thoughts, struggling with their feelings for one another and wondering what the future held.

THE MILLER HAD returned that same evening from his trip into Willowglen. The next morning, Cate walked the path from the cottage that she shared with Fiona to prepare his meals for him. When she went now, though, she left Andrew with Fiona and each day when Cate returned, Fiona took her place and worked beside the old man at the mill or tended his little garden beside his house.

After George's visit to Willowglen, Fiona and Cate pressed him for news of what was happening in the town. All he could tell them, however, was that the priests were still there. They had stopped asking Will about Cate and her child, he had said, and Will hoped they had forgotten about her.

For the next few days, Cate and Fiona spent their evenings in quiet companionship. Neither woman spoke again of what had happened between them the day the miller delivered his grain to Willowglen, but there was an undercurrent of strain between them that hadn't been there in the past. Fiona accepted it as something she must endure for Cate's sake, because she understood now that she truly loved this woman.

EACH DAY THAT passed saw Fiona struggle to reach a decision about returning to Willowglen to let her family know that she had not come to any harm. Finally, her desire to test the mood in the town for herself helped make the decision. As Fiona mounted Brilley and set off, Cate stood in the cottage doorway watching her go, with a forlorn look on her face.

FIONA TOOK THE shorter route back to Willowglen, entering the town by St. Stephen's Gate. She stopped at the Grouse and Pheasant to ask after Mistress Catherine Hawkins and was told that Mistress Hawkins had left earlier in the day. The proprietor didn't know her destination, so Fiona made her way to her grandfather's house to be greeted with enthusiasm by her entire family.

She apologized for her absence and explained that she was on an urgent errand for a friend. She asked to be excused from the family gathering for a while longer so that she could attend to her obligation. Her mother's probing looks did not escape Fiona's attention, but she said nothing more about her undertaking. Her father informed her that they would only stay in Willowglen a few more Sundays. He asked her to return in enough time so that she could travel with them to Glenculley. Since she felt that she could do nothing else for the moment, she agreed that she would try her best.

Once again at the Grouse and Pheasant, Fiona ordered a flagon of mead and took her place at a table in a quiet corner of the Inn. Since it was early in the day, the place was almost empty and she was glad of the quiet. After the serving girl delivered her beverage, Fiona poured the liquid into the cup she wore tied to her waist and drank it empty. She poured herself a second cup and removed the leather folder from her pack. She sat writing on the handmade pages until Catherine came in.

Seeing the young Scot sitting in the corner, Catherine approached her. She kept the conversation light, finally asking if Fiona had been successful in her endeavor. Fiona nodded and Catherine breathed a sigh of relief.

"I've only come to tell my family that I am well and that I have an errand to perform for a friend. They did not ask what the nature of the task was or where I went to do it. I am grateful that they are not prone to probing my actions too keenly. The friend that I am with..." Fiona gave Catherine a knowing look and Catherine nodded her understanding. "has asked me to return before nightfall. So I must be on my way soon."

"I see."

"How are things here?"

"Little has changed since you left." Catherine looked around and saw that everyone had left the hall except the two of them. When she spoke again, she whispered. "The Churchmen have hounded Will, asking where his daughter is."

The look on Fiona's face betrayed her disbelief. "My friend's uncle said they no longer asked. That it seemed that they had forgotten about her."

"Yes, Sarah told me of the visit they had from an old friend.

She told me that Will told him that so that he wouldn't worry, or carry his worry home, for that matter."

"I see," Fiona said. "So what has Master Pritchard told the priests, then?"

"He has told them that she ran away and that he has no idea where she has gone. They seem to have taken her actions as just another of his daughter's willful measures, but they pester him almost every day wanting to know if she has returned. There is talk of sending out the constable's men to search for her. I'm not sure this would be a good thing, Fiona. I am troubled. If my idea was, indeed, successful, then perhaps our friend should come back and prove to these men that there is no mark on the child and stop this madness once and for all."

Fiona nodded and answered in low tones, matching Catherine's. "Our friend has begun to think that she would like to return for that very reason. She is still afraid, though. I will see what I can do to help her make a decision." Fiona looked deeply into Catherine's eyes as a new thought came to her. "Of course, if she decides not to return, I could always suggest that she travel to Glenculley with my family and me."

"Knowing our friend, I think that it might be difficult for her to be away from her family."

Again, Fiona held Catherine's gaze. "Families are sometimes made by circumstance rather than by birth."

"Very true." Catherine checked the hall again and found that they were still alone. "I think it wise to let our friend make her own decision. Don't you?"

A nod, then Fiona drained her cup and tied it at her waist again. She gathered up her papers and pushed them into the leather folder, which she stuffed into her bag. As she tossed the bag over her shoulder, Fiona said loud enough for anyone listening to hear, "It has been good to see you Mistress Catherine. I'm glad to hear that you are enjoying your stay in Willowglen. I must be off. I hope I will see you again." With that, Catherine watched Fiona stride out of the Grouse and Pheasant. When she disappeared from view, Catherine decided that she would do well to go to see her friends, Sarah and Will Pritchard.

THAT EVENING, WHEN Cate heard that not much had changed in Willowglen and that the Churchmen still pressed her father, she thought about returning. The ink treatment on Andrew's hair had held up well. They would need to do another before they left because the hair closest to his scalp showed white again as it grew, but Cate felt confident that another application of the ink mixture would last long enough to present her and her son to the Churchmen to show them that he had no mark that they could use as an accusation. She was torn between wanting the nightmare to be over and her desire to make the peaceful, tranquil days with Fiona last forever.

ANOTHER FEW DAYS passed before Cate finally made the decision to return to Willowglen. The evening before their departure, Cate and Fiona took the lamp black out and coated Andrew's hair with it again, making sure to cover any white hair. Their own preparations to return to town were easily finished afterward.

The next morning, just before sunrise, Cate and Fiona stood by the river. In the gray of early morning, the fragile lilies-of-the-valley and violets were only visible as delicate shadows.

Fiona sighed. "I find it difficult to leave this tranquil place."

"I know what you mean. If it weren't for the possibility of being discovered, I wouldn't want to leave myself. Especially with you here with us." Cate looked down at Andrew so as not to meet Fiona's gaze. "But I do want to get it over with."

"Yes, well, we should make a start. If we can get you home before the town stirs, it will cause fewer questions and less gossip."

Cate wondered if, once they reached Willowglen, she would ever see Fiona Smith again. The young Scot had maintained a distance between them since the day Cate had run off with her clothes. It saddened her to think of the bond that had grown between them coming to an end. She plucked up her courage and asked, "Do you not want to be seen with me, then?"

Fiona raised her eyebrows at the question. "No, not at all. It's you that I am concerned about." *You are all that I care about.* Her look radiated with love and compassion. "We'll take our time, then. Let's have a good morning meal, and then we'll go. Shall we?"

Cate smiled, and Fiona felt the now familiar weakness in her legs at that disarming look.

Chapter
Eleven

CATHERINE LEARNED OF Cate's return just as the sun had begun to touch the rooftops of the town on its way toward the west. She met Fiona in the Market Square and Fiona informed her that she had deposited Cate and Andrew with Cate's parents, assuring Catherine that both of them were well and safe.

"And our plan has remained..."

Fiona smiled. "Successful."

Catherine breathed a sigh of relief. "I'll be off then. I'd like to see Cate and meet this little man."

"Yes, you go ahead. If you'll excuse me, I'll make my way to the Grouse and Pheasant. I was just on my way there since I haven't had anything to eat since early this morning, and I'm ready for a good meal."

"Oh, Fiona. My manners. Please, let me take you there. You must be my guest."

"No, no, Catherine. You go and see Cate. I'll make my own way."

"I'll agree to that on one condition. I'll go and visit with the Pritchards for just a brief time. Will and Sarah will want to spend time with Cate and their grandson. I won't be long, then I'll catch up with you at the Inn and you will be my guest. That is, if you'd like the company. I shouldn't presume."

"I shall be glad of your company, Catherine. I can tell you all that has happened." Fiona gave Catherine a look that implied that she had confidences to share.

The two women parted. Fiona headed down Market Street leading Brilley. Catherine made her way across the Market Square toward Bookbinders Row, excited to see Cate and meet Andrew for the first time.

Fiona bedded Brilley for the night and found a table in a quiet corner of the Inn's main hall. She requested the serving girl bring food and mead for two. She gulped down the mead and had poured a second cup when Catherine entered the hall. Fiona stood in greeting and told her that she had ordered food and drink for her. Catherine thanked her, noting again Fiona's borderland attire, the striking deep blue cloak that she wore with the subtle yellow tunic brought out the blue of Fiona's eyes. Catherine admired the beautiful embroidery on both the tunic and the vest she wore. The sleeves of her linen tunic hugged her muscular arms.

Fiona stepped around the table, helped Catherine remove her traveling cloak, and hung it on a hook on the wall nearby. Catherine couldn't help but appreciate the dark-haired young woman. As Fiona returned from hanging her cloak, Catherine marveled at her long legs and her tall, strong form. Fiona gestured for Catherine to join her and she poured a drink into the cup that Catherine offered.

Leaning across the table, Catherine looked into Fiona's eyes and whispered, "Tell me all about your time with Cate. She would not say much to me about it." When Fiona's mouth widened into a broad smile and she said nothing, Catherine decided to try a different approach. "You said everything went well, earlier. How can I ever repay you?"

"No need, I've had ample repayment." Fiona's cheeks reddened.

Catherine wanted to ask what she meant, but the serving girl appeared with a bowl of spiced parsnips, yams and onions and a small leg of mutton. She lifted the lid of the flagon and glanced inside, noting that it was not yet empty before moving away from the table.

Almost in a whisper, Fiona told Catherine about her encounter with the miller, and how he finally acquiesced, letting her see Cate, and how together they had applied the ink mixture to the baby's hair. They had done the procedure twice—when she first arrived and again just before returning to Willowglen. She noticed Catherine glancing at her hands and said, "I was careful."

Fiona then told her about her time spent with Cate in the granary and later in the miller's son's cottage.

Catherine smiled and nodded. "George's son died many years ago. He has not been able to admit it to himself for all this time. He has always talked as if he were coming back from some great adventure any day now, but of course it will never happen."

"It is truly sad," remarked Fiona. "But I must say that I'm glad the cottage was there. It made our stay a little more pleasant and gave Cate a respite from the duties the miller imposed on her. Of course, I tried to help where I could, but he had grown used to Cate in the short time she was there and expected quite a bit from her."

She thought she would say nothing about her feelings for Cate, but when she was done with her narration, she held Catherine's gaze for a long while without speaking.

Finally, Catherine said, "Is there something else, Fiona?"

Fiona's chest heaved as she drew in a deep breath. "I wonder if you could tell me something about Cate Pritchard?"

Catherine surveyed the young Scot for a while before she responded. "You just spent more than two weeks with her. Surely you've learned something about my goddaughter in that time. Still, what would you like to know?"

"This troubadour, the father of her child, was he the first man she had...interest in?"

As Catherine looked into Fiona's eyes, she hoped to decipher what it was that was in her heart that prompted the question. Unsure of how to answer, Catherine said, "He is the first that I've heard about. But as you have come to know, it was all for naught, anyway. From what Sarah has told me, I'm sure he's gone for good. Evidently, he was for pleasure, but not for responsibility. Why do you ask?"

"I...well..." Fiona took a long sip of mead, then, stared into the cup in front of her on the rough-hewn table. She ran her long, sturdy finger around the rim slowly several times, and then looked up at the ceiling.

"Fiona?" Catherine was surprised to see tears in her eyes. She reached out for the hand trembling on the rim of the cup. "What is it?"

Fiona looked squarely at Catherine and blinked. "She's a beautiful woman."

"Oh. I see," Catherine whispered.

The two women ate in silence after that. Fiona mostly pushed bits of orange and yellow around on her trencher, the platter from which they had served themselves still mounded with food. The women looked up from their meal at a loud bang when the door to the Grouse and Pheasant hit the wall with force. Hubert of Middleton stepped over the threshold and looked around the room.

As soon as Hubert spied Catherine in the corner, he gestured to someone outside and Lydia stepped through the doorway wearing a worn purple hooded cloak. Catherine almost spilled the contents of her cup when she saw her. Without explanation to Fiona, she sprang from her seat and ran to Lydia, embracing her as she whispered in her ear, "What are you doing here, love? You weren't supposed to come until I told you it was safe."

"I had to come," Lydia answered with a tremor in her voice. "Something peculiar has happened. I had to make sure you were not in danger."

Catherine held Lydia at arm's length and smiled, genuinely glad to see her. "I'm fine, as you can see." Then, looking over at

Hubert, Catherine said, "Thank you for escorting Lydia here, Hubert. Tell the innkeeper that you will stay the night, and inform him that Lady Lydia will stay with me."

Hubert bowed grim-faced, and went to find the proprietor of the Grouse and Pheasant.

"Come," Catherine said. "I want you to meet someone. Then I'll tell you all about what's been happening here and you can tell me your news."

As Catherine escorted Lydia to the table where her friend sat, Fiona turned to the couple. Fiona met Lydia's gaze. Catherine couldn't tell what passed between them, but it didn't feel comfortable. She cleared her throat. "Lady Lydia Wellington, I'd like you to meet Fiona Smith of Glenculley. Fiona is the daughter of a childhood friend of mine, Duncan Smith, John the silversmith's older brother."

Lydia nodded. Her cool retort sounded as if she were snapping a lid shut on her feelings. "Mistress Smith."

Catherine looked at Lydia with raised eyebrows. She had never seen her behave thus. She wondered what was going on, but thought that this was not the time to discuss it. Instead, Catherine said, "Sit with us, Lydia. We have plenty of food. If it's not to your liking, then I'll have them bring something else."

She caught the serving girl's eye and beckoned her to the table, telling her that they would need more mead to drink and another trencher.

"I'm not hungry, Catherine. I'll just go upstairs."

Fiona stood suddenly, towering over Lydia. She looked back and forth from one woman to the other and said, "I really should let my family know that I'm back. Thank you for the meal, Catherine. I do appreciate it." She glanced at Catherine, knowingly as she added, "...and for the conversation."

She lifted her cup, drank it to the dregs, whipped it beside her to clean any last drops from it, and walked directly out of the Grouse and Pheasant without even hooking the cup onto her belt.

"What was that about?" Catherine said.

"Perhaps she felt it was too crowded in here," Lydia chided.

Catherine looked around at the quite empty room, puzzled. When she looked back at Lydia, she saw fire in the gray-green eyes, and thought she finally understood.

"Lydia, you are not jealous, are you? Of Fiona? Of me?" Lydia's pained look told her she was right. Lydia stood to leave. "Love, this is absurd. Sit down, please. Let's talk." Catherine pleaded. "I need to tell you what's been going on."

Tears welled up in Lydia's eyes. She blinked them away. "I'm tired. I need to rest. The journey was long."

"Please, Lydia. You need to eat; then you can rest. This won't take long. We need to talk."

Lydia sighed. It would be no use arguing. She was tired, but she was hungry, too, although she would not admit it just moments before.

"All right, Catherine. Have it your way." She sat in the seat that Fiona had previously occupied. The serving girl appeared with a flagon in her hand. Lydia lifted her drinking cup from her belt and held it out to the girl, watching the amber liquid stream into the vessel. As the girl walked away, she sighed again and looked coldly into Catherine's eyes.

Catherine had never seen Lydia look that way before and she shivered in response. Catherine chose her words carefully as she began to speak.

THE FIRE IN the fireplace in the hall of the Grouse and Pheasant was nothing but dying embers as Catherine and Lydia continued to talk softly. The mutton leg had been stripped clean. Only a few remnants of the roasted vegetables remained, clinging to the platter like withered leaves. During the course of the evening, the hall had filled with people crowding in to enjoy a meal, some mead or ale and a good time. The noise had built to a crescendo and died down again as the crowd thinned. During that time, Catherine told Lydia everything that had happened, from the birth of Cate's child to learning that Cate and her son had been the object of the Spanish priests' attention. She told her that Will had sent Cate from Willowglen a little more than two weeks earlier, just as Catherine was leaving Briarcrest, in an effort to protect his daughter and her son. She told Lydia about meeting Duncan and his family and enlisting Fiona's help.

Shyly, Lydia said, "When I saw her here with you, I didn't know what to think. More than a fortnight without word and the probing that Alfred experienced by this peculiar monk had me very upset." Her eyes wandered to the doorway of the Inn before looking down at the mutton bone. "She's very beautiful, this Fiona."

"But surely you didn't think..." Catherine's eyes widened. "Lydia, look at me." Lydia slowly raised her head and met Catherine's eyes. "You didn't think..." Catherine sputtered. "that she—and I? Oh, Lydia." She lowered her voice and leaned across the table until Lydia could feel her breath on her cheeks. "I could never do such a thing. You are all I have ever wanted, you and only you, are my heart's desire. Please, tell me that you believe me, Lydia. I could not bear it if you thought otherwise."

A small sob escaped from Lydia.

Catherine noted that Lydia's once bright auburn hair had dulled a little with the gray that now threaded through the strands here and there, but she was still beautiful, and she was still the love of Catherine's life. Catherine knew it. Now she must make Lydia believe it was still true.

She whispered softly, "Lydia, she's a child, and she's in love with Cate. Fiona, like Cate, has become like a daughter to me." She tried to convey the sincerity she felt as she continued. "There is nothing to be concerned about, Lydia. It is you, and only you, that I love."

Lydia looked deeply into Catherine's eyes. She knew that everything she had just been told was true and straight from Catherine's heart, that there was no reason for her to worry about losing Catherine. They were meant to be together. Always. It was ever so and nothing had changed. Her racing heart slowed to a more normal cadence. She knew, now, with certainty that Fiona was exactly what Catherine said she was—a friend, a daughter. "I'm sorry, Catherine," she said, her voice trembling. Tears moistened her eyes. "I don't know what came over me. I was sick with worry after not hearing from you and then, when I saw her...I don't know what happened."

"Let's not dwell on it. As long as you understand now, that's all that matters. Fiona is a strong woman. That she is has served us well. She is a true friend. We should see to it that she remains a friend, but we won't concern ourselves with that until tomorrow."

"I agree, and I promise, I'll make it up to her as soon as I see her."

Lydia's eyes danced as she spoke next. "What about Cate? Do you think that she might have feelings for Fiona?"

"I have no idea, but I think we have other things to worry about right now. We still need to make sure those priests are satisfied that the rumor of Andrew's birthmark was untrue and there is nothing for them to bother with here." A look of concern crossed Catherine's face. "But you are tired and so am I. Let's go to bed."

The women climbed the stairs to the upper floor of the Grouse and Pheasant and Catherine opened the heavy curtain to the tiny room where she had been staying. The bed was small. They would need to sleep very close together. Catherine smiled as she drew the curtain.

Chapter
Twelve

THE NEXT MORNING, when Catherine and Lydia emerged from their small room and stepped down the narrow stone staircase leading to the main hall of the Grouse and Pheasant, they saw a familiar form at one of the tables in a quiet corner. Fiona sat hunched over, with a pot of cassia tea in front of her.

As the two women approached, they could see that she was scribbling something. At her left elbow, a stack of crudely bound papers stuck out of a worn leather binding. The page she worked on was half-filled with script that bordered a little sketch of a granary complete with waterwheel. Her small bottle of ink sat poised above the page and she held a short quill balanced gracefully between thumb and fingers.

"Good morning, Fiona." Catherine spoke first.

Fiona lifted her head and pulled the bound sheets over to cover the page of new writing. Her eyes moved from Catherine to Lydia and, as she gave the smaller woman a wary look, her neck muscles tightened visibly.

Lydia smiled tentatively before she spoke. "Good morning, Fiona. I do hope you will forgive my rudeness last night. I'm afraid I was too tired and out of sorts to allow my usual graciousness to shine."

Fiona's left eyebrow rose slightly. Then she brightened and her mouth curled into a smile. "Do not trouble yourself, Lady Lydia. It is understandable. I hold no grudge. I only want to be your friend." Then with emphasis, she added, "As I am friend to Catherine, which I hope she has already explained. Please, sit down." She gestured with her quill to the bench opposite her.

"And a good friend you've been, too, I hear." Lydia sat down and looked her in the eye. "I must add my gratitude to Catherine's." She looked up at Catherine and smiled an endearing smile. Catherine returned a look full of relief and took her place beside Lydia.

"Will you join me in breaking your fast?"

"Thank you, but no, we don't have the time," Catherine replied. "We're on our way to the Pritchards. Lydia is anxious to get there to see Cate and to meet little Andrew. He is such a dear. We only stopped to greet you when we saw you sitting here." She glanced at Fiona's papers. "Working on your writings, I see."

Fiona's cheeks reddened a little. "Yes. Much has happened in these past weeks and I have not had much chance till now to write it all down in any detail."

"That reminds me," Catherine said, "I did talk to Will about printing your work. I had forgotten."

Fiona looked eager. "What did he say?"

Catherine shook her head. As she did, she saw a visible slump in Fiona's shoulders. "He's too afraid right now. Concern for his family clouds his judgment. When the priests came asking about his print shop and his books that was bad enough, but when they came asking about Cate and her child... Well, he's just being cautious. Perhaps when all this is over, he may be more willing."

"I don't know how much time I have. My father talks of needing to start for home soon. Our cousins are caring for the land and our livestock, but father is eager to get back. My brothers, too, grow restless with not much to occupy their time, although my elder brothers' wives seem content enough. No doubt Willowglen, with its fine markets and wares, has been occupying a great deal of their time." Fiona grinned. "But then again, that may well be my brothers' reason for wanting to leave soon. They may fear that all their silver will soon be spent if they don't cart their wives back to Glenculley soon."

Catherine and Lydia laughed. Then Catherine asked, "Will you go with them?"

Fiona's eyes seemed to deepen as she met Catherine's. Her voice cracked when she answered. "I—I don't know."

"Do you...want me to talk to Cate?" Catherine asked.

"No!" Panic filled Fiona's widened eyes. She looked away from Catherine. "I mean...I don't know. I don't think she..." When Fiona looked back at Catherine, her eyes were full of pain. "Do you think she..." She looked down at her hands.

The silence thickened as time passed. Then, Lydia spoke. "I have something to say, if you'll allow me, Fiona." Fiona nodded and Lydia continued. "When Catherine and I..." She glanced at Catherine, hoping for some acknowledgement of what she was about to convey as well as a willingness to allow her to continue. Catherine understood and nodded. "When Catherine and I discovered that we cared for each other, we didn't let on about our true feelings for one another for a long time. This led, shall we say, to unnecessary complications. It made for many unhappy hours for us both. From this, we learned that it is important to speak our minds to one another."

Catherine squeezed Lydia's hand under the table and added, "Like last night."

Lydia met her lover's eyes. "Like last night," she said before looking back at Fiona.

"Express your feelings sooner rather than later, Fiona. Think of the worst thing that can happen if you do. What will it be? That you don't gain Cate's favor? You already lack that as far as you know. But if you tell her of your feelings, you may be surprised at what you hear from her in return. I don't claim to know what she may answer. I don't think Catherine has any idea herself." Catherine nodded her agreement. "You are the one who needs Cate's answer. You'll never have it, unless you speak to her in all honesty."

Fiona stared at the quill in her hand as she twisted it between her fingers. "You're right, Lydia, of course. I shall go to Cate. Perhaps I shall even stay in Willowglen for a time. Perhaps we just need more time. Then I shall ask her the question that burns in my heart. I admit that I am afraid of what her answer might be, but then, as you say, I know nothing of her true feelings now anyway."

Fiona's resolve would have to wait, however, for at that moment, Will Pritchard burst into the Grouse and Pheasant looking as if he had seen a ghost.

WILL PRITCHARD'S EYES were wild, his hair disheveled. His cap sat askew on his head. An edge of his shirt was tucked into the waist of his leggings. Catherine looked down at his feet to see that he only wore one shoe and wrinkled her brow in dismay. In his hand, Will clutched the other shoe like a strangled rat. His chest heaved in an effort to catch his breath.

Catherine couldn't tell whether his panting was from running all the way from Bookbinders Row or if some terror that he had witnessed had caused it. She shuddered. *Perhaps it's both.*

Will surveyed the hall frantically, searching for someone. His gaze came to rest in the corner where Catherine and her companions sat. Recognition dawned across his pale face and he stumbled over to the table and stood, trying to catch his breath. The women could see him trembling.

Catherine stood up as Will approached. "Will, what's wrong?"

"Cate," he panted. "They've taken Cate." His eyes were wide with fear.

Fiona jumped to her feet, towering over Will. Gathering up her papers and writing instruments, she stuffed them in her sack. "Where have they taken her?" she growled.

Will, befuddled by this large stranger, blinked up at her. "Who — who are you?"

Catherine came to his rescue. "Will, this is Fiona, Duncan Smith's daughter. She is a friend. She's the one who brought Cate and Andrew back."

"Why?" Will bit his lip as tears welled up in his eyes. He put out a hand to steady himself against the table. "Why did you do it?" he whimpered. "Why didn't you leave her where she was?"

"Will," Catherine cried. "Please, Fiona did nothing wrong. Cate made the decision to come home. Fiona was only trying to help."

Will's eyes grew dark and brooding as he looked up at Fiona. He spat out his next words. "Well, you didn't help at all. You only made things worse. Now the constable's men have dragged her off before those priests. As soon as they found out that she was back, they were on her like a pack of hungry wolves. Someone wasted no time getting the word to them. Her mother is beside herself with worry and grief." He turned to Catherine. With an angry edge to his voice, he whispered, "And I am afraid for Cate's life."

Catherine held his gaze for a long time. "If anyone is responsible for Cate's return, I am, not Fiona."

"Wh — what?" Will cried. "What do you mean?"

"I enlisted Fiona's help to bring Cate back to Willowglen should she choose to come. Don't you see, Will? You couldn't hide her forever. If they wanted her, they could have easily found her. I brought her back so that we could prove this rumor of birthmarks and dealings with the devil were all lies, once and for all."

Will looked from one woman to the next, puzzled. Catherine's words made no sense to him. *Why had Cate returned and put herself and her son in danger? What was Catherine babbling about rumors and lies about birthmarks? It was the truth. The boy had a shock of white hair that was the cause of all this trouble — that and his mother's indiscretion that had brought him into the world in the first place.* He turned to Catherine, pleading in his eyes. He could only whisper. "It is not a rumor, Catherine."

Catherine smiled knowingly. "Have you looked at the child's hair since he's returned home?"

Will frowned as he shook his head.

"Trust me, Will. It is a rumor...and a lie."

His brows tightened even more in his growing confusion. "But I saw it."

"Birthmarks disappear all the time, Will," Catherine explained gently. "Children come into this world with blotches and all manner of marks on their little bodies and, in days, they are gone."

Fiona could stand it no longer. She interrupted, repeating her demand. "Where have they taken her? Where have they taken Cate?"

Will's shoulders sagged, his face, tired and drawn. "They took her to the Governor's Hall."

"And Andrew?" Catherine asked.

"They insisted that they wanted Cate first. They said they'd deal with the child later. They ripped him from Cate's arms and insisted that Sarah take him. Poor Cate was mad with anguish. They dragged her off. Sarah wanted to go with her, but she thought that if she stayed she could keep Andrew safe for a little while longer. Sarah is so distraught, Catherine. I came looking for you in the hopes that you could do something."

The pleading in Will's eyes caused Catherine's heart to ache. Fear and dread for Cate and Andrew pushed their way toward the surface of her emotions. Fiona, unable to wait any longer, turned and strode toward the door without another word.

Catherine looked at Lydia and said, "One of us should go to Sarah."

"I'll go," Lydia said. "You go with Will and Fiona. Send word about what's happening as soon as you can. I'll try to calm Sarah."

Catherine nodded, gratitude and relief evident on her face. Then she turned Will around and pushed him to a bench. "Will, put your shoe on, for goodness sake." She pulled his tunic out of his leggings and fixed his hat on his head. When he had donned his shoe, she urged him toward the door of the Inn so that they could catch up to Fiona.

As they hurried down Market Street, Will turned to Catherine and said, "Thank you. I'll not forget your help." Looking to Fiona, who took long strides in front of him, he added, "All of you."

"Never mind about that now, Will. The important thing is that we help Cate."

Chapter
Thirteen

BROTHER IAGO KNOCKED on the doorframe of Father Gaspar's room located along a dark corridor of the Governor's Hall.

The response was more of a snarl than a question. "Who is it?"

Iago could barely contain his excitement, and failed to notice Gaspar's tone. "It's Brother Iago, Father. I have news."

He heard shuffling, followed by the sound of something bumping against the wall. Finally, the thick tapestry covering the opening moved the width of a man's hand revealing Gaspar's long hooked nose. The priest looked tired and forlorn. Dark circles hung beneath his eyes.

"Father, what is it? Are you ill?" Iago asked.

Gaspar swatted at the air in front of him and shook his head. "No, not ill. Only sick at heart." His chest heaved in a sigh.

Alarm spread through Iago, the heat of it searing in his chest as if he had just taken a strong drink. He recognized the signs of Gaspar's melancholy for he had seen them before. It had not happened since they had left Spain. He thought that the new surroundings had served to ward off the oppressive demons from which Gaspar suffered. Now, his mind screamed out. *No, not now. Not when things are finally starting to go our way.* But he was careful. He knew that he had to choose his words with care or the old man could easily bolt.

Gaspar watched Iago staring at him through the small opening. He whispered, "I have no joy, Iago. No elation. I have lost my faith again, little brother."

Iago's insincere smile was meant to sustain the priest, to portray what he hoped would be viewed as his genuine concern for the man. It was far from what he actually felt. "It will pass, Father. It always does. These trials are meant to make your faith stronger." Even as he spoke, he felt a surge of excitement at the girl's return. He licked his lips and wondered if he should tell Gaspar about it. He decided to take a chance. "I have good news, Gaspar."

Again, the old priest waved his hand in front of his face. "I cannot abide it now, Iago. I must rest. My legs are leaden. I am very weary. I have no vigor at all."

Gaspar let the curtain drop. Now only one of his eyes was visible through the opening. Desperation drove the next words from Iago's mouth.

"Father, we will go to the chapel and pray. Later, when everything is quiet." He saw Gaspar's eye widen just a little.

Relief washed over the monk. "But for now, my news. They have found the printer's contemptible daughter."

Interest sparked in Gaspar's dark eye. He made no reply for a long time. Finally, the curtain opened a little again and he spoke. "Where did they find her?"

"She returned to her parents at nightfall yesterday. I have had the constable's men bring her here. We should question her as soon as possible."

Gaspar sighed again. "I cannot. It will have to wait a little, Iago. I am not myself." The curtain began to close.

"No!" Iago caught himself. "I mean, you must not let this trial overcome you, Father. God will help you. *I* will help you. Delay could mean problems with the chief constable. It is said that he is a friend to the printer. We should question the girl now, while Godling is out of town. His men do not dare defy us."

After a long silence, Gaspar replied, his tired voice trembling. "You think this is best?"

The monk nodded, trying not to look too eager.

"I will need your help, Iago. You know that when I start to lose my faith, I am unable to counter during the questioning as I should in these types of matters."

Iago nodded, realizing for the first time that Gaspar's dilemma could have advantages for him. He would be allowed to make more of a contribution to the trial and questioning. He ran his tongue over his fleshy lips. "Perhaps we should go *now*," Iago suggested.

"Do you think so, little brother? I don't know. I am so tired."

"Father, the constable is returning soon. He said he had business with the sheriff again, but they were going to meet at that inn only a day's ride from here. He could be back tomorrow for all we know. We must use this time to our advantage. We have the girl. We must act."

Gaspar's thin chest rose again as he drew in a tired breath. "Give me a moment. I shall meet you in the main hall. We will use it for an inquiry room."

As Iago made his way across the main hall, he couldn't help but laud himself. Now, it would finally begin. His waiting was over. This was the first step of his plan. His patience had paid off.

He would succeed. He pulled his cowl over his head more and his face disappeared into the black shadows, his wicked smile not visible to anyone he might encounter.

THE PRIEST SAT at a long table raised on a dais. Several tall, narrow windows framed him on either side. Behind him stood the Dark Monk, seemingly made even more shadowy than usual by the morning light streaming through the window. Lines and furrows tracked from the tall priest's nose to his taut, thin lips suggesting that something was wrong. He narrowed his small, black eyes as if trying to stare through the woman standing before him, believing he could look into her very soul.

Cate stood in the middle of the room, her hands clenched in front of her, her knuckles turning white, her shoulders slumped.

Gaspar stared at her, saying nothing, until his concentration was broken by a commotion that erupted at the entrance to the hall. Outside, one of the constable's men raised his voice. From among a group of people that had just arrived, a man shouted loudly that he would, indeed, enter the chamber. Someone else, a softer voice, a woman's voice, said something that could not be recognized. After more grumbling, three people entered the room.

Will ran in first. He tried to approach Cate, but another of the constable's men stepped in front of him before he could get there. He was gestured toward the perimeter of the room. He staggered toward the wall and leaned against it to keep from collapsing. Catherine and Fiona followed him. They took up their places beside Will. As they stood waiting, Catherine looked up at Fiona and saw her jaw pulsing with anger at the sight of Cate slumped before the thin priest.

Gaspar looked away from Cate and his eyes came to rest on Fiona. He looked down at her with contempt.

A local cleric sat off to the side of the room with a large book in front of him, a quill and inkpot at the ready to record the proceedings. Pressed into service because he was literate and would be able to take the account of what was about to take place, his face betrayed no emotion. He knew the Pritchard family well.

Gaspar now peered down his nose at Cate and said in a thin, nasally voice, "State your name, girl."

Cate looked up, hesitant. Then she pulled herself up to her full height and said, "I am Catherine Lydia Pritchard, daughter of Will Pritchard, the book printer of Willowglen. I am called Mistress Cate by most."

Trying to quell his anger at the girl's insolent tone, Gaspar took a deep breath before continuing. "We have been waiting to ask you some questions, Mistress Pritchard. Where have you been?"

Cate stifled a shudder. She knew that she mustn't reveal who had given her shelter during her absence, for the miller would be in great peril for doing so. If they hauled him before these priests it might come out that he didn't follow the way of the Church, but rather the old religion that worshipped the goddess and looked to nature for signs and portents. No, she would not mention the miller. He must be repaid for his kindness, for offering Cate and her son some measure of protection while she was gone from Willowglen. She said, hesitantly, "I have been alone in the countryside." As she spoke, another thought struck her and she added quickly, "I was alone...in — in prayer."

"Prayer, you say?" Gaspar squinted one eye in disbelief. "How is it that a woman who has befriended the devil himself goes off to spend time in prayer? Do you want us to believe you have repented of your sins?"

Knowing she couldn't say that she had no sin to repent, she tried a different defense. "I have had nothing to do with the devil, sir," Cate said, sticking out her chin. "I have done nothing wrong."

Gaspar's pale face colored. Cate trembled as she saw his anger rise. Gaspar seethed, "Do you deny that you bore a child without the benefit of the Church's blessing on your union with the child's father?"

The mention of Nathaniel Mistlewaite caused the hair to stand up on the back of Cate's neck. Why wasn't he here to defend what had happened between them? Why wasn't he here to defend her and his son? "Apparently, my child's father didn't care for the Church's blessing, or for us, as much as I thought he did."

"You admit, then, that the child's father is faithless." It was not a question.

"I know nothing of his views of the Church, sir. We never spoke of them. I only know that he did not want to remain with us as soon as he heard that I was with child."

"So, what *do* you know of the child's father, Mistress?"

Cate took a deep breath and, although anyone who knew her well could tell that she was nervous, she spoke clearly. "That he was a wandering minstrel, a bard who travels the land singing songs and telling stories to those who will listen and give him food and shelter in return."

"Where is this minstrel from?" the priest asked.

"He made his way to Willowglen from London, so he said, sir."

"Do you know his family?"

"No sir. I know nothing of his family. He did not speak of them."

"So, you are to have us believe that you knew nothing of this man, neither his views of the Church nor his faith, to say nothing of his family or his origins, yet you consented to lay with him and came to bear his child?"

Cate flushed with embarrassment. She lowered her eyes and answered softly, "Yes, sir."

The Dark Monk stepped forward from his position behind Gaspar. His hands were hidden inside his voluminous sleeves. As he leaned toward the priest, it looked as if his hood would swallow half of Gaspar's head. Catherine shifted her position, hoping to hear their exchange, but even as she strained, she realized that they were too far away to hear anything they said.

When the monk pulled away, Gaspar said, "Do you deny that you have lain with the devil himself who planted his seed within you?"

Cate straightened visibly and said with certainly, "I do deny it." The room, which had filled with other people during the questioning, buzzed at Cate's assertion. When the murmuring died down, Cate added, "Nathaniel Mistlewaite is a lot of things, many of which I would not dare to call him in your honorable presence, but he is not the devil." The murmuring started up again, but Gaspar quelled it with a look.

"How can you assert this? Do you know the devil, girl?

Cate's shoulders sagged again. "N—no. I've never had anything to do with the devil."

"How can you be so sure?" Gaspar sneered. "The evil one comes in many guises. Perhaps he has come in the guise of this bard called Mistlewaite."

Cate answered, trying to keep the angry edge from her voice. "My child is not the child of the devil. He's good and pure and sweet. Nathaniel Mistlewaite did us hurt by running out on us, but he is nothing but a churl and a mucker of a man."

Gaspar's brow contorted. He seemed hesitant. Iago sensed his uncertainty and stepped forward. He leaned toward Gaspar and spoke in a low, rumbling voice. Then, he stepped back into the shadows once again.

The monk's words seemed to put Gaspar back on course. The questioning continued long into the afternoon. Questions were repeated over and over and presented from several different approaches. As the proceedings progressed, everyone felt the burden of fatigue, most of all Cate, standing under the scrutiny of the priests who held her future in their hands, although by whose authority, no one could quite say. Several more times, Gaspar seemed to lose his train of thought and fumble a little. Each time that it happened, the Dark Monk stepped forward to put it right, and they continued on. At last, Gaspar came back to the line of questioning he had previously posed by asking about the child's father and Cate's supposed association with the devil.

After another long conference between the two Churchmen, Gaspar's voice conveyed confidence when he said, "It has been said that the child born to you was marked by the devil himself. Do you deny this?" He challenged her to deny it with his look.

Cate's voice trembled, but she would not allow this man to accuse her of ungodly acts when she was innocent. She tried to sound strong and sure when she answered, but her "I do" came out far softer than she had hoped it would.

"What? Speak up, child. Do you deny that the boy was born with a mark?"

Cate mustered as much courage as she could find and tried to sound more confident when she spoke this time. "I do deny it. There has been a mistake, sir." She challenged Gaspar with her look as the room filled with soft mutterings again, and she added, "He's just an ordinary little child. He has no mark."

Gaspar raised his eyebrows.

Will pushed himself from the wall now, unable to hold his tongue any longer. "If I may speak, holy father?"

Gaspar gave Will a penetrating look. "You are the girl's father, are you not?"

"Yes, sir.

"State your name and position in this town."

"I am Will Pritchard, Cate's father. I am a bookbinder and seller on Bookbinders Row in the east of town."

"What is it that you wish to say, Master Pritchard?" Gaspar sighed as if bored with this interruption.

"I wish to ask of you who it is that has spread this gossip about my daughter and her child. If we knew that, we could, perhaps, realize how these accusations came to be made. There are some in this town who are jealous of our family. This could prove the source of such rum—"

"Sir," Gaspar bellowed, "how we came to this knowledge is no concern of yours. We are privileged to this information without any need to reveal who your daughter's accusers are. You are out of order to make this demand. Unless you want to find yourself under questioning, as you have been in the past," he added with emphasis, "I suggest you resume your place as observer to these proceedings and keep your remarks to yourself. Otherwise, I may have you ejected by the constabulary and you will not be allowed to return. Do you understand, Master Pritchard?"

Will's shoulders drooped as he murmured, "Yes, good father" and he stepped back, slamming against the wall. His frustration clearly visible on his face, his eyes darkened as he glared at this supposed man of God.

Gaspar slowly turned his gaze from Will back to Cate. His countenance changed to what looked like a cat toying with his prey.

"So, Mistress Cate, you deny that the child has any mark on him?"

"Yes, sir." Cate brought herself to her full height. She had to defend Andrew. With strength of conviction, she said loudly, "I do deny it. He has no mark on him."

Taken aback momentarily, Gaspar seemed to falter at her certainty. He turned his head slightly, and Iago stepped close to him again, exchanging words that, again, could not be heard by anyone else in the room. When Iago stepped back, Gaspar asked, "Where is the child?"

Will, Catherine, and Fiona, standing behind Cate, took in a collective breath and held it. It was bad enough to have Cate brought here, but to see Andrew brought before these priests and put under their scrutiny would be frightening. Still, each admitted, it was also inevitable. In order to prove that the gossip was no more than that, the priests would need to see for themselves that the baby did not have the mark that had been part of the accusation.

"Constable," Gaspar ordered, "take the girl to one of the holding rooms and lock her away."

Will pushed away from the wall and opened his mouth to protest, but said nothing when Gaspar glared at him.

"We cannot risk that the mother possesses some wicked powers with which she may bewitch us when the child is brought before us." Then he added, "We will not examine the child now, however. Have him brought and held here."

He sighed, visibly fatigued from the ordeal of questioning Cate. "I am weary. I will rest before examining the child. See to it that he is brought and held here under guard so that no one has access to him until we have had a chance to see the boy for ourselves. But make sure that he is kept away from that woman." He pointed at Cate with a long, bony finger.

As he let his arm fall wearily, Gaspar arose from his seat and walked with some effort toward a door to the left of the dais. The Dark Monk followed close behind without looking back.

Two of the constable's men came to stand beside Cate. Her face was white with fear when they led her away. When Catherine looked over at Will, his pallor matched his daughter's.

As Cate disappeared from sight, he staggered and fell back against the wall again, unable to control his legs. Catherine put her arm out to steady him and he whimpered a wordless cry as he thrust his face into his hands. She guided Will out of the hall. Fiona followed behind, but not before glancing back toward the doorway through which Cate Pritchard had disappeared.

Chapter
Fourteen

THREE PEOPLE HURRIED into Market Square from the Governor's Lane. Before turning up Bookbinders Row, Fiona put her arm out to stop Catherine. Will continued on ahead of them.

"I'm going back," Fiona said.

Catherine looked at her questioningly. "Do you think that's wise?"

Fiona's response was emphatic. "Whether it is wise or unwise doesn't matter. I have to go back."

Catherine understood. Fiona wanted to try to make contact with Cate. She doubted that she would succeed, but she understood her need to try. She nodded to Fiona and whispered, "Please, be careful." Then she turned and quickened her step to catch up to Will as he forged ahead, his fists clenched against his anguish.

When Will and Catherine arrived at the Pritchard home, they found Sarah clutching Andrew tightly to her chest as one of the constable's men argued with her.

"I have nothing to say about it Mistress. They want the child. I'm just doing what I'm told."

Sarah's voice betrayed her fear and anger. "Sam Cooper, I would have thought that you knew better than to do what strangers to this town tell you to do. Have you no mind of your own? How will Andrew survive the night without his mum and her sustenance? It was bad enough I've had to go asking for help of Margaret Poole. Since she's just had a child and has plenty of milk, she was good enough to feed him until Cate comes back from the scrutiny of those Churchmen. You just leave him here until Cate returns."

"I'm sorry Mistress Pritchard." Sam's face contorted as if what he was about to say gave him a stomachache. "She's not coming back. At least not tonight."

Sarah brought Andrew tighter to her breast. "What do you mean?"

"Them priests have ordered your Cate be held at the

Governor's Hall. She's not coming home tonight. And I'm to take the child to be held there at the priest's orders."

Sarah didn't know whether to feel fear or relief. At least if Andrew were to be taken to the Hall, he would be with his mother. She said as much. When Sam didn't respond, Will added the details of Andrew's fate as he had heard them at the Governor's Hall. Then he, too, pleaded with Sam, begging him to leave the child.

Will stood by his wife's side now, clinging to her and the baby as if he could stop Sam from doing the bidding of the priests. When Catherine joined her friends, Sam put up a hand and said that there could be no further discussion. He needed the child and he needed to get back to the Governor's Hall. The child would be kept under guard there, separate from his mother, as he had been bidden.

"This is overmuch, Sam," Sarah cried. "How can you do this to a child? He needs his mother."

"Look," Sam said, "I'm only doing what I'm told. I can't risk going against them priests and with Ben Godling away from Willowglen, I'm to do their bidding in his place." He stepped closer to the group and lowered his voice as if expecting the walls to be able to hear what he said next. His eyes implored them to believe him. "I don't like this whole business any more than you do. I think Ben left just so he wouldn't have to deal with those priests. He thinks they have no business here, as most of us do, but there isn't much to be done about it, now, is there? They've commanded the child to the Governor's Hall. I have nothing to say about it. With Ben gone, it's left to me. So, what am I to do?"

Sarah stepped closer and looked at Sam with a fierceness in her eyes that made him tremble. "Have some backbone, Sam Cooper, that's what you can do. For goodness sake, have some backbone." Her chest rose and fell with her anger as she stared at him.

Will finally pulled Sarah away as Catherine said, "We cannot stop you, can we, Sam? There is nothing that we can do that will change your mind?"

He shrugged, helplessly. Sarah glowered at him for a long while. Finally, Sam held out his hands and said soothingly, "Give me the child, Sarah. I'll see he's taken care of."

Sarah didn't move. Catherine whispered softly in Sarah's ear. "This will get us nowhere, Sarah. Sam doesn't want to take the child by force, that's obvious. Let him have Andrew."

Sarah knew she was right. There was nothing to be done. If Sam didn't return to the Governor's Hall with Andrew, he, too, would be suspect. How many more people would be falsely accused of being in league with the devil before they all awoke from this awful nightmare? Sarah looked at Sam's outstretched hands for a long moment before reluctantly handing the baby to him.

He took the baby gently in his arms and smiled at him. Then, holding Andrew close to his chest, he hurried away from the shaken group and out into the street.

AS THE SHOCK of what had just happened started to wear off, it dawned on Catherine that Lydia wasn't there as she had expected. Looking around the Pritchard house, she asked Sarah, "Where is Lydia? I thought she came to stay with you while we went to the Governor's Hall."

Sarah blinked, trying to recall the events that had taken place before Sam Cooper's arrival. "She was here most of the day. She helped me to calm myself after they took Cate, and it was she who suggested that we go to Margaret Poole and see if she would be willing to feed Andrew in Cate's absence. Margaret was hesitant at first for she had heard the gossip around town that Cate had done something to produce a child with an evil sign. She finally said she'd let him suckle when we allowed her to examine him and she saw that he looked like a perfectly normal child after all. Later, as we sat by the fire and Andrew slept, Lydia and I talked a little more about the events leading up to this day and, when I told her that I had my suspicions that the accusations about Cate and Andrew came from that Isobel Pewsey, she just stood up without a word and ran off."

"Oh, no." Catherine's eyes widened. "I hope Lydia hasn't done anything foolhardy. I'd better go find her." Removing a shawl from the hook by the door, she then wrapped it around her shoulders. She shouldn't have needed it, for the afternoon air was warm and mild, but thinking about the possibilities of what Lydia was up to had chilled her. She stepped outside onto a still bustling Bookbinders Row. She walked briskly toward the Pewseys' shop. As she approached, an unshuttered window allowed her to confirm her suspicion. She spied Lydia alone with the Pewsey sisters at the front of the shop.

As Catherine opened the door, the aroma of ink and oil met her as it wafted over the threshold. It smelled much like Will's shop, only stronger, with the addition of a musty odor of wet pulp drying to make paper.

She smiled apologetically at Winifred Pewsey, closing the door behind her. Winifred seemed almost relieved to see her.

When Lydia turned to face Catherine, she had a determined scowl on her face. Catherine noticed that Isobel Pewsey fidgeted where she stood and would not meet her gaze.

"Lydia, we need you at the Pritchards. Please come with me." Lydia made no move. "We need to go now. Please."

"Not yet, Catherine. I'm not through questioning these two about the accusations that have been made regarding Cate."

Catherine held Lydia's gaze, hoping to convey the pleading she dared not allow into her voice. "Lydia, let's leave it for another time. Come back with me."

Lydia's lips tightened in determination. "I've just been having an interesting talk with Isobel and Winifred. I'm merely inquiring about what they might know about this whole situation, nothing more."

Catherine stepped in front of Lydia, blocking her from Isobel and Winifred's view and whispered to her. "We need to go back to the Pritchards' *now*, Lydia. We have more pressing matters to discuss. Please." The look on Catherine's face told Lydia that there could be no more discussion.

Something had happened. Lydia realized that she needed to end her conversation. She wasn't getting anywhere with them anyway. She had accomplished what she intended. All she had really wanted was to let the Pewsey sisters know that she suspected them of having some part in what these priests were up to. She peeked around Catherine and addressed the sisters. "Well, thank you for the information. I see that you don't know much about what's been going on in Willowglen these past days at all, and it's just as well."

Looking back over her shoulder as she reached door, she added, "Best to stay as far from this troublesome state of affairs as possible, I think. Don't you?"

Isobel looked as if she might cry. Winifred put her arm around her sister and smiled sweetly at Lydia and Catherine. "Yes, I agree with you, Lady Lydia. It's best not to be in dealings such as this. I assure you that my sister and I have had nothing to contribute in this matter."

Lydia nodded to the two young women. As she and Catherine left the shop, they heard Winifred cooing to her sister, telling her not to worry, that she had nothing to hide and that everything would be fine.

On the short walk to the Pritchard house, Catherine quickly whispered a recounting of the events at the Governor's Hall and told Lydia that Andrew had been taken as well. By the time they entered the Pritchard house, Lydia was livid.

"I've not had any dealings with the Pewseys before, but I can tell you this: those two are up to something. I knew it as soon as I started talking to them. Isobel really isn't very bright and she admitted to me that she didn't like Cate at all and that she thought that Cate was mean to Nathaniel Mistlewaite and that's what drove him off. She's also jealous of Andrew. I think the poor thing knows she'd never be very appealing to any man in Willowglen or elsewhere, for that matter, even though her father has some means to pay for a good dowry for her. The girl's a simpleton. Her own sister admitted as much. I think the only way she'd find a husband would be by some treachery on her father's part. Her sister said that she harbors delusions that Mistlewaite really wanted *her* and was only using Cate to get to her. Can you imagine?

"The sister, Winifred, on the other hand, is very bright, so much so that I don't trust her at all. I don't believe for a minute that the sweet smile she had for me while I spoke with them is genuine. She cut her sister off more than once when I asked about the accusations made about Cate. She was obviously trying to keep her from talking too much. I think that Sarah is right in thinking that Isobel Pewsey may have been the one to accuse Cate. Jealousy and spite have caused people to do such things in the past."

"I wouldn't be surprised." Sarah sighed. Her eyes had a deepening sadness about them. "Anyway, we have no proof. Besides, how does knowing that help us to defend Cate?"

"I'm not sure," Lydia said.

"Well, every bit of information we can gather may prove helpful later, so I'm glad you went to talk to them, Lydia," Catherine chimed.

Lydia looked at her with a sly smile on her face. "Really? I thought you were cross with me when you came into that shop."

"I guess I was. I wasn't sure what more trouble you might have been stirring up. But I see now that we have, at least, a little more information about what's going on and that has to be valuable. I'm just not sure what the importance of it is yet."

Will sat at the table near the fire with his head in his hands. "We should go back to the Governor's Hall. If they decide to examine Andrew, we should be there."

"I think you're right, Will," Catherine said. "You and Sarah go on ahead. Lydia and I will be there shortly. We've something we must do first."

Chapter
Fifteen

FIONA MOVED ALONG the cobbled street back toward the Governor's Hall. Before reaching the main entrance, though, she turned and walked along the side of the structure. This was the part of the building into which Cate had been escorted. She didn't know exactly where Cate had been taken, but at least there was a chance she could discover her location if she kept alert. She had to try.

Away from the main street, Fiona slowed her pace, examining each window as she passed. The Governor's Hall was a two-story building painted pristine white. Even in the waning daylight, she could still see its shining dome, which proclaimed Willowglen was an independent borough. As Fiona's eyes darted from opening to opening in the edifice, she thought about her father's stories of how progressive Willowglen had been while he was growing into manhood. What had happened to that town? The city no longer seemed so advanced now that it let the likes of Father Gaspar Maria de Salvadore and his phantasmal companion wield their power over its citizens. She thought Constable Ben Godling must be a mouse of a man to let these Churchmen take over as he had. She shook her head, then turned another corner and stopped.

Now standing at the rear of the structure, she saw an area where the earth dipped and undulated. Undersized windows set below the main floor level almost looked as if they perched on the ground. She approached, trying to look as if she were out for an early evening stroll through this public land. Coming closer, she noticed a dim light coming from one of the small, barred windows. She bent over and looked in. Then she hiked up her leine and knelt down. The rough grass felt cool under her knees. The Governor's Hall possessed all the rich trappings of a building funded by the good citizens of Willowglen. Even these lesser windows had glass panes in them, no doubt an effort to show off the affluence of the town. Unlike the larger windows that graced the building, these were barred.

As she peered through to the coarse glass, she thought she

could just make out the shadow of someone pacing back and forth. Looking down the row of windows, she saw all but this one was in darkness. She decided to act. Plunging her hand through the bars, she rapped on the window. The movement below stopped. Head movement seemed to indicate someone looking up in the direction of the sound. Fiona tapped again. The figure moved toward the window and stopped before moving away.

Disappointment washed over Fiona. If it was Cate down below, perhaps she was too frightened to investigate the source of the tapping. She pushed herself up from the ground, but as she did, the figure came back into Fiona's line of sight. She heard a scraping sound and watched as the figure pulled something dark and heavy. The form disappeared again as it approached the wall below the window. A moment later, Fiona spied the fingertips, barely grazing the side of the window frame. It took several attempts to reach the latch. At each attempt, Fiona pushed on the window to see if it would open. Finally, it swung inward.

"Cate. Cate, is that you?" Fiona whispered.

"Fiona?" It was Cate's voice.

"Yes. Cate, are you all right?"

"Yes. Except—"

"What? Have they hurt you?" Fiona felt the tension rise between her shoulders. If they hurt Cate, they would pay.

"No. No one has hurt me. But I hurt. I need Andrew. I need to feed him."

"Oh." Fiona sighed in relief. Yet she noted, ironically, that she couldn't seem to get away from images of Cate Pritchard nursing her son. "I don't know how we can get him to you, Cate. Maybe if I could cut these bars I could hand him down to you."

"No, not that." Cate refused adamantly. "I can barely reach the window. You'd have to drop him down. He could be hurt. We can't risk it."

They were silent for a long time. Finally, Cate's moans sent Fiona into action. "Cate? I'm going to see what I can do. Maybe one of the guards can be bribed to let you have the baby. I'll be back as soon as I can." When Cate didn't respond, she called out in a hoarse whisper, "Cate. Did you hear me?"

"Yes," Cate said. The discomfort in her voice was clear. "Hurry, please."

Fiona jumped to her feet. She didn't bother circling back to the Governor's Lane. Instead, she took the more direct route, cutting across the grounds straight to New Gate and on to Bookbinders Row. Just as she reached the narrow bridge that crossed the River Willow, she pulled up. Sam Cooper rushed along bearing a tiny wailing bundle. He looked worried. As Sam approached, Fiona held up her hand and, surprisingly, he stopped.

"Is that Andrew Pritchard you have there?"

Sam looked warily at Fiona. "Who wants to know?" he said above Andrew's cries.

"A friend of Andrew Pritchard's, that's who. The babe is obviously hungry."

"I know that. Don't you think I know that? I've brought up four of my own, you know."

"Then you know he's wanting his mother."

"I know that, too."

"You should give him to his mother." Fiona took another step forward. She towered over Sam Cooper.

He stared up at her. "The priest said he wasn't to be with his mother. She might bewitch him."

"She's already bewitched him, wouldn't you say? Otherwise, why would he be yelling so?"

Sam Cooper stared into the little red face and his face softened. He looked back up at Fiona. "I hate to see them cry. I was always fussing with me own when they cried like such."

Fiona saw beads of sweat forming on Sam Cooper's forehead. "Take him to his mother for feeding. Then, you can take him away for guarding. The priests need never know. They're probably at their prayers anyway, pious, holy men that they are." She defied him to contradict her. He looked away toward the Governor's Hall. She could tell he was thinking. Then he looked down at the babe crying plaintively in his arms.

"I can't," he said almost wailing himself. "What if they see me?"

"They won't see you." Fiona pinned him with her look. "I'll tell you what. I'll go with you. I'll watch for you to make sure that you aren't found out. No one has to know."

He shook his head, unsure.

"You know this is right, constable. You must do it."

Sam stared at her. If she could have read his thoughts, she would have heard her own words echoing beside Sarah's. *Have some backbone, Sam Cooper,* he heard the desperate woman say again.

"All right, all right," he said between clenched teeth as the baby continued to squall. "You come with me and make sure no one sees. If we get caught, it's you who made me. I'll say you pulled a knife on me."

"Fine, say whatever you like, constable, I don't really care. Just do this for the sake of the child and his mother." She stepped aside, then, and fell in beside him as Andrew wailed for their entire journey. Fiona couldn't help but allow a small smile to cross her lips. The situation was dire, indeed, but at least she could alleviate Cate's immediate suffering as well as Andrew's discomfort. She slowed her pace so that Sam could keep up with her, still smiling.

SAM COOPER WOULDN'T let Fiona see Cate. He said he couldn't take the chance, that he had taken risks enough allowing Cate to nurse Andrew. If the priests found out, he would be a dead man. Of that he was certain.

Instead, he left Fiona at the top of the stairs that led to the storerooms below while he brought Andrew to Cate. When Fiona heard Andrew stop crying, she knew that Cooper had delivered the boy safely to his mother's arms.

A short while later, Cooper emerged at the top of the stairs carrying the baby. He looked down at the child and smiled, obviously captivated by the tiny boy. He looked at Fiona and said, "Had four of these meself. All grown up now. Don't have a concern." He lowered his voice and looked around before adding, "I don't think we have to worry about them priests in the middle of the night. They like their comforts. I've never seen them roaming these dark, cold halls at night all the while they've been here. They each have a fire in their room that they want to stay close to. I'll take good care of him," he said nodding toward the baby. "I'll give him to his mum again when he wakes up."

Fiona clamped her large hand on Sam's shoulder. "You're a good man, constable. No matter what, you can feel content that you have done right by Cate and her son."

"Yeah," he said, a grim look on his face. "Maybe I'll find me backbone yet."

"What's that?"

"Nothing. It's not important. You'd better get out of here. Wouldn't want anyone to see you in our company. I might have to tell them that you pulled that knife on me still."

Fiona looked him in the eye and said, "I don't think you'd do that. I believe you'll always do what's right."

"Maybe. Maybe not. You'd better not wait around to find out. Go down the hall." He nodded in the direction he wanted her to go. "You'll find a small side door. No one will see you leave that way."

Chapter
Sixteen

GASPAR STOPPED AS he walked away from the main hall and looked at the Dark Monk. "Iago, take that cowl away from your face. I would look at you when we speak."

"I told you, Gaspar, I have my reasons for keeping my identity hidden. It's better this way."

"I do not understand you sometimes, Iago. Yet..." Gaspar thrust an outstretched hand into the blackness of the monk's hood and stroked his cheek before continuing, "Yet, I am enamored of you." Iago tried not to flinch at the man's touch.

Gaspar tried in vain to keep the pleading from his voice. "You promised me earlier that we would pray together. I've done as you have asked. We've questioned the girl. She is in custody, which is what you wanted, I think. Will you come with me now and pray for my faith to be restored?"

Iago said nothing. Instead, he pushed past Gaspar toward the chapel that was part of the Governor's Hall.

THE TWO MEN dressed in the black and white robes of Dominic the Preacher stood before the side altar in the chapel. Both stared straight ahead, focusing on the cross above them. Christ hung slumped, the weight of his body pulling at the flesh on his hands, his head, plaited with thorns, slumped forward. The taller of the two men said, "I am like Christ on the cross, Brother Iago. I am still sick with torment."

"It is the same as before." It was a statement, not a question, for Iago already knew the answer. His hood buried his face deeply within the fabric as always.

"Yes, my brother. I fear I have lost my faith. I cannot feel His presence. It was so difficult when we questioned that girl. If you hadn't been there to help me when I faltered, I don't know what I would have done. How can I do his work when I wonder if He even exists? It causes me much anguish. It is such a distraction."

"Have you prayed, Father Gaspar? Have you prayed that your faith be restored?"

"I have prayed, Little Brother. I have prayed and I have wept to no avail. I have started to wonder what I am doing here. I question whether or not we should just leave this place and go home, back to Spain."

Trying not to let panic overcome him, Iago quickly said, "But your work is not finished here, Father. There are evils in this place that we must root out. We are making progress. We have the girl. We will prove that she has taken up with the devil and that the child is his issue. This town needs to be cleansed. Let us continue to seek out anything and anyone else that may need the salvation that we bring."

Gaspar looked down at the smaller man. Sadness filled his eyes. "You are so sure, aren't you, little one? Your faith in Him never wavers, does it?"

The monk smirked within the darkness of his hood. If only Gaspar knew. His faith had left him so long ago that he hardly remembered what it was like to believe any more. Of course, he could never let the priest know. He wouldn't understand. No, his suffering was his own. He had no desire to share it with this man, but he needed Gaspar, and he needed him here in Willowglen. He couldn't let him entertain the idea of returning home. He would not be able to carry out his plans without this pawn of a priest.

He had to admit that, without Gaspar, he would never have been able to return to England — would never have been able to wield this much power in the town of Willowglen. He had them all running now. They were afraid of him. He saw it in their eyes every time he looked at one of the townspeople. The look of fear made him shiver with pleasure.

He wasn't about to give all this up, now that they were finally making progress. He had to make sure that Gaspar didn't give in to this current perception that he couldn't carry on. He had to get him to banish these thoughts of returning to Spain before they ruined his plan. Months and months he had lain awake at night trying to come up with a way to get his due. The girl was in his grasp. The next step seemed inevitable. The one he really desired would come. He could feel it.

It was easier than he had imagined and more than he had hoped for. The printer was a friend to Briarcrest. His daughter was a harlot. How convenient. One of the women of Briarcrest already walked among them. The two were inseparable. They always had been. He could be patient. After all, he had waited years to come to this point. However, this talk of loss of faith and returning to Spain just wouldn't do. He had to put a stop to it immediately. He knew

Gaspar's weakness better than Iago knew his own. He could make him stay in Willowglen and he knew it. What he would have to do repulsed him, but he would do it. He would do whatever it took.

"I am sure that if we pray together, Father, your faith will be restored. You will feel God's presence, I'm sure of it."

"Oh, I long to feel His presence, Brother. It is pure ecstasy, you know. Have you felt it, Iago? Oh, but I don't have to ask. I know that you have. You are so filled with His presence." Gaspar heaved a heavy sigh. "I am ready, Brother. Let us pray."

Iago turned to look around the tiny chapel. Candlelight gave it a soft glow. The setting sun spared a few remaining rays to shine though the small colored windows set into the western wall. Iago saw no one.

"Let us pray," Iago said as he turned back to face the altar.

Gaspar closed his eyes. The men began in unison: Pater noster, qui es in caelis, sanctificetur nomen tuum — *Our Father, who art in heaven, hallowed be Thy name...*

Gaspar drew in a sharp-sounding breath. Ecstasy. Iago's hand was on him. Gaspar's voice grew weaker, sounding like a whimpering kitten as he continued. Adveniat regnum tuum — *Thy Kingdom come.* Gaspar felt his soul take flight. His body tingled. Fiat voluntas tua, sicut in caelo et in terra — *Thy will be done on earth as it is in heaven.*

Is this what the presence of God felt like, Gaspar wondered? Yes, he was sure of it. Iago continued to stroke him through the thick robes. Exhilaration filled the tall priest. He could hear his blood as it coursed through his veins, whooshing and pounding in his ears. His chest heaved as his breath became labored. Now, only Iago's voice could be heard echoing throughout the small chapel. Gaspar mouthed the words as they continued, but no sound came from him. His chest rose and fell as his excitement grew. *Forgive us our trespasses as we forgive those who trespass against us...*

Iago felt Gaspar's hardness beneath the old man's robes. He firmly grasped the now prominent organ and moved his hand faster. Gaspar felt that he would cry out with sheer joy, but he knew he should not. This moment was not for the world to know. It was between him and his God, and dear little Brother Iago. God was with him. Soon, his darkness would end. The pleasure he felt was exquisite.

Et ne nos inducas in tentationem — *Lead us not into temptation...*

Iago sneered from within the darkness of his cowl as he felt Gaspar start to tremble, heard him gasp as he fell away from his hand. He looked over just in time to see the priest crumble to his knees, whimpering like a child, making unintelligible sounds.

With a booming voice, larger than one would think such a

small man could possess, Iago pronounced the final words of the prayer. "...sed libera nos a malo—*Deliver us from evil.*" The collapsed man with the beatific smile on his face whispered, "*Amen. Amen.*"

Iago looked down at him with contempt. Then he turned from the heap that was Father Gaspar Maria de Salvadore and walked out of the chapel. There would be no more talk of returning to Spain.

Chapter
Seventeen

AS CATHERINE AND Lydia stepped over the cobbles of Bookbinders Row, the sun glowed red and gold against the clouds dipping below the roof lines of the houses of Willowglen Township. Lydia, smaller in stature than Catherine, had trouble keeping up. As her legs pumped below her layered skirts, she asked breathlessly, "Where are we going, Catherine?"

"To the Governor's Hall. I want to get there before Will and Sarah do. This situation is foolishness. I'm going to talk some sense into that priest and get him to see that Cate is just an imprudent young woman who let herself be influenced by the wrong man."

"Do you think he'll listen? You'll have to get him alone. From what I've heard, the priest seems tied by some invisible bond to that one people are calling the Dark Monk. I don't like the sound of him, that's for sure."

"I've seen him. He is worrisome. There's something about him. And you're right. While the priest questioned Cate, he faltered more than once and the Dark Monk intervened to put him right. It was almost as though the monk were the master pushing and pulling that priest to make him go in the direction of the monk's choosing. He gave me the shivers, it's true, but I don't trust either of them. Still, we have to do something to put a stop to this. I'm hoping to try to get the priest alone. Perhaps if he's not under the influence of that monk, I can talk some sense into him. If I have to promise him a large donation to his coffers, I will. But this nonsense must stop."

As Lydia gasped for breath while she tried to keep up with Catherine, she wondered whether her idea was rational. First of all, could they get the priest alone? Second, would he listen to reason as Catherine hoped? Perhaps even money might not make a difference.

As the two women entered the Governor's Hall, Sam Cooper walked across the room crooning to Andrew. No sound came from child asleep in his arms.

Catherine blocked the man's path. He stopped short of walking into her and gave her a surprised look. "Sam Cooper," she said sternly, "I only ask one thing of you. Take good care of this child while he is your responsibility."

Sam's expression softened. "I will, Mistress. You know I love little ones." He glanced around to make sure that they were alone in the vast hall before adding quietly, "He's already fed and I'm sure the priests are already tucked into their nice warm rooms with their supper by now. We never see them at night."

As he said this, another of the constable's men entered from a door on the other side of the room. Having heard Sam's remark about the priests, he said, "Not tonight, Sam. I guess the good fathers are feeling very pious. I saw them go into the chapel a while ago. Maybe they went to pray for all of us. That Dark Monk seems to think we're all of the devil, I'd say." He touched his cap and said, "Good eve, Lady, Mistress," as he continued toward the main entrance of the hall to leave.

Without another word to Sam, Catherine grasped Lydia by the wrist and started toward the chapel. "Come on, Lydia. Perhaps we'll get our chance yet."

"Wait." Sam called after them, his words echoing around them in the hall, but they took no heed. "Mistress, I wouldn't disturb them. They're a funny lot, you know. I'd just leave them be. The less said to them the better."

The women were already into the chapel hallway before Sam finished speaking.

QUIET SURROUNDED THEM as Catherine and Lydia slipped into the chapel. When they saw the two figures standing at the side altar, they moved soundlessly into the shadows, hoping that the monk would leave before Gaspar did, so that they could speak to Gaspar alone. From behind a pillar, they watched as the men started to pray. *Pater noster, qui es in caelis...*

Catherine felt disoriented when the monk brought his hand across Gaspar's abdomen. What was he doing? Then she saw the motion of his arm, rubbing up and down. She looked at Lydia and raised her eyebrows in disbelief. Lydia, too, realized what was happening and her face darkened with embarrassment and anger. Catherine thought that she might not be able to control her own rage at the hypocrisy of these men. How could they accuse Cate Pritchard of lying with the devil when they stood before the altar praying to God the Father while they did such things? What manner of depravity was this?

Catherine caught Lydia's arm just before she stepped out of the shadows toward the altar. With her lips pressed together firmly, she shook her head hoping that Lydia wouldn't move to confront the two men. Lydia was panting visibly and a scowl darkened her face.

The monk's voice boomed, "*...sed libera nos a malo.*" The old priest collapsed on the steps of the altar and whimpered his *Amen*, barely audible to the women. The monk turned and started down the center of the chapel toward the door.

Catherine and Lydia both moved behind a pillar in an attempt to stay out of sight. As the monk passed them, Catherine shuddered. Dark memories flooded her mind — a hooded creature attacking on a Hallows Eve night long ago. Catherine had felt helpless. She had called on some deeply hidden strength because Lydia's life had been at stake. She had no idea why these images came to her now, but she found she could do little to stop them from assailing her.

Finally, Lydia's voice roused her from her nightmarish thoughts with an uncharacteristic oath as she whispered, "God's wounds."

Quickly, Catherine put a trembling finger to Lydia's lips to silence her. Lydia grabbed her hand and held it gently in her own. Then, she peeked out tentatively from their hiding place. From behind her, Catherine peered over Lydia's shoulder. The monk was gone. Having quieted her uneasiness, Catherine stepped in front of Lydia and motioned her to follow her out the chapel door. The hallway was empty. Trying to step as lightly as they could to keep their footsteps quiet, they fairly ran the length of it. They kept going when they reached the main hall, where they encountered no one this time. Outside, the crisp night air cooled their reddened cheeks and calmed their distress at the scene they had just witnessed.

Lydia's anger faded slowly. "Those men are depraved and yet they accuse others? We should have gone to Gaspar, just then, Catherine. We should have let him know that we saw what just took place. We could have used it against him for Cate and Andrew's benefit."

"No, Lydia. Now we know the true measure of them, I think they are even more to be feared. There is no telling what they will do to Cate, to Andrew, to any of us. I think we have to be very careful."

"That monk gave me gooseflesh when he walked past," Lydia said. "For a brief moment, I thought he had seen us and was going to stop. It was almost as if he sensed our presence there."

"Yes, I saw his hesitation, too. I thought he had seen us. It was a very small gesture, but I feared as you did. My breath caught in my chest because of it. I was so grateful that he moved away quickly after that." Catherine shivered. "I didn't trust that Dark Monk before, but now, after what we've seen tonight, I think he is to be avoided at all cost."

"What do you think we should do now?" Lydia asked.

"I'm not sure," Catherine answered. "Perhaps it would be best if we went back to Will and Sarah's. Obviously nothing more will happen at the Governor's Hall tonight."

The two women walked back toward Market Square, then headed in the direction of New Gate, up Bookbinders Row to Will and Sarah's house. When they reached the Pritchard's, Sarah and Will told them that they had gone to the hall and were turned away. They said they had been told that the priest and his monk companion were in prayer for the evening. The two women said nothing about what they had witnessed in the chapel in the Governor's Hall.

Chapter
Eighteen

FIONA LEFT THE stairway as instructed by Sam Cooper and found the side door just where he told her it would be. The doorway was so low that she had to crouch down to exit it. On the other side, she found herself just a few steps from the corner of the building that would take her back to Cate. When she reached the window, it was still open. She knelt down as she had earlier and called softly, "Cate? It's Fiona. How are you faring?"

Fiona heard sounds of scrambling. She couldn't see Cate. She must have stationed herself just below the window again.

"I'm much better. Thank you. They wouldn't let me keep Andrew, though. I'm worried about him."

"The constable's a good man. He'll take good care of him. He promised he'd bring him back to you in the middle of the night."

"He told me. And yes, he is a good man. Our family has known Sam Cooper for a long time. He loves children. He wouldn't let my Andrew suffer. Still, I miss my baby. I know the only reason he dared to bring him to me was because you persuaded him. Thank you."

"I couldn't let you suffer, either of you."

After a long pause, Cate's voice trembled when she spoke. "I'm afraid, Fiona, afraid of what will happen to us."

Fiona thought her heart would break at the words and her feeling of helplessness. "I don't know what more I can do," she said in desperation.

"Don't leave me."

"I won't. I'll be right here."

"You're a very caring woman, Fiona."

Fiona blushed. "You're worth caring for."

"Please keep talking to me, Fiona. Your voice is a great comfort."

"I don't know what more to say. What would you like to hear?"

"Tell me about your homeland. Tell me about where you live

and what you do. I want to hear it all."

Fiona talked long into the night, telling Cate about her family's land and their crops and livestock and about her own little stone house that she and her father and brothers had built on a hill. She told her about her writing, although she did not mention anything that she had written about Cate Pritchard since she had met her. She told her of her dream to have her writings and her drawings published one day. By the time Sam Cooper brought Andrew back to Cate to suckle again, Fiona's voice had grown gravelly, unaccustomed as she was to so much conversation. She kept quiet when they heard Sam enter and was grateful for the rest while Cate nursed her son.

When Sam had taken Andrew away again, Cate said, "Tell me more, Fiona."

Fiona told her stories of the border wars and of her father and brothers fighting against the English. Now the Scots befriended the English, Fiona noted, remarking on the fickleness of men in their search for land and power. She wondered aloud at how long the peaceful relationship would last and she asked Cate what she thought of it. Cate said that she didn't understand the differences between men who inhabited the same land and that she wouldn't hazard a guess as to what would happen in the future. Fiona told her more stories of the beautiful land to the north. When she felt as though she had run out of words, she took a deep breath and launched into tales her father had told her about his journey of an adventurous quest and how he came to meet and fall in love with Fiona's mother.

"I don't know if I'll ever find someone to love that way," Cate remarked.

"You will, Cate. You will." And Fiona couldn't help but wish it could be she who would be allowed to fulfill Cate Pritchard's dreams of love.

"I didn't love Nathaniel Mistlewaite, you know. I know that now."

"Oh?" Fiona's heart pounded within her chest as she wondered at Cate's admission.

"No. I didn't love him at all. He held some mastery over me that I cannot explain. When he spun his tales and sang his songs, he seemed to hold me in his power. He loved to hear himself tell his stories, too, but you tell yours much more beautifully from a woman's perspective. It turned out that his lovemaking was much like his songs, more for his own pleasure than for that of those who experienced them. I realize now that his attention made me feel good for a time, but the feeling soon faded as did his stories and songs."

Fiona silently detested the man who had duped Cate into allowing him to have his way with her. "I'm sorry that your first experience was not one of true beauty and love. You deserve better. I'm sorry that he ran out on you. He should have been more of a man. He should have been there for you and for Andrew. You deserve someone who wants to care for you, both of you."

"Thank you for saying that, Fiona. It's kind of you."

"I say it only because I..." Fiona wondered if she should finish her thought.

But what did it matter? She might never be able to see Cate Pritchard face to face ever again. Her future was so uncertain. She recalled her conversation with Catherine and Lydia in the inn that morning.

Was it only hours ago that she had sat contentedly breaking her night's fast and penning her feelings for Cate plus all they had experienced while at the miller's homestead? Lydia had said that she and Catherine had known that they had feelings for one another when they first met, but they had hesitated to express them. Fiona recognized a tinge of regret in Lydia's eyes when she admitted it. She had then disclosed to Lydia and Catherine that she would consider not wasting time by waiting to express her feelings to Cate. But was this the time to do it? When else, she thought? With things as they are, who knows what tomorrow shall bring and what fate awaits Cate and her son? No, she would not wait. She could not let this moment pass and chance never having the opportunity again. "I—I say it only because I...well, I...care for you, Cate. Very much. You must know that."

Cate's response was barely more than a whisper. "I—I care for you, too, Fiona. I hope you know that also."

Fiona held the statement in her heart. She didn't want to read too much into it, hope for things that could never be. Finally, she decided to throw caution to the wind and said, "You are more to me than a friend, Cate. I love you. *I* would be the person to take care of you and Andrew. If only you would allow me to do so."

A long silence ensued.

Tormented that she had misspoke, Fiona cried out, "I'm sorry, Cate. I shouldn't have said those things." Softly, Cates words floated up through the barred window. "Do you take them back then?"

"No. Only if you want me to. Do you?"

"Never. For I feel the same way about you, Fiona Smith. I know what true love is. It is what I've felt for you since the first day I saw you in Uncle George's cottage. I love you, more than I've ever loved anyone in my life, save for my son."

"I would never want to diminish your love for Andrew. You

know that, don't you?"

"Yes. And I love you for it all the more."

Fiona smiled broadly.

"Tell me another story," Cate pleaded.

Fiona thought for a few minutes. "Shall I tell you a child's tale, then? One my mother used to tell me when I was just a wee young lass?"

"Yes, that would be lovely," Cate sighed.

So Fiona started with, "Once, there was a lovely princess..." When she finished the story and asked Cate if she enjoyed it, she got no answer and she knew that Cate had fallen asleep. Fiona, also exhausted, wrapped her brat around her tightly and, not wanting Cate to waken and think she had abandoned her, stuck her hand though the open window into the room where Cate slept. Then, Fiona fell into a weary, fitful sleep lying on the ground outside the room of Cate's confinement, wondering what the morrow would bring for all of them.

Chapter
Nineteen

OLIVER PEWSEY COULD not help but register distress when he opened the door to his living quarters behind the ink and paper shop and found the Dark Monk standing there. He quickly hid behind what he hoped was a welcoming smile.

Iago saw easily that his presence caused the man some fear and discomfort. The monk liked that. It gave him a feeling of power. He grinned to himself from within his dark cowl, knowing that Pewsey would not be able to see his satisfaction.

"Holy brother, you grace my home with your presence." Pewsey's voice quivered, betraying his nervousness. "Please come in. Come in."

Iago pushed past the rotund man, entering his home. The dwelling was aglow with the fire that was lit in the fireplace. A pot of stew bubbled as it hung over the flames. Oliver's wife just stared at the stew and stirred without stopping, refusing to acknowledge the monk's presence.

In the far corner of the room, the Pewsey sisters sat, a forgotten game of cat's cradle lying tangled around Winifred's hands like broken spider webs. Iago had a fleeting thought about her beauty, but let it slip from his mind. He had more important things to attend to tonight.

The older girl, Isobel, sat like a lump of pudding beside her more attractive sister. Her mouth hung open and her eyes were as big as overturned pots, all bulging and round.

The monk approached the girls without another word to their father. Their mother continued to move her spoon in circles in the cooking pot, as if no one at all had come to call.

When Iago spoke, he kept his voice low so that only the girls could hear. "I have come about your testimony. Tomorrow, we will examine the Pritchard boy. I must be sure, without a doubt, that you have seen the mark. Tell me that you know he has the devil's mark upon him."

Isobel stared at a stain on her skirt. The dark brown mark

looked like a snake, long and tapered with a large head, slithering down her substantial belly. Iago turned his attention to Winifred.

Through clenched teeth, he seethed, "Has your sister become mute?"

Winifred turned to Isobel and crooned softly, "Isobel, tell the good priest what you saw through the open window that night after Cate had delivered her child." Isobel looked into her sister's eyes. Winifred saw fear there, but she continued, insisting, "Tell him, Isobel. He wants to know so that he can rid our town of evil." She softened her voice and repeated with an encouraging nod, "Tell him."

Isobel continued to stare into Winifred's eyes. As she spoke, she found courage in her sister's gaze. "I looked into the window of the Pritchard house. I had heard from Jack, the fishmonger's helper, that the baby was probably born that day. I wanted to see him. I wanted to see if he looked like Nathaniel Mistlewaite." She took a deep breath and, still locked in Winifred's stare, she said, "I saw his grandmother holding him, rocking him. His wrap had fallen from his head. I could see the white blob on the side of his head. When I told Win..." Winifred's eyes grew large and Isobel started again. "Some—someone told me it was because Cate—Cate Pritchard— had fornicated with the devil himself, not with Nathaniel. The child was evil and shouldn't be allowed to live and Cate has to be a witch to have done such a thing."

Winifred gave her sister an almost undetectable smile. Isobel breathed a visible sigh of relief and went back to staring at the serpentine stain on her skirt.

The monk let out a low guttural sound. "Are you certain that you saw this? You must be certain. It could not have been some trick of the eye from a distance?"

Isobel traced the stain's slithering pattern as if stroking a pet. Finally, Winifred looked into the blackness of the monk's cowl and said, "She is certain. The child is marked by the devil himself."

Iago stood silently staring at the sisters. Only the interminable sound of a wooden spoon scrapping the bottom of the kettle broke the silence—that, and the sound of Oliver Pewsey's wheezing breath coming from a corner of the room where he sat as if nothing out of the ordinary was happening in his house.

Once again, Iago had a fleeting thought about Winifred's beauty and he allowed himself the luxury of lingering over it. She reminded him of another young woman that made his need grow and throb within him. The old wound on his back ached when he thought of her, and he recoiled silently.

He had had her that night. She had been in his grasp. His member was hard with the excitement of it. Keeping his hand tightly around her arm as she pleaded with him to let her go, he managed to pull his leggings down around his knees. She struggled against his grip protesting, but that only thrilled him more. He knew she would be like this. It pleased him that she did not give in too easily. He yanked up her dress. He was so close. In an instant, he would push his way into her and fulfill years of longing.

But the terrible, excruciating pain stopped him. It had filled his body, radiating from between his shoulder blades, and he dropped to his knees unable to catch his breath. Even in the blackness of the night, he saw flashes of light from behind his closed eyelids, like a thousand stars in the sky. They burst in time to the throbbing pain that wracked his body. His now flaccid member ached at the lack of the fulfillment that he had just been anticipating. Every time he tried to draw a breath, the pain kept him from doing so. Dizziness overwhelmed him. He steadied himself with his hands and crawled away from his attacker to save himself from any further assault. As he scuttled away like a rodent, he caught a glimpse of the taller woman throwing down a large piece of wood, grabbing the other woman by the hand, and dragging her down the alley.

It took him long, long moments to recover. During that time, he thought he might die from lack of air. When he finally gulped a huge deep breath, it hurt between his shoulder blades so badly that he thought he would faint. He crawled off down the alley until he found a dimly lit window. He pulled off his tunic and saw blood. She had broken the skin with her blow. "Wretched cow!" was his last thought just before he passed out.

He didn't wake until the next morning as the town itself stirred. When he moved, the dried blood on his tunic tore from his flesh with agonizing pain. He couldn't let anyone find him there, not in his condition. He would be suspect. For all he knew that dim-witted herbalist had gone to the authorities and they were already searching the streets for him. If they found him, the woman might be able to identify him. Surely his injury would be enough to implicate him. He twisted his neck as if to ward off the feeling of a rope around it as his punishment. No, he wouldn't let them find him. With his body still crippled with pain, he lifted himself from the ground and tried to keep his balance. The dizziness almost overtook him again, and he put his hand out on the wall to steady himself. He managed to recover enough to limp toward the road that led out of town. As he staggered away, several people saw him and called after him. Unsure whether they were friend or foe, he hobbled on more quickly until he left the wretched town of Willowglen behind him. He would have to look for another way to fulfill his craving.

"Good brother. Sir Monk." Oliver Pewsey stood between his daughters and Iago, looking into the blackness of his cowl with concern and fear. Iago shook off the memory as Oliver asked, "Are you all right?"

"Do not concern yourself," the monk barked. "It is nothing."

"You would not answer my inquiries. You cried out."

Uncertainty welled up in Iago and a fire burned in his chest from fear. "What...what did I say?"

"It was...well..." Oliver stared at him, wondering if it would be possible to use this outbreak as a means to protect his family.

"I cannot say. Or perhaps I should say that I will not say." He watched the monk for signs of anger. There didn't seem to be any, so he pressed on. "Perhaps...if I had some...uh, assurances...yes, assurances that my family will be protected in all of this business."

Iago stared at the man for a long time before he growled an answer. "You have my word, Master Pewsey. Your family will come to no harm from this."

"Ah. That is most gracious of you, sir."

"Now tell me, what is it that you heard when I cried out."

"I'm sure it is nothing." Oliver stared pointedly into the blackness where the monk's face should be. "Nothing that should be spoken, in any case."

"I see. Then it is of no consequence at all, is it?"

"To be sure, sir. As long as we have...an understanding." He would not let on that all he had heard were the words *breathe* and *cow*, which told him nothing. But as long as the monk didn't know that, he had perhaps bought a safeguard for his daughters by the monk's peculiar conduct. Oliver conjured up a look of concern that he did not feel. "But, are you sure you are not unwell?"

"What I am is of no concern to you." Iago tugged his cowl further over his head. "I have the information I need from your daughters. I suggest you keep them in the house until this nasty business with the Pritchard strumpet and her wicked son is over if you know what's good for them."

Oliver's eyes quickly gazed down at the floor as he took in the monk's warning. The monk walked across the room toward the door through which he had entered earlier. Without another word, he walked out, slamming the door behind him, causing every Pewsey to jump. Oliver Pewsey stared at his daughters and wondered what business the Dark Monk had with them, but both of them started to wail when he asked them, so he thought it best to leave it for another day.

Chapter
Twenty

EARLY MORNING DARKNESS surrounded Catherine in her tiny room at the Grouse and Pheasant. After a restless night, she awoke to a feeling of dread. The Churchmen couldn't be trusted. Cate and Andrew's fates were in their hands and the Pewsey sisters were suspect. Sarah and Will were beside themselves with fear and grief. Catherine agonized over what she could do to save Cate and her son, but try as she might, she could think of nothing that would get them released from custody. It had become clear to her that the Dark Monk possessed power over the priest, Father Gaspar. Nothing she might say to the tall Churchman would influence him should the Dark Monk choose to intervene.

Lydia stirred in the small bed that they shared. With barely room for each of them, Lydia turned over with some difficulty and faced Catherine, whispering, "Catherine, are you awake?"

"Yes." A feeling of protectiveness overwhelmed Catherine and she wondered how she could keep Lydia from going to the Governor's Hall this morning. She didn't understand why, but knowing what these priests were like made her want to keep Lydia away from them, and she knew that such strong thoughts of this type were always to be trusted when she had them.

"What are you thinking about?" Lydia asked.

What to say? These thoughts would only provoke another argument, yet she had to rely on her instinct. She knew that Lydia would not accept her feelings as a reason to stay away. An idea formed regarding the Pewseys. She whispered her scheme to Lydia, letting it take shape as she spoke. "I need you to do something for me today."

"I'm going with you to the Governor's Hall."

"No, listen, this is important. Someone needs to watch those Pewsey girls. I think you're right. They are up to something, and I don't trust them. One of us should go to Bookbinders Row and keep an eye on them. You should do it."

Lydia's voice became louder. "Why me?"

Fear gripped Catherine, but she couldn't explain it. Instead, she put a finger to Lydia's lips. "I've got to try to keep everyone calm when we go to the Hall. Sarah and Will are so upset that they can't be responsible for keeping a level head. Fiona is beside herself about Cate's captivity and someone has to speak on Cate's behalf."

Lydia's whisper cut her off. "How can you think anything anyone has to say will keep those men from deciding anything other than that she is guilty of some abomination? After what we saw last night, I should think you would not even attempt such a thing. I think that you should go and spy upon the Pewseys and I should go to the Hall. That way, you won't say something that you'll regret later."

Catherine's heart pounded in her ears. She would lose this battle if she kept on this way. In desperation, she said, "If I promise to hold my tongue, will you go to the Pewseys?"

Lydia said nothing for quite a while, then, "Promise on your father's soul, Catherine Hawkins."

Conflicting emotions warred within Catherine. All she had to do was promise on her father's soul that she would not speak at the Governor's Hall and Lydia would do as she asked. But could she do it? Could she promise on her father's soul and not mean it? Her father was long dead. Would it trouble him if she broke her promise? Whether he was in heaven or hell was already a foregone conclusion. The larger question was could she knowingly lie to Lydia? Well, she supposed, she didn't know if she was actually lying. Whether or not she opened her mouth in the Governor's Hall would depend on how events unfolded this day. She would do what must be done. She would make the promise. Then she would see what the day revealed.

"I...I promise," she whispered.

AT MID-MORNING, LYDIA stood up from her seat on the low stone wall where she had been sitting since soon after she and Catherine parted company in Market Square. Lydia had gone to Bookbinders Row, but not before reminding Catherine of her promise, and not before watching the effort with which her beloved walked toward the Governor's Hall. Lydia was concerned that the burden of grief Catherine bore over Cate's plight was what weighed her down and she felt helpless to do anything about it.

Nothing had happened at the Pewseys all morning. The shutters in the shop had been thrown open since the spring morning carried a refreshing breeze. Lydia saw Oliver Pewsey come into his shop shortly after she arrived, but she had seen nothing of his wife or his daughters. An eerie quiet permeated the street. At this time of the morning, it should have been filled with people going about their business. Where was everybody?

No doubt they had all gone to the Hall. She had heard the whisperings of people as they passed earlier that day. Word had spread quickly that Cate Pritchard and her son were in custody and that the priests would examine the boy for the devil's mark. Anger welled up in Lydia. She could picture the whole town milling about outside the Hall, waiting for word of what had taken place inside, looking for sordid details of Cate's fate and particulars of Andrew's supposed evil mark. Maybe Catherine wasn't so far from wrong to verbally attack the Church for its hypocrisy. While she was at it, Lydia thought, Catherine should probably assail the townspeople for their treachery, too. They were no better than the priests. Or perhaps it was the other way around. Perhaps the priests were no better than the common people, looking for imagined evils and scapegoats.

As she stood there, wrestling with these thoughts, she saw someone else come into the shop from the living quarters. She recognized the silhouette as that of Isobel Pewsey. She watched as father and daughter engaged in animated conversation. Lydia was too far away to hear their words, but she mused that she didn't think Isobel capable of such liveliness. As she watched the interaction, another form appeared in the room behind Isobel and took part in the exchange. Lydia recognized the smaller shape as Isobel's sister, Winifred. Oliver Pewsey's hand flailed as he spoke. Winifred threw her hands up in the air. Isobel stood with hers on her hips. What could they be arguing about? Perhaps the girls had heard what was happening at the Governor's Hall and wanted to be with the rest of the town to participate in the excitement. As she watched Oliver, hands waving as he spoke, both girls turned and stomped toward their living quarters. Oliver Pewsey's chest heaved. Then he went back to his worktable.

A short time later, Lydia heard footsteps approaching at a quick pace down the empty street. When she looked in the direction of the sound, she saw one of the constable's men running, face reddened from the effort. Lydia slipped behind the wall and crouched down, only peeking around the opening when she knew that the man had reached the ink and papermaking shop. As he entered, he called out breathlessly to Master Pewsey. Then the heavy door slammed shut and she could hear no more. A few minutes later, Isobel and Winifred ran into the shop. Another animated conversation took place among the four of them.

Lydia wondered if the man had come as a result of the goings-on at the Governor's Hall. There had to be a reason why the Pewseys had locked themselves away from all the excitement. She ducked back behind the wall wrestling with a feeling that she should go to the Hall instead of hiding out spying on the Pewsey family. When she poked her head above the wall to look into the shop across the street, the four people inside were still talking, arguing from the look of their movements. As the moments ticked away, she realized what she had to do.

Stepping around the opening in the stone wall, Lydia quickly made her way to the road that led to the Governor's Lane.

CATHERINE FOUND THE scene in the Governor's Hall to be exactly as it had been the day before. The tall priest sat on the dais with the Dark Monk behind him. The early morning sun made the monk seem even darker than he was in his black robe and cowl, just as it had done the day before. The only difference this morning was that the room was filled to capacity with townspeople. Their presence angered Catherine for she knew that they had only come to gape and to be privy to the proceedings so that they could carry gossip to their friends and neighbors. In the corner of the room, sitting at a small angled desk, again sat the local cleric with a quill poised over his paper, ready to write down an account of the proceedings. Catherine balled her fists as she stood stoically beside Will and Sarah listening to the priest.

"...because you have been accused of such things, we are come here this morning to examine the child born to you." Gaspar motioned in the direction where Sam Cooper stood. "Bring the boy here."

Sam elbowed his way through the crowd until he stood in front of the priest. Andrew appeared to be sleeping contentedly.

The priest nodded toward the bundle cradled in Sam's arms. "Is this the child of Mistress Pritchard?"

"Yes, Your Excellency, it is. His name is Andrew."

"And can you swear that this child has been under your watchful eye all night?"

Without hesitation, Sam said, "Yes, sir, he has."

Gaspar's expression changed to a smug smile. "Bring him closer. I would examine him for the devil's mark."

The crowd shifted, nervous at the mention of such evil portents. Sam approached the dais and held Andrew out toward the priest. As he did, the Dark Monk leaned forward to get a better view.

"Remove his wrappings," Gaspar commanded.

Sam did as he was ordered. When the wrap fell away from Andrew's head, Catherine could see that it was covered with thick black hair. No white patch could be seen. She breathed a sigh of relief.

The tall priest looked down his nose and let his eyes wander all over Andrew's head. Gradually, his expression changed from confidence to disorientation. He turned his head slightly and the Dark Monk moved to his side, whispering to him as he had done the day before. The priest seemed to recover. He snapped, "Turn him over. Let me see the back of his head."

Sam gently turned Andrew so that his stomach rested across his thick forearm. He pulled the blanket back and patted Andrew reassuringly.

Black. All there was to see on Andrew's head was thick black hair. The priest squinted at the child. Then he gestured brusquely for Sam to turn him face up again and he peered into the baby's face. Catherine saw the priest's expression become confused again, and he turned slightly toward the Dark Monk.

The monk's hood engulfed the left side of Gaspar's head while he spoke in low tones into the priest's ear. In spite of Catherine's position at the front of the crowd, she could not hear him.

As the monk stepped back, Gaspar's head became whole again. He sat for a moment, pursing his lips. Then he glared at Cate. With a voice full of contempt, he asked, "Has this child been baptized?"

Cate hesitated. "No, sir, he hasn't." A low murmur filled the room. Cate quickly offered, "I had no way to have him baptized. I said yesterday when I spoke that I spent my time away from Willowglen, alone in prayer. There was no one to give him the sacrament."

Gaspar stared at Andrew again. Then, he looked up and said to no one in particular, "Bring water. I shall baptize him now. The child must not be allowed to remain a heathen."

The hall buzzed as the people speculated as to why the priest had decided on this course of action, but Catherine had no doubts. He wanted to prove that Andrew's hair had not been changed by some means. She felt her heart beating rapidly in her chest, hoping that the ink would not run. Andrew's life depended on it. She looked over at Cate whose face was so white that she looked as if she had seen an apparition. Over Cate's head, she glimpsed Fiona towering over the crowd, her eyes filled with terror.

Catherine turned her attention back to the priest just as someone appeared out of the crowd and handed Gaspar a ewer filled with water. The man held out a basin. Gaspar motioned for Sam to hold the baby over the vessel and the priest began to pour methodically over the child's head.

"Ego te baptizo—*I baptize you*...in the name of the Father...and of the Son..." The priest poured water liberally, getting the child's head wet all over. Andrew opened his mouth and wailed. Gaspar raised his voice and continued, "...and of the Holy Ghost." The

Dark Monk and a few others added their "Amen" to his prayer.

Gaspar stared at the water in the basin. Catherine stretched her neck to see. The water was clear, and she breathed a sigh of relief. Andrew continued to howl.

The Dark Monk stepped forward and engulfed Gaspar's ear once again. When the monk stepped back, Gaspar raised his voice over the sound of Andrew's crying and pronounced, "Clearly, this child objects to us giving him this sacrament. If he is not the child of the devil himself, he is certainly possessed by the evil one. Why else would he protest this way?"

A ripple of whispers hissed around the hall. Catherine felt sick to her stomach.

Gaspar's face contorted into a twisted, angry visage as he continued, "Although I cannot say how, the mother has bewitched us. Clearly, she is a witch. She has lain with the devil and used his power to trick us all into believing that the child of this union has no mark. Yet you hear him yourselves. The child objects to being baptized into the Church. He rejects God's grace." He looked down at Andrew with loathing and pronounced, "He cannot be allowed to live."

The crowd gasped. Andrew stopped crying. Gaspar lowered his voice and continued, "Neither can the woman responsible for this issue. They shall both die at the stake." At that, both Cate and Will fell on the floor in a faint.

Gaspar watched Cate crumple, a look of contempt on his face. He turned to Sam and, with a fierce look in his eyes, he said, "Give that *thing* to someone else to hold." Another of the constable's men pushed his way to Sam's side and held out his arms to take the baby. Then Gaspar wheezed between panting breaths, "Now...bring me...Isobel Pewsey."

At that, someone screamed, the crowd pushed forward, and chaos broke out in the room.

TO CATHERINE, TIME appeared to have slowed. Frozen to the spot where she stood, she looked down at Will lying on the floor just in time to see Sarah slowly drop to her knees by his side. In heavy, elongated words Catherine heard her say, "You've killed my husband!" It took a great deal of effort for Catherine to turn her head in the opposite direction, but when she did, she saw Sam stomping off at a snail's pace through the crowd and assumed that he moved so slowly because of the crush of people pushing against him as they moved toward the center of the room. She saw Cate stir and sit up as if slowly drawn with invisible ropes. Fiona reached her in one long stride and bent down to scoop her into a standing position.

Catherine herself wanted to shout, to tell Gaspar that he was making a terrible mistake. She thought about the scene she had witnessed the night before in the Chapel in the Governor's Hall, and she considered accusing the priests of terrible deeds before the altar of God, but she couldn't. The heavy air that surrounded her pressed in on her chest and she couldn't take in enough air to speak.

As Fiona steadied Cate, the man holding Andrew handed the baby to Cate. As she clutched him to her breast in a protective gesture, Catherine saw tears slide down Cate's cheeks. And still Catherine could not draw a breath.

At the very moment when she thought she, too, would faint for lack of air, a familiar voice shouted from the back of the room, bursting the oppressive bubble that engulfed her. She drew in a huge, redeeming breath that sent a searing pain into her lungs. Time resumed its normal passage as she turned in the direction of the outburst. Lydia emerged from the crowd.

Lydia opened her mouth to speak, her face ablaze. "What absurd folly is this? The child has no mark. You have seen for yourself. The accusation is false. The mother is no more than a young girl who fell under the influence of a honey-tongued wandering minstrel. She is not the first and she will not be the last. If you must, put her in the stocks for her indiscretion, but do not condemn an innocent child." She stood at Cate's side now. "And if I were you, priest, I would look into my own life to see what evils there are for which I must repent. You would do well to consider what you do while at your prayers."

Gaspar's eyes widened at the same moment that the Dark Monk's head came up and his body stiffened.

Lydia pressed on with her railing. "Perhaps you should take a lesson from your own preaching and think about the hypocrisy of your own actions in the chapel last night." Gaspar stared, looking as if he'd seen a specter. The Dark Monk started to move forward. "Compared to you, these two have done nothing. They do not deserve such punishment as you have decreed." She pointed an accusing finger at Gaspar. "Think on your own life before you pronounce judgment on others, priest."

As Catherine let out her breath, she screamed, "Lydia, No!" And with a look of torment in her eyes, she pleaded, "Please, say no more."

But Lydia would not be silenced. She ranted on. As she spoke again, Gaspar found his voice and called for her to be still, but she refused to listen. Andrew started to wail again and both Cate and Sarah cried loudly.

"Silence!" Gaspar hurled his command into the din and

pounded his fist on the table. "All of you, be quiet!" Everyone stopped, including Andrew. Gaspar blinked into the room, his chest heaving, his angular face reddened in anger. When he composed himself enough to speak again, he pointed to Lydia. "Lock this woman away. I'll have her at the stake with the other one. How dare she say such blasphemous things against us? We are doing God's work here. Surely this shows that you, too, are filled with wickedness and sin." He waved them off as if they were flies at his food. "Take them all way. Prepare for a burning. We will purge this infernal town of its evil. Clear the room. Everyone out. Out, I say." Then looking around, he shouted, "Where is that Pewsey woman?"

No one answered. Only a scuffling sound could be heard as the occupants busied themselves trying to get out of the room. The press of the crowd, however, was too great to exit through the door with any speed. As they joined others in the street who were not able to gain entry to the Hall, they were assailed with questions. At the back of the crowd, Catherine saw Sarah supporting her still unsteady husband out the door. She looked back at Cate with wild fear in her eyes.

When the hall finally emptied, only Fiona and Catherine remained with Lydia, Cate and Andrew. Gaspar dropped into his seat, exhausted by his own outburst. The Dark Monk stood like a statue behind the priest. When Gaspar looked up and realized that Catherine and Fiona were still there, he looked at them with disdain and said simply, "If we are building a fire, we surely can add a few more sticks to accommodate the two of you."

Fiona's cheeks burned with indignation. "I will not leav—"

"No!" Catherine shouted. She glared at Fiona, willing her to come to her senses. What good would they be if they, too, were imprisoned? They would gain nothing and possibly lose everything. Still looking at Fiona, Catherine said, "We will leave. We want no more trouble. Come, Fiona."

Out of the corner of her eye, Catherine saw the look on Cate's face. It nearly broke her heart. Lydia's eyes burned with anger. Catherine wondered if she was angry with the priest's unjust accusations and rantings or at what appeared to be Catherine's cowardly attitude. She realized that arguing with a man who had lost his senses was fruitless. She needed time to think, time to plan. She was certain that she and Fiona were Cate and Lydia's only hope. In order to help, she had to get Fiona out of the Governor's Hall.

She turned on her heel and headed for the now empty doorway that led outside. Fiona didn't follow. Catherine stopped, turned back, and demanded, "Fiona. Now. Please. We must go."

Like a sturdy oak, Fiona stood rooted by Cate's side. Catherine saw the muscles of her jaw contract and twitch. She looked at Gaspar, who only stared, fuming, saying nothing. In desperation, Catherine stormed back across the room. Without looking at either Lydia or Cate this time, she grabbed Fiona by the arm and pulled. The large woman didn't budge. Panic welled up in Catherine. She looked into Fiona's eyes and said, "Fiona, please, come with me."

A look of understanding appeared across Fiona's face. She, too, now refused to look at Cate. Fiona and Catherine bolted for the door.

THE CROWD OUTSIDE the Governor's Hall buzzed with gossip. When Catherine and Fiona emerged everyone stopped talking and stared at the two women. Catherine, desperate to be away from the prying eyes of the townspeople, plunged through the crowd. Fiona followed on her heels. Ripples of whispers resumed, closing in around them. In several long strides, the two women turned into the lane, away from the curious onlookers. As they hurried along, Fiona asked, "What is your plan, Catherine? I perceived that you have one and are in need of my help again."

Catherine refused to meet Fiona's deep blue gaze. Instead, she kept her eyes on the cobbles as they picked their way over them back toward Market Street. Finally, she said, "You are correct, Fiona. I do require your help, but I have no idea what we are going to do to get Lydia, Cate and Andrew out of this predicament. All I knew was that we had to get out of there before that mad priest condemned us to burn, too. What good would we be to our friends if we were locked away with them?"

Fiona stopped and stared, a puzzled look on her face. Catherine slowed her pace as Fiona asked, "Do you mean you don't have a plan?"

Catherine stopped and looked Fiona in the eye, saying with a confidence she didn't feel, "Just because I don't have a plan now, doesn't mean I won't have one later. I need some time to think. And I needed one less person to worry about. I couldn't have them lock you away, too. I thought I had made sure that Lydia would stay away from the Governor's Hall today. I don't know what she was doing there. She was so concerned that I would say something that would get me into trouble, and yet, she's the one we should have been worried about."

Catherine stopped speaking. A crowd had gathered around her and Fiona as they spoke. When Catherine realized that they were there, she gestured for Fiona to walk with her again. The onlookers didn't follow. "That priest is truly mad. I have a feeling that he is no more than a puppet to that Dark Monk. If there is evil in Willowglen, it came to town with those Churchmen. If we figure out how to get rid of them, we'll be able to free Cate and her son — and Lydia. Catherine's voice cracked with emotion when she said Lydia's name.

They kept walking, not really knowing where they were headed. When they arrived at the living quarters where Edward and John, the silversmiths, lived, they went in and resumed their discussion.

LYDIA SAT IN a storeroom no more than the size of a small pantry. The door was bolted from the outside. She slumped down onto a storage crate and tried to slow her breathing. Anger still burned within her against the injustice that she had witnessed. Slowly, the realization came to her. The priest was mad. He wasn't in control at all. He obviously took his cues from the Dark Monk. Lydia shivered when she thought of the monk, and a feeling of dread came over her — and something else that she couldn't put her finger on. It was almost as if she felt that she should recognize him, but how could she with his face buried deep within his monk's hood? She shivered again and rested her back against the cold, damp wall of her confinement. What was it about that monk?

AT THE BIDDING of the priests, the constable's men returned Cate to the larger room she had occupied the night before. She looked up at the open window high above her head hoping she would hear Fiona's voice, but she heard nothing.

That was it, then. Fiona hadn't cared for her as much as she said she did. She could understand that, but to think that Catherine didn't care what happened to Lydia, she could not understand. Cate struggled to contain her anger. Would her godmother abandon Lydia, her and her child? She could not bring herself to believe it. Perhaps they were trying to do something now, as she sat there in this cold, bleak room. In spite of her attempt to remain confident, a dark mood filled with hopelessness overtook her.

Cate understood the way of the world when things got difficult. After all, Nathaniel had abandoned her without a thought when she told him she was with child, and that was a much smaller thing than being condemned to burn. She looked down at the tiny boy cradled in her arms. A painful sadness settled on her chest. If only she could save him, she would be willing to give up her own life. She saw no hope. Tears streamed down her face again as she wondered how long they had to live.

Chapter
Twenty-one

CATHERINE PACED ACROSS Edward's living space as the old man dozed in front of the fire. Thankfully, he seemed oblivious to the anxious conversation that took place among Fiona, her family and Catherine. When Fiona informed her father and brothers of what had happened, they were appalled, but they insisted it was unwise to interfere with a priest as unstable as Gaspar had apparently become.

Duncan shrugged and said, "No offense, Catherine, I know these people mean a great deal to you, but I'll not put my family in harm's way to come up against a radical priest and that menacing monk I've heard about."

As much as Catherine would have liked to have the help of Duncan and his sons, she understood that he had no vested interest in these terrible events, and she resigned herself to the fact that Duncan would be of no assistance to them. Fiona, however, couldn't control her anger at her father's refusal to help. She tramped from the house to the garden without another word. Catherine found her chopping firewood, each fall of the blade an expression of her frustration and rage.

"Fiona."

Fiona raised the heavy ax high over her head and let it fall with such thrust that it embedded itself halfway into the large log on which she was splitting the wood. She had to tug several times to free the blade.

"Fiona, you must stop. We have to talk."

Fiona reeled toward Catherine letting the momentum of the weapon twist her around. Her eyes were so dark that they looked purple and they shone with tears.

"What is there to talk about?" Fiona snapped. "They've got Cate. They've got Andrew. They've got Lydia. My family refuses to help us. We have nothing. We are powerless against them. They will kill them, Catherine. Don't you care?"

Catherine couldn't control her own anger any longer. She

pushed forward and stood close to Fiona. Eye to eye, each could feel warm breath on her face from the other. Catherine stared at Fiona through hooded eyes.

"Understand this, Fiona Smith." She poked Fiona with a long finger. "I care with all my heart. Cate Pritchard is very dear to me, so her son could not be otherwise. Lydia is my life. Too many times in this lifetime have we been parted from one another. I will *not* allow that to happen again. If we could have secured aid from your father and brothers, it would have been very helpful, but they are not our only source of support. You forget. At Briarcrest, we have men pledged to protect us. Those men are trained in the art of battle. They would not hesitate to kill for us if our lives were in danger. I think this qualifies as one of those times. I suspect that we may only have a day or two to act. Those priests will be in a hurry to see this deed done. If we are to have any hope of preventing this dreadful thing, I must get word to Hubert. Unfortunately, he has returned to Briarcrest and it is almost a full day's journey there."

For the first time since the distressing events at the Governor's Hall, Fiona saw a glimmer of hope. Of course. Briarcrest has the resources. With Catherine's men, they might just be able to do something. "When do we leave?" Fiona asked.

"I think we should not hesitate. I fear if we do not leave now, we may be followed. After all, it is clear from Gaspar's remarks that we are now suspect as well."

Before Catherine had finished her last sentence, Fiona had set the ax down and made for the street in several long strides. She turned back to Catherine and, in her husky voice, merely said, "Let's be off, then."

BY THE TIME Catherine appeared at the blacksmith's stables dressed in leggings and a tunic covered by her traveling cloak, Fiona already had the horses ready. Brilley pawed the ground, her muscles tense with anticipation of the ride. Catherine's own horse nodded and whinnied as if to say she was ready to take her mistress wherever she needed to go.

Catherine hoped that they had not waited too long to start their journey. If the priests had the sense to have them followed, they might be stopped on the road and detained or worse. Catherine shivered at the thought. Was she doing the right thing involving Fiona in this? Perhaps she should go alone. But the road to Briarcrest was fraught with perils. A rider might come up against bandits and robbers. The ride was not easy, especially as quickly as they needed to go. They couldn't lose any time if they hoped to make it back in time to rescue Cate and Lydia.

To avoid being seen leaving Willowglen, the two women walked the horses along a footpath behind the rows of houses on Market Street. At one point, Fiona had Catherine take Brilley and continue on while Fiona doubled back to make sure that they were not being followed. When she caught up to Catherine again, she said that it appeared that they were alone. As they neared the Market Gate, they mounted. Fiona turned on Brilley and looked up the road behind them. She still saw no one following them. The two women nodded to one another and urged their horses into a gallop. Moments later, they turned onto the Old Roman Road in the direction that would take them to Briarcrest.

Chapter
Twenty-two

THE USUALLY PROPER priest slumped in his chair on the dais. The Dark Monk spoke to him in low, soothing tones. Concerned about what Gaspar intended to do to Isobel, he hoped that he would only reproach her and be done. The stupid girl had been mistaken, that's all. There was no mark on the boy. There was nothing to be done for it now. Anyway, it didn't matter. Iago had what he wanted, and it had come to him earlier than he hoped. The thought of Lydia held in a room below the Governor's Hall excited him. It took every ounce of control for him not to leave Gaspar to his own devices and go to her, but he thought better of it. He was so close. He couldn't let the disturbed priest spoil things for him now.

Gaspar seemed to recover a little while they waited. When Iago told him that he should question Isobel, but then let her go, Gaspar resisted, his anger rising again. The only way that Iago could get him to calm himself and agree to the monk's suggestion was by promising to pray with Gaspar again. This time, though, he knew he wouldn't go through with it.

One thing Iago was certain of was that they couldn't risk involving any more townspeople. Killing the printer's daughter and her son would be enough. He had other plans for Lydia.

He was through with his clandestine manipulations of Gaspar. The monk himself needed to take charge. The priest had served his purpose. He watched Gaspar as he sat muttering under his breath, fully aware that the priest hovered on the edge of madness. Gaspar would be dangerous now. Iago stared into the old man's unseeing eyes. The black centers were large with almost none of the surrounding dark brown color visible. Iago would have to be careful.

SAM COOPER ARRIVED with a frightened, sniveling Isobel Pewsey in tow. Looking at the pathetic girl, Iago realized that she, too, could easily be pushed over the brink to total irrationality.

What did it matter in this case though? The girl was already an ugly simpleton. He should do the town a favor and let Gaspar burn her, too. Yet he knew that if the townspeople became aware of Gaspar's unstable condition, they would rebel against his actions. Taking one prominent merchant's daughter might be allowed, but inflicting harm on two probably would not be tolerated.

The townspeople might take matters into their own hands if that happened. The priests would be powerless against an angry mob, especially since that coward of a chief constable, Ben Godling, had fled with half his men before the proceedings had even begun. At the first sign of trouble in the town he had sworn to keep safe, the man had run like a rat with a starving cat in pursuit. Iago sneered at the thought. Godling's cowardice had left Gaspar and Iago in a position to easily take command of the rest of Godling's men. The remaining constabulary feared the power and influence of the Church enough to allow Iago and Gaspar to command them. Thus, they were able to pursue the printer's daughter. Of course, the Dark Monk only wanted her because he hoped that she would bring Lydia to Willowglen.

When Iago realized that there was a connection between the printer and Briarcrest, he had hoped that, with the presence of the spice vendor in the town, he would be able to attract Lydia to the proceedings. He had thought that he would have to have Gaspar throw the Hawkins woman into the fire to cause Lydia to come to her harlot's rescue. But it had all turned out to be so much easier than he had anticipated. Lydia had appeared, railing in the printer's daughter's defense. Gaspar, already unstable, played right into Iago's hand without even knowing it.

The monk licked his lips as he thought of Lydia so close and within his grasp. Tonight, he finally would have her. By the morning, he planned to be gone, taking her with him. She would finally be his forever. Months of pining and waiting would be over. The dream he had hoped to realize all those years before would finally be his.

GASPAR ROUSED FROM his babbling stupor when Isobel appeared before him. He fired question after question at her. Did she, or did she not, see that the boy had had the mark of the devil on him? Did he have a mark of white hair indicating where the devil's member had touched him at conception? Hadn't Isobel told the Dark Monk as much? How could she have been so sure, and yet, when they examined the child, his head was a black as soot? Had she lied? If she had lied to a priest, she, too, would stand in the fire in which her accused was about to die.

With that, Isobel, tears rolling down her fat, misshapen face, looked down at the floor and muttered unintelligibly.

Iago knew that he had to do something. He couldn't deal with two people infected by madness. He thought about the promise Oliver Pewsey had elicited from him. Just as he was about to intervene in Gaspar's incessant assault, Winifred burst through the door of the Governor's Hall with her father hobbling and panting behind her in pursuit.

Winifred ran to her sister and Isobel fell into her arms. "There, there," Winifred cooed, patting her on the shoulder. "Don't let these men frighten you, Issy. It will be all right. I'll take care of you."

Oliver Pewsey stumbled to a place beside his daughters and tried desperately to speak, but he was too winded. He looked on as Winifred continued to comfort her sister.

"A touching scene," Gaspar said with contempt, "however, the fact remains. You, Isobel Pewsey, have lied to us and the Church condemns your mortal soul to hell forever for lying." Isobel whimpered at the condemnation. Oliver sputtered a protest. He looked to the Dark Monk, who said nothing.

Winifred's body tensed and she looked at Gaspar and stammered, "Leave her alone. Can't you see that my sister isn't as quick as most people? How can you say such things to her?"

"Quiet, girl, for I hear you have had a hand in these falsehoods as well. I shall condemn your soul to hell along with this one." He pointed to Isobel, who did not make eye contact with him.

"Go ahead," Winifred screamed. "I don't believe in your stupid condemnations anyway. You're all like the Pharisees that you preach against. You say there are lessons to be learned from the way that they acted in Christ's time, but you don't heed your own teachings. Now, leave my sister alone."

Calmly now and quietly, Gaspar stood up and made his next pronouncement. Pointing at the Pewsey sisters, he shouted, "Burn, burn. You shall all burn. The Pewsey sisters will now also burn. It will be a grand fire, purging this hateful city of all of its evil."

Red-faced Oliver Pewsey, beside himself with anguish, tried to defend his daughters, but couldn't get the words out. Gaspar looked him in the eye and said, "Careful, Master Pewsey, or you shall join your daughters on the pyre."

"Brother Monk, please," Oliver cried out then. "Remember your promise. Please. I have kept my own counsel and have said nothing of your words in my own house. Protect my daughters."

Iago knew that he had to intervene quickly. From deep within the cavern of his dark cowl, he soothed, "Father Gaspar, perhaps we should not be too hasty. After all, Isobel was only trying to help.

She tried to be a good Christian by telling us about the child. Perhaps she was mistaken in what she saw. Surely we can forgive this error."

Unfortunately, Isobel found her tongue. "I didn't make a mistake. I saw what I saw. I thought it was funny that Cate Pritchard's baby had a white spot on his head and I told Winifred. She was the one told me I should come and tell you, that you would know if it was a bad omen or not. She's the one who doesn't like Cate Pritchard anyway. She wanted Nathaniel Mistlewaite for herself and she knew she had no chance with him. She had me spy on the two of them all the—"

"Isobel!" Winifred's face contorted into a look of scorn as she spoke through clenched teeth. "Why don't you be quiet, sister, dear. You're too stupid to know what you're talking about—"

"Fathers," Oliver interrupted, "forgive my daughters. This is nothing more than a childish disagreement. Pay no attention to them. They are distraught. They don't know what they're saying."

"I do so know what I'm saying, father," Winifred cried. "I'm tired of always having to look out for this one." She pushed Isobel away. "I'll never get a decent husband until you can marry *her* off to someone who doesn't realize what a simpleton she is. Otherwise, who will have her? Look at her! She's nothing but a fat ugly chit."

Isobel looked down at the floor, unable to meet her sister's gaze. "I can't help it. I'm not pretty and smart like you, Winifred."

"What did you hope to gain by sending Isobel to us, then?" Iago demanded.

Winifred answered, "I wanted to be rid of Cate Pritchard. If she wasn't around taking the attention of every young man that comes to town, maybe my father could finally interest some dullard of a man in Isobel. Then, at last, I might have my turn. I want a man between my le—"

"Winifred!" Beads of sweat formed on Oliver's brow. He pleaded, "Please, Winifred, let us not burden the good fathers with our family problems." He smiled weakly at Iago. "With your permission, please good monk, I beg of you, remember your promise. Have mercy. Let me take my daughters home."

"No," Gaspar said.

Iago leaned in toward Gaspar and whispered, "Father, let us pray about this. We will go into the chapel together."

Gaspar brightened. He looked into the blackness of Iago's cowl and said, "If you wish, my brother, we will pray."

"Let them go, Gaspar." Iago hissed. "We have no further need of them. You have made your decision about what will happen to the printer's daughter and that other woman who dared to defy you. That is enough. That is all the Lord requires of us here. I am certain of it."

Gaspar squinted into the dark cowl for a long moment. Finally, he sighed. "As you wish, brother," he said. "Let us go to the chapel to pray, then."

Iago turned back to the Pewseys, his triumphant smile unseen. "Master Pewsey, take your daughters and leave...*now*," he commanded.

The rotund man quickly herded his daughters toward the door of the Governor's Hall. As he did, he whispered to Winifred, "I don't know what's gotten into you. We shall have a long talk when we get home, my girl." Winifred shrugged his hand from her shoulder as she stormed ahead. Isobel lagged behind, so Oliver turned his attention toward his older daughter. "Come along, Isobel. Let us get home. Our business is done here. No one will be prodding you for any more information about Cate Pritchard or her baby. It's over, Issy." He took her by the hand and followed Winifred from the Hall. As he left, he heard Gaspar whimper, "Can we go to the chapel to pray now, brother, p-l-e-a-s-e?"

"Not now," Iago snapped. "There is a more important matter that requires my attention."

Chapter
Twenty-three

LYDIA STIRRED AND sat up at the sound of wood being drawn across the door. As it creaked open, she blinked, holding up her hand in an effort to ward off the blinding lantern light that flooded the small dark room. She couldn't make out the figure standing in the doorway. When her eyes finally adjusted, she shuddered. The lamplight lit up faint features in the depths of the Dark Monk's cowl. Light and shadows played off cheekbones and chin. Once more, she had the feeling that she should recognize the man, but she couldn't place him. He stepped into the room and pushed the door closed behind him. He stood in front of her, saying nothing for a long time. She watched his chest rise and fall, almost unnaturally, and she wondered if he was having difficulty breathing.

When he finally spoke, his voice was hoarse and strained. "I have waited a long time for this moment."

Lydia cocked her head, trying to place the voice. She couldn't. Her question came out in a whisper. "Who are you?"

"Lydia, Lydia, I'm shocked that you don't recognize an old friend."

She tilted her head in the other direction. Who was it? She should know. This voice was from a long distant past, but where in the past, and to whom did it belong?

The monk put the lantern down beside him, his breathing somewhat eased, his voice stronger now. "I'm very happy that we can renew our long lost friendship. You and I are going to spend a great deal of time together. We shall make up for all the time we've lost. This time, no one will interfere. This time, I'm going to teach you many things."

Teach her? Lessons. She stuck her neck out a little more to try to get a better look at the face. An icy fear crept through her body. She knew now. "Isadore," she hissed. "I—I thought you were...dead."

"I could say the same about you. That is, until I found out

otherwise from someone who traveled this way not long ago. When I heard of the two ladies who lived at Briarcrest, I wondered that those old hens had somehow managed to survive after all this time, but when I was told one used to have a shop in Willowglen, I knew immediately that it was that spice merchant and I hoped that her companion was the beautiful Lady Lydia. But let us not dwell on the past. We should turn our attention to the present and to our future."

Lydia felt the sweat forming on her brow and upper lip. Her mouth was dry.

Isadore continued, "We've been apart a long time, but we'll be together for the rest of our lives. Have no fear, my fair Lydia. I have a plan. I've been thinking on it for a long time." He tapped a plump finger to the side of his hood at his temple area. "Ever since I found that you were not dead. We are going away, just you and I, together." He smiled a tortuous smile at the thought.

"You have no right..." Anger rose within her. She clenched her fists in an effort to control it, knowing that she had to be careful.

"Right? Do not speak to me of privilege. I have had to compromise and give concessions all my life, first with your father, then with that cow of a nurse, not to mention that aunt of yours who ruled Briarcrest. She, too, was most determined to keep you from me." The tension in his face was evident, even in the low light. "Do you know that I have had to spend more than two decades pretending to care about—in more ways than I'd care to enumerate—that pathetic, arrogant priest who condemned you?"

His face relaxed and his tones were almost cooing as he said, "But don't worry, my Lydia. I'll rescue you from the jaws of death. Gaspar will not be able to send you to the fire because we shall be away together long before it happens."

"I'm not going anywhere with you." She choked back her rage. "I loathe you. You tried to kill me."

"Only because you wouldn't listen to me when I tried to teach you how to be an obedient woman," he whined. "You were on the road to hell with your independence and your heedlessness. I blame that woman, that nurse of yours, and your aunt for your godless behavior. Those women were too influential. They should never have been allowed to have such a hand in your upbringing. They all behaved far too much like men. They needed to be stopped, but I was powerless against them. Your father never listened to me. He had no use for me. He only allowed me to remain in his household because I had some ability to read and write, and he wanted you to learn these things. I wanted to teach you how to be a virtuous woman, to teach you to be obedient and to listen to the men who had your best interest in mind. If I could teach you, if I could show you how much I cared for you, then you would become a much more malleable woman. You needed someone to mold you."

"You were never the one to teach me anything," she snapped. "Not then, not now. Leave me. I want nothing to do with you." Her mind darted around the room looking for some means of escape, the search fruitless. It took all the control she could muster not to lunge at him, pummel him with her fists. Even in the dim light, he saw her eyes blazing.

"I see that the years have only made you even more unruly. We shall have a great deal of work to do, you and I. But have not a care, my Lydia. We will have time."

Lydia folded her arms across her chest. How could she defend herself against this man? She had to find a way. Unfortunately, she had not yet explored this room in which she was held captive. She had no idea if it contained anything that might be used as a weapon against the threat that Isadore posed. She turned away from him in scorn.

Isadore sighed into the silence. How could he win her over? He hesitated. "I—I never meant to hurt you back then, you know. I only meant to teach you a lesson." As he said it, he regretted his attempt to explain himself. Through clenched teeth, he added, "But you made me so vexed by your resistance."

Then in softer tones again, he added, "I was glad to hear that you lived, though. I truly was. Once I heard the news, I began to make my plans. It was just a matter of time until I could get Gaspar to see the way that we must follow. He came to understand that we must root out the evil in this town. I did it all for you, you know."

A joyless laugh left his lips. "Once we set foot in Willowglen, it was easy to prey upon the printmaker. Knowing that he had an association with Briarcrest gave me hope that one day I would encounter you and from there, it would be easy to make you mine. I knew, in truth, that we would have this sweet reuniting someday."

She turned to face him again, her face red with fury. "I have a truth for you, Isadore. This is no pleasant meeting as far as I'm concerned. I want no part of you. This whole thing is a mockery. That you would allow an innocent young woman and her blameless child to go to their deaths to get to me is detestable," she spat. "Have you no scruples?"

"Scruples?" His face contorted as he spewed out his next words. "I left my scruples by the docks of Bristow a long time ago. With the hounds of Briarcrest nipping at my heels, I left everything behind."

"After you tried to kill me."

"When I tried to teach you a lesson," he insisted. "I had to get on that ship to save my life and this was a most unpleasant thought to me. I was afraid of the sea, you see. I had long avoided it all my life. But with the dogs of Briarcrest on my trail, I had no choice. Once again, other men made a decision for me. What choice did I have? I had no one to defend me. The men of Greencastle had deserted me. I was not trained to fight. All I know are the ways of the Church, not warring. So you see where that left me. The ship was there. The captain was willing. I left for Spain that night. But that night, I also knew that I would do whatever it took to ensure my own survival. So, yes, I left any sense of right and wrong on the dock that night, along with a great deal more."

Listening to him, Lydia knew full well that Isadore had abandoned his sense of propriety long before that night. If he hadn't, he would never have tried to hurt her as he had done. Her chest rose and fell as she gulped back her resentment.

On what came to be a most dreadful night, Lydia had been distraught. After finally declaring their love for one another at the May festival at Briarcrest, she and Catherine were separated not knowing if they would ever see each other again. Marian, her nurse turned companion, had died quite suddenly compounding her grief. Her father had wanted to send her to France to marry a stranger. She wanted no part of his plan. She had no choice but to flee when she heard that Isadore was coming to Briarcrest intent on taking her back to her father.

In her anguish, she had been foolish enough to leave without preparation or plan. She fled to the Abbey of St. Nicholas where she intended to ask for refuge from her plight. She never made it.

When Isadore overtook her on the road, he had insisted that she accompany him. She refused and broke from his hold, running toward the Abbey, which was within sight. He caught up to her and, removing his rope from around his waist, he started beating her. She warded off his terrible blows as best she could with her hands, but he tripped her when she broke away, attempting to make for the Abbey again. As she hit the ground a searing pain surged through her head and everything went black. Still, this did not stop him. He ripped off her cloak and continued beating her. Frenzied, he commanded Greencastle's men to run her through with a sword, but they all pulled back, refusing to obey his command.

Lydia awakened from her stupor and tried to crawl free of him, but the rope came down across her back again as she scrambled on her hands and knees toward her sanctuary. Finally, something harder hit her and she went down again.

The next time she awoke, she thought she was in heaven. Women dressed in white surrounded her in a room bathed in the soft glow of candlelight. They moved their mouths as if they were chanting, but she heard nothing. She knew she wasn't dead when she tried to move and felt the pain that burned through her body. There was no pain in heaven, she thought just before everything went black again.

When she awoke later, Hilary's troubled face came into view as she bent over her. Her mouth moved, but Lydia couldn't understand her words. In the end she slumped back, deciding that it really didn't matter because she knew that she wouldn't be able to answer anyway. The pain in her head and her body was excruciating. As she stared into Hilary's face, it started to blur, then darkness engulfed her again. The next time she awoke, she was at Briarcrest and Catherine was with her, nursing her back to life and health.

Isadore spoke, bringing her back from her reverie. His voice had softened again. "Come here to me, Lydia. We've been apart for so long."

"No!" She shrank back onto the wooden crate until her back touched the wall. "Leave me alone, Isadore. Better still, let me go."

"Let you go? Oh, no, you won't be going anywhere until we leave together, my dear. I'm going to save you from burning with your little harlot friend. The printer's daughter and her wicked offspring will die. It will give Gaspar something to do. He needs something to keep himself occupied. You and I, however, will be long departed before he ever realizes what has happened." Isadore took a step closer. "Now, though, we shall have a little prelude of what is to come for us."

Isadore lunged for Lydia and she heaved his bulk from her. He charged her again, his face twisted in rage. As he neared, she rammed her knee up between his legs with all the power she could gather. He screamed and fell back, writhing on the floor, clutching himself, his knees drawn up tightly to his chest.

Lydia saw her chance. She jumped over him, made for the door, and pushed it open. She charged into the passageway just as two of the constable's men came running from around the corner and blocked her path.

Quickly sizing up the situation, one of the men grabbed her by the arm and shouted, "What have you done to him?"

Lydia looked him in the eye and said, "Given him a taste of his own medicine."

Isadore's continued shrieks brought the second man into the storeroom. When he finally calmed down, the man helped him as he struggled to stand. Half crouched and stumbling, Isadore raged, "I tried to help you, you offensive wench! No more," he sputtered. "I had thought to spare your life, but I shall see that you die with the others now."

He held himself as he hobbled from the passageway to the stairs to make his way up to the Governor's Hall. Halfway up the steps, he stopped. He grimaced and called back, "Lock her up. I'm going to see Gaspar."

The two men stood in the narrow passage, blinking in dismay. They looked from the now-empty stairway to each other and then at Lydia. Finally, one of them said, "In with you," as he thrust her back into the room.

"Fine," Lydia snapped as she stumbled over the threshold gaining her footing after a few steps. She stopped and smoothed her dress, then pushed her disheveled hair behind her ears and said, "It's better than the alternative."

She stomped toward the box and sat down with a thump. As she stared blankly back into the passage, one of the men scooped up the lantern from near the doorway and swung the door shut. Darkness engulfed her again. She heard the wooden bar scrape into place and men talking to one another for a brief while, then, everything went silent. She clambered up onto the box, raised her knees to her chest and wrapped her arms around her legs. Was there no way out of these horrible circumstances for her and Cate and her helpless baby? Had Catherine really abandoned her?

Chapter
Twenty-four

THE SUN HAD long set when the outline of Briarcrest, lit by a full moon, came into view. The horses chuffed as they galloped along the road. Exhaustion had overtaken Catherine hours before, but she insisted that they press on, not wanting to waste any time in reaching Hubert and his men.

Fiona intently watched the road before them, grateful for the light in the sky to help them on their way. Only fools and brigands were out at night, she thought. They weren't thieves, so they must be fools. Yes, she admitted to herself now, she was a fool and would always be so — a fool for Cate Pritchard.

As they rounded a bend, they were surprised to see a rider coming toward them from the opposite direction. He approached them at a gallop. Fiona glanced quickly at Catherine. She showed no recognition of the person, but she also noticed that Catherine seemed to be staring at the road ahead, unseeing. Fiona reached for the reins of Catherine's horse and pulled Brilley and Catherine's horse to a stop at the same time. They were out in the open with no place to hide, no way to avoid the approaching rider. They might as well hold up and wait for him.

Catherine realized that they had stopped as if she had been roused from a sleep. "Why did you stop?" she demanded. "We're almost there."

"Do you not see him, Catherine?" She pointed to the approaching horseman.

"Oh," Catherine said, the fatigue evident in her voice. "No, I didn't."

"No place to get away from him now. I thought we might just as well wait here and have a wee rest. We'll have the advantage if we're ready for him. Here, take this." Fiona handed Catherine a thin dagger from within her boot. Catherine dismounted and took the weapon. The two women stood side by side between their horses, leaning against their flanks. Fiona drew her sword, and the horseman halted a short distance from them.

The rider slid from his horse. As he walked toward them, he cried, "What in name of all the saints are you doing out here in the middle of the night?"

"Hubert." Catherine lowered the dagger and breathed a sigh of relief. Fiona sheathed her sword. "I'm so glad you've come, but how did you know?"

"I couldn't sleep. I decided to walk the old ramparts. It's a lucky thing that the moon is full tonight. I saw your horses approaching. As you came closer, I thought I recognized your horse Dancer's odd gait, Catherine. I couldn't believe my eyes. For a moment, I thought, no, it can't be, but the more I watched that horse, the more certain I was that it was you. So let me ask again, what are you doing out here in the middle of the night without an escort?"

"We've come for your help, Hubert. It's a long story, though, and I fear my legs won't hold me much longer. Please, let's get to Briarcrest. We can continue this conversation there."

Hubert held Catherine's gaze for a long while. Finally, he said, "Catherine, you're very tired, so are the horses. I know it will take longer, but let's finish the journey at a slower pace."

"No, Hubert. We cannot waste any time. If I did not have need of others to help us, I would turn around and head back to Willowglen now. However, we must go to Briarcrest to get more help, so let us do it quickly."

Hubert knew when to argue with his Ladies and when not to do so. He could tell that this was one of those times when it was best to do as Catherine commanded. They mounted their horses and sped off toward Briarcrest at a full gallop again.

WHEN THEY REACHED Briarcrest Hall, Hubert went off to find a kitchen maid whom he instructed to bring water for Catherine and Fiona to wash the grime of the road from their faces. He also had her bring food and drink for them. As they sat eating before the banked fire in the huge stone fireplace in the Great Hall, they told Hubert what had taken place in Willowglen since he had returned to Briarcrest.

"I knew I should have stayed," he said, pounding his fist into his other hand. "I had a feeling that something was not right in that place."

"Don't trouble yourself, Hubert. You couldn't have known, and I did insist that there was no reason for you to stay. The important thing is that you return with us and bring all the help you can. We must make a plan."

Hubert tried to talk Catherine and Fiona into staying behind, promising to gather his men and head to Willowglen at first light, but neither woman would hear of it. When it became apparent that they would return to Willowglen, whether with him or on their own, he said, "It will take me a little time to gather the men and make the horses ready for the journey. I've sent someone to tend to your horses, but it would be prudent to use fresh ones for the return trip. In the meantime, I'll send someone on ahead to find out what has happened since you left Willowglen. My man can meet us back on the road and give us a full report. With that information, we should be able to make a plan. For now, you two look as if you could do with a good sleep. There will be nothing more for you to do until we're ready to leave. Why don't you rest a little?"

Fiona and Catherine looked at one another and saw their own weariness reflected in each other's eyes. "Yes, I could do with a brief sleep," Catherine admitted. "Wake us as soon as you've assembled everyone. I want to get back on the road as quickly as possible. I don't think we have much time."

"I'll have someone call you. You have my word. We should be ready before daybreak."

As Hubert turned and hurried down the length of Briarcrest Hall, Catherine beckoned Fiona to follow her. They climbed the staircase leading to the upper chambers of the house, and Catherine showed Fiona to a room containing a large tapestry-enclosed bed. Then she left for her own room. Both women had fallen into their beds, fully clothed, and were asleep before Hubert had reached the outer courtyard. As he started for the village to rouse his men, he wondered just how many he would need to rescue the captives from the clutches of Churchmen.

Chapter
Twenty-five

IN A VOICE filled with anger, Isadore shouted, "That woman kicked me with immense force." He limped around the room still hunched over, holding himself.

"Iago, please calm down," Gaspar beseeched. Iago had come to Gaspar's room to tell him what had happened. He hoped someone would offer him sympathy for what had happened, even if it was only this half-crazed priest. "What were you doing with that woman, anyway? They are both wicked. You shouldn't soil yourself with them. Let the constable's men deal with them." He watched Isadore pace around the room. When he started shouting again, Gaspar pleaded with him to temper his voice. "You'll have everyone wondering if it is I who has done you harm."

Isadore gave Gaspar a look of contempt. In the end, he knew full well that all Gaspar cared about was himself. He wondered if he should yield to the burning rage within him and tell him to stop calling him by that fabricated name he had gone by for so many years in Spain. He thought better of it. It could lead to a whole list of questions he'd rather not have to deal with at the moment. Best to hold his tongue, he decided as he swallowed his anger. He turned to muttering to himself quietly.

One of the constable's men, a man named Martin, who had come to Isadore's rescue, pushed aside the tapestry cover across Gaspar's door. He watched Isadore hobble across the room and then asked Gaspar, "Is he all right?"

Isadore turned on the man and snapped, "No, I am not all right. I am in pain still from that despicable woman's attack. I want her dead. How long will it take you to prepare the fire?"

Taken aback, Martin said, "I—I—don't know, sir. Sam Cooper is in charge with Ben Godling gone. I'll have to ask him."

"There is no need to ask him, constable. It is my decision, not his, and I am telling you I want those women and that child of the devil ready to burn by tomorrow afternoon."

Gaspar broke in. "Brother Iago, please. Let the men do their work. The pyre will be ready soon enough." Gaspar licked his lips and looked hopeful as he added, "Meanwhile, let us go to the chapel to pray."

Isadore blinked at Gaspar from within his dark cowl and wondered how the priest had managed this moment of reason before he dismissed the thought and turned back to the constable. "Go back to your man and be quick about it," he barked. "I want you to report back to me as soon as you know when the pyre will be ready."

"Yes, good fathers," Martin said softly. He put his head down, not wanting Isadore to see his troubled expression as he backed out the door.

He didn't believe that Cate Pritchard, whom he had known from childhood, was guilty of anything that deserved death. Catherine and Lydia had taken turns sitting by his wife when she was on death's door after their own daughter had been born. If it wasn't for them, he knew his wife would be dead. These were good women. He couldn't understand how Lydia had incurred such wrath so quickly from the old priest. Truth be told, he didn't understand what either of the Churchmen were doing in Willowglen in the first place, nor did he understand how Ben Godling had given up his authority to them so easily.

He went quickly to find Sam Cooper. The two men had already had a discussion about Cate and Lydia and Martin knew that he and Sam were of like mind. Somehow, they had to hold off these men as long as they could in the hope that they could come up with a plan to help them.

Martin found Sam in the main hall staring out a window into the blackness of the night. When Sam turned and saw the look of distress on Martin's face, he knew that more trouble was brewing. Sam looked around and determined that they were alone. "What is it?" he whispered. "What's happened now?"

"It's the Dark Monk," Martin panted. "He wants the fire by tomorrow. What are we going to do?"

Sam looked around the hall once more. *Damn you, Ben Godling,* he thought. *When are you coming back? Everyone thinks you a coward for disappearing instead of realizing that you've gone for help.* Uncomfortable talking about such matters in the Governor's Hall, he motioned Martin to follow him. They walked outside into the cool spring night, heading for the Governor's Lane as if they were out for a stroll. Once he was sure that they couldn't be heard, Sam spoke. "I've been thinking about it. The only thing I can come up with is the problem with the wood."

"The wood?"

"Yes, you know, the wood." Sam said it as if his friend should understand completely.

"I don't understand, Sam. What are you talking about? What about the wood?"

"Well, first, we'll need every available man to gather the wood, won't we?"

Martin looked wary as he replied, "Yes."

"So we can't very well start tonight, can we? Everyone's gone home. It would take us the better part of the night to round everyone up, wouldn't it?"

Martin knew that the constabulary left in Willowglen consisted of about eight men. Ben Godling had taken four with him when he left. It would take no more than an hour to rouse them all from their homes, but he knew Sam wanted him to agree with his assumption that it would take hours, so he nodded his agreement.

"So in the morning, after we've rounded up everyone, then we have to go and gather the wood, don't we?"

Again, Martin agreed.

"And after that, we have to stack the wood, don't we?

Martin nodded.

"And then, we have to prepare the whole thing and we have to be ever so careful, don't we?" Once Martin had again agreed, Sam shrugged. "Could take days."

As he thought about what Sam had just said, Martin's face lit up like a lantern. "Yes," he said, thinking about ways that they could ensure the preparations took long enough that, perhaps, something might happen to save the women and the child from their condemnation. "Yes, indeed." The corners of Martin's mouth turned up, and his eyes brightened. "Could take days and days."

Sam returned his smile. "Let's go to the tavern. We'll need a tankard to help us think clearly." The two men started for the tavern as Sam finished his thought. "We've got to plan where we'll get the wood. I'm thinking it needs to be quite a ways out of town. We'll need to hire a wagon to bring it back to the Market Square. That could take a whole day in itself, don't you think?"

Martin grinned broadly and slapped Sam on the back as they continued on. "You're a born leader, Sam Cooper."

Sam nodded his thanks to his friend shyly.

"IAGO, PLEASE, WE should pray for the souls of those who will burn. Come to the chapel. You'll feel better."

Isadore barked at Gaspar, "I will not feel better. As for their souls, let them rot in hell for all I care."

Lydia would pay for rebuffing him. He had planned to spare her and secret her away, but when she hurt him — and he still could feel the sting of her assault between his legs—he lost all attraction for her. Years of yearning for Lydia melted in an instant. Now he would make sure she felt plenty of pain when she and that little harlot friend of hers and her wicked son all burned. A contorted sneer appeared across Isadore's lips.

"You said you'd pray with me," Gaspar squeaked.

Isadore looked at him with scorn. He had to be free of this man. He could no longer pander to him, but he also knew that he had to be cautious. "I am not feeling well, Gaspar. I am still hurt. I need to go and lie down."

"But, Iago…"

In his mind, Isadore screamed, *don't call me that. It's not my name. Iago is the name you gave to that ragged, destitute man who showed up at your door all those years ago in need of food and shelter. I am not that man. My name is Isadore and Isadore I will be called.* However, wisely, Isadore kept his thoughts to himself.

"I cannot, Gaspar. Do not ask it of me. I must go and lie down."

Gaspar seemed to come to his senses for a moment. "Forgive me, brother, of course, of course. You must go and tend to your ills. Perhaps," he looked into the blackness of Isadore's hood with hope, "later."

Isadore did not respond. Instead, he hobbled off to the hallway that led to his room. As he did, he heard Gaspar whisper, disappointment evident in his voice, "I shall go to the chapel and pray for your recovery, brother."

Chapter
Twenty-six

SAM TRIED HIS best to avoid the monk, but when he finally was summoned to the main hall, Sam knew he could no longer put it off. He and Martin had already discussed the predicament with the rest of the men at great length. At first, some had not been sure about the course of action that the two men proposed, but Sam's argument had been convincing. They all knew Cate Pritchard and the Lady Lydia, and even though Cate had acted imprudently and had lain with a man, he had said, she was not the first woman to have this happen to her. It did not mean that she had lain with the devil and the child was nothing more than an innocent babe. He reminded them that they knew nothing about these Churchmen who had presented themselves to Ben Godling weeks ago and had acted as if the King himself appointed them. They finally agreed that they didn't think that either Father Gaspar or the Dark Monk had the authority to act as they did. In the end, Sam had gotten all of them to consent to his plan, although some were more hesitant than others. If they proceeded slowly, cautiously, they would have more time to assess the situation.

Sam stood before the Dark Monk as he questioned him about the pyre. In answer to his question about when it would be ready, Sam explained that the men had already been gathered at great sacrifice to Martin and himself who had stayed up all night in order to rouse a group of workers and prepare to start the effort. In truth, Martin and Sam had spent a good deal of the night in their own beds, sleeping peacefully, after several tankards of ale. They had roused the men early that morning and discussed their situation before Sam had been called to this meeting.

Sam explained that he would need to hire a wagon to transport the wood needed for the fire into the square, and that the blacksmith could not be located on this particular morning. Isadore had shrieked at him to find another wagon and get on with it. Surely there was more than one in the whole of Willowglen. Sam agreed to try to find another means to transport the wood. Isadore then insisted that Sam should enlist more of the townspeople to gather the necessary fuel for the fire and that they should carry it on their backs, if need be. Sam remained calm as he explained that he would do everything he could to hurry the preparations along, knowing that Isadore would not accept any more excuses.

"I want that fire ready by tomorrow morning. If it is not ready, I shall find other men who are willing to work faster and build an even bigger fire, and you, Sam Cooper, and all of your men will join those women and that child." Isadore raised his voice. "Do you hear me?"

Sam knew it was over. His shoulders slumped as he nodded. They would have to comply. He couldn't risk the lives of four good men to try to spare the condemned women and baby. They would have to speed up their cutting. He bowed to the monk and left the Governor's Hall.

OUTSIDE OF TOWN, several men cut and shaped tree limbs. They took their time, stopping often to share a flask and talk quietly. The pile of wood they had accumulated by the middle of the day was meager. When Sam Cooper arrived, he informed the men of what had taken place when he met with the Dark Monk. They would have to pick up their pace and ready the fire before morning.

In less than an hour, they had the first wagonload of wood in the square and had started back for more. As the wagon rumbled over the cobblestones heading back out of town, the Dark Monk stood at the edge of the square, watching. He glanced down Market Street and smiled wryly at the thought of the spice vendor and her friend from the borderlands. The two women had run like scared rabbits, had they not? In a way, he was a little disappointed. He had thought that the two women would have been more trouble, would have put up more of a fight for the sake of the condemned. It was unfortunate. He would have liked to have seen Lydia's ally damned, too. After all, she deserved punishment for what she had done to him all those years ago. The scar across his back tingled at the thought of that night long ago and he grimaced. Ah, well, he thought, perhaps she would suffer more knowing that Lydia had died an awful death and she did nothing to try to help her. By now she had probably taken refuge back at the old cow's fortress called Briarcrest. He sneered and turned his attention back to the wagon disappearing around the bend on its way out of town.

If all went well, he would be rid of Lydia and the other woman and her screaming child by the middle of the next day. Then, he would be away from Willowglen before Gaspar even knew he was gone. Once he was free, he would make his way to London, where no one knew him and he could live as he pleased. He felt for the concealed purse hanging at his side under his robe. Gaspar was a fool. He didn't even know he had taken it. The contents would allow him safe passage and a good life for quite some time to come. Perhaps it was better that he would be on his own, he mused. His money would go further and he wouldn't be tied down. Yes, perhaps everything had happened for the best. He licked his lips in anticipation of the future.

Chapter
Twenty-seven

SIR HUBERT MIDDLETON and his best men had traveled from Briarcrest, setting out at dawn, accompanied by Catherine and Fiona. They had set up camp several miles outside of Willowglen in a sheltered, chalky outcropping of a hill and waited for the arrival of another of Hubert's men who had been sent to Willowglen shortly after Fiona and Catherine had arrived at Briarcrest.

As the sun sank behind the ridge, Fiona paced like a caged animal. Catherine sat watching her, sipping liquid from her tankard, until she could stand it no longer. She spoke gently. "Fiona, why don't you come and sit down. Your pacing does no good."

"I can't stop, Catherine. I'm too uneasy. Are you sure that this man will be able to find out what's going on in Willowglen? How can you be sure that he won't give us away as we sit here waiting for him to come back?"

Catherine smiled a wry, crooked smile. "I'm very sure. The man who has been sent to Willowglen has a talent for slipping in and out of places without being noticed. He also has a knack for picking up information. I am confident that he'll return with everything we need to know and he would never betray us. Once he returns, we'll be able to make a final plan. We'll save them, Fiona. I know we can."

"I wish I could have your confidence. I'm so worried about Cate. I can't stop thinking about what I'd like to do to that Dark Monk and his priest puppet. That monk has the other one in his control. He is responsible for the priest's rage. He made sure that Gaspar would condemn Cate. You know that, don't you?"

Catherine raised her cup to her lips and took a drink before she answered. "Yes, I saw it, too. But trying to get to them would do no good. If we would have reacted when we were in the Governor's Hall, the constabulary would have been bound to protect them, and you would have had your wish to remain by Cate's side. However, the difficulty would have been that you would have been with her in eternity, for I fear you would both be dead."

Fiona stopped her pacing and stared at Catherine. "How can you speak so and remain calm, Catherine?"

Catherine laughed, but it was not a happy sound. "I am far from calm, Fiona. I am very deeply troubled by all this. First, I am afraid that we will be too late. If we are not too late, then I fear that we will not be successful and those most dear to us will be lost. I can barely keep my wits about me. But I know that if I give in to those feelings, I will be of no use at all in our endeavor to save our friends. I must admit, though, that I have help. Here." She held out her tankard to Fiona. "Drink this."

Fiona took the cup and sniffed, pulling away from the contents with a jerk of her head. "What is it?"

"Amantilla," Catherine replied. "Also called Valeriana. It has soothing powers. It will calm you and help you to keep your wits about you."

Fiona thrust the cup back at Catherine. "I have no desire to be stupefied."

"It will not be so, Fiona. It merely calms you. Your senses will not be dulled. You have my word. Please, drink a little."

Fiona reluctantly pulled the cup back and smelled it again. Once again, she turned her nose from it. Then, she held her breath and took a sip. She found it wasn't as foul tasting as she had thought it would be. She quickly drank several more large mouthfuls and handed the cup back to Catherine wiping her mouth with the back of her large hand.

Catherine watched the Scottish woman as she waited to feel the results of the brew. Fiona resumed her pacing, although less briskly than before. After a few trips back and forth, Fiona sat down on the log beside Catherine.

"I can feel it," she said, an amazed tone in her voice. She looked at Catherine with eyes wide. "You said it wouldn't make me dull witted. I feel as if I have taken strong drink. I don't want to feel that way."

"It will pass. You drank too quickly. Do not worry, Fiona. You will be fine."

Fiona sat staring into the hillside before her. Finally, she took a deep breath and said, "Yes, you are right. It is passing."

"Calmer?"

"Yes, I think I am."

"Good," Catherine pronounced.

After a little time, Fiona ventured, "Do you have any idea how we can go about rescuing them?"

"I'm afraid that our only chance may be to get to them out in the open. That means we may have to wait until the very last moment. I've spoken to Hubert about this. He feels it may well be our best chance, too, but he wants to hear what Roger has to say about the situation when he returns."

Fiona sighed. "You may be right. It will be too difficult to get into the Governor's Hall and try to get them out undetected, but waiting until the last minute has its own perils. We will need a good plan."

When her father spoke of the battles that the Douglases had fought to keep the borderlands of the Scots from the English, he attributed the clan's success to the fact that the leaders had kept their heads and determined a definite course of action. Fiona's brothers had only seen a few skirmishes as they came into adulthood, and Fiona, herself, had taken part in a couple. By that time, they were no more than annoyances from intruders onto their land, but she still had some measure of familiarity in battles. Hubert and his men must have had ample experience in defensive arts, too. Catherine had once told her that she, too, knew how to use a sword. Perhaps they would be successful if they had a good plan. She looked over at the group of men from Briarcrest and felt grateful for their help. It saddened her to think that her father had refused to come to her aid. It would have meant so much to her if her family would have been willing to help. Perhaps it was for the better, though.

Fiona turned to Catherine and asked, "You said you are able to use a sword?"

"Yes, Hubert and I have practiced with the sword for years. It helps me keep myself nimble."

"Have you ever been in a real battle?"

"No."

"Do you think you could stomach one?"

"For Lydia, Cate and Andrew's sake, yes, without a doubt."

Fiona's eyes darkened as she quickly considered various rescue attempts. As each possibility emerged, she discarded it as unusable. As she planned, she found that clarity returned. So did her confidence—and some measure of hope.

Catherine watched Fiona. When her expression changed from dark brooding to illumination, Catherine gave her a questioning look.

"Perhaps I have a plan," Fiona replied.

Catherine smiled. "Then we should go and discuss it with Hubert."

Their conversation, however, had to be delayed, for as they approached Hubert from one direction, a rider approached from the other. It was Hubert's man, Roger Malmsbury, returning from Willowglen.

ROGER SPOKE IN clipped sentences. A small, wiry man, he could blend into his surroundings and not be given a thought by anyone.

"Constables are agin' it," Roger said. "Moved as slow as they could but couldn't take no longer. That Dark Monk, he's a trickster. Wants it over with, so tomorrow it is."

"Will it be in the square?" Hubert asked.

"Already piling up the branches."

"Good man, Roger. Have you eaten?"

"This morning."

"Go have the men get you some food."

Roger smiled and turned to walk away, but Hubert called to him. "Roger, thank you. You did well." Roger flashed a big, toothy smile and he hopped toward the other men from Briarcrest. Once he was gone, Hubert turned to Fiona and Catherine and said, "Now, let's hear your plan."

As Fiona spoke, both Hubert and Catherine nodded. They commented here and there as the proposal was refined. When all three felt that the details were sufficiently worked out, Hubert pronounced, "I think it will work, especially because, from what Roger said, we probably will get little interference from the constabulary. Get some rest. We'll move camp before dawn and steal into town before they're ready to begin their terrible deed." The women nodded, and Hubert walked over to his men to inform them of the plan.

Fiona and Catherine settled on the ground beneath their cloaks for warmth. Catherine listened to the low drone of the men's voices as she drifted in and out of sleep. The Amantilla was working. She could hardly feel the dull aching in her chest, which was the fear she couldn't shake. What if she lost Lydia? She couldn't bear the thought. No, the plan had to work. The prospect of failure was not something she wanted to think about. She let her mind wander to a May feast long ago, thoughts of a first kiss, Lydia's supple mouth on hers, their first tentative touches, making love for the first time. Catherine let out a deep sigh and fell fast asleep.

Before dawn, Hubert roused her. Surprised at how rested she felt, she looked over at Fiona, still sleeping under her deep blue cloak. She stood up quickly and put her finger to her lips. Leading Hubert away from the area where Fiona slept, she whispered, "Let's let Fiona rest a little bit longer."

FIONA AWOKE TO stirrings in the still darkened camp. When she looked over at the spot where Catherine had lain and saw that it was empty, she shot up and grabbed her sword. As she sheathed the long weapon into its scabbard hanging at her side, she saw Catherine approaching. To Fiona's surprise, she was dressed in battle gear. Over leggings and tunic, Catherine wore a fine chain mail coat that came almost to her knees. A broad sword was sheathed at her side. Protective plates covered her boot tops and shins and she carried a helmet in her gloved hand.

"Did you sleep well?" Catherine asked.

Fiona stretched her back. "Well enough. I think your drink helped. Also, I felt much better knowing we have a plan that might just work. I only hope that Roger is right about the constables not sympathizing with those priests."

"He's never been wrong yet."

"Good," Fiona pronounced.

Hubert walked up to the two women and held out a mail coat. "You'd better put this on," he said as he handed it to Fiona.

She thought about refusing. She wasn't used to fighting in such gear and feared it might restrict her movement. Catherine read her thoughts and said, "Please, wear it, Fiona. What good would it do to free Cate only to have you die gaining her liberty?"

Fiona blushed and took the garment. Once she had donned the mail, she tested her movements, surprised by the lightness of it and the ease with which she could move. The mail was of fine quality, indeed.

THE COMPANY FROM Briarcrest stole in through Market Gate making little noise. An eerie quiet permeated the town of Willowglen. Market Street was deserted. As dawn broke over the distant hills, they contained their horses within the cattle pen beside the cobbled path and quickly divided into three groups making ready to penetrate the town on foot.

Roger Malmsbury appeared out of nowhere again and informed them that the constabulary had worked all night to prepare the pyre at the bidding of the Dark Monk, who still insisted that the burning would be today. Malmsbury had managed to find out that Ben Godling had gone to the sheriff for help. Apparently, the town blacksmith had overheard Godling informing the men who rode with him that he feared that these Churchmen would bring nothing but grief to Willowglen and he thought that the sheriff might help him stand up to these men. He knew they were trouble, but he had difficulty getting beyond the fact that they were men of the Church. His last encounter with the sheriff had left him to his own devices in protecting visitors and inhabitants of Willowglen from the robberies that troubled travelers on the Old Roman Road outside of town. Still, he hoped that the man would grant him some authority to act against the Church in this matter.

Catherine breathed a sigh of relief when she heard this. "I knew Ben Godling couldn't be such a coward."

Hubert raised a thin eyebrow. "Well, let's not count on Godling just yet, Catherine. You never know how people will react in these kinds of circumstances until you're actually in the midst of them. Perhaps Godling has other reasons for abandoning his post."

"I agree. It doesn't matter what his motives are. We have our plan and we'll carry it out no matter what Ben is up to. Fortunately, we don't need him to be successful. We'll be fine." Catherine wished that she felt as confident as she hoped she sounded.

Hubert looked around at the men who had gathered. "Ready, men?" he asked. Mail clinked softly as they all nodded. "You have your assignments. Let us away, then." Without another word, the groups started into Willowglen.

Chapter
Twenty-eight

LYDIA AWOKE FROM a troubled sleep on top of the wooden crate. She rubbed her shoulder and twisted her neck from side to side trying to rid herself of stiffness. *What did a few little aches and pains matter?* Compared to what she would soon be experiencing, these were nothing. She shivered and her thoughts turned to Cate and her tiny son, innocent people being used as pawns. Her brow furrowed as she struggled to try to figure out how she could expose Isadore and his diabolical plan.

When one of the guards had brought her a meager meal late at night, she had tried to inform him about Isadore, but he was a stranger to her and he wouldn't listen. He wanted no part of anything that would pit him against these Churchmen. She pleaded with him to let her escape, begging him to leave her door unlocked as if by accident. She promised him that, should she be caught, she would never divulge how she had managed to obtain her freedom. The more she spoke, the greater was the fear she recognized in his eyes. Finally, he said what she already knew. He wanted no part of it. He couldn't risk it. He had a family. Surely she understood.

Disheartened, she had left the food he had offered in the corner of the room and had finally succumbed to sleep after much angry railing and cursing into the darkness of the little room in which she was confined. Where was Catherine, she wondered? Why hadn't she done something to get her and Cate out of this terrible situation?

For a fleeting moment, she thought of the tall Scot and doubt clouded her mind again. *Perhaps Catherine and Fiona... No!* She couldn't allow such ideas to invade her mind. Catherine loved her. Catherine had insisted that Fiona was no more than a friend. She had said that it was Cate that Fiona cared about. Was she lying? She conjured up an image of Catherine's face and felt a pang of loneliness. No, Catherine would not abandon her. She whispered into the ether, "I know she's working out a plan to win our release. She would not do otherwise."

Lydia took a deep shuddering breath. She smoothed her hair, which she knew was a tousled mess. The cap that she had been wearing had long ago fallen off, perhaps in the scuffle with Isadore. She had not bothered to try to find it. As she glanced around once more, it occurred to her that she wasn't in total darkness. She could see by some dim light, the source of which was unclear to her. Examining her surroundings, she looked up toward the ceiling.

The source of light, she discovered, was a small opening in the wall high up near the top. It let in just a sliver of light. The room next to her, the one into which she had seen them take Cate, must have a window in order to allow light into her area of confinement, she concluded. She stood up on the box on which she had been sitting, but she couldn't reach the hole. Looking around, she found a smaller crate. Trying to lift it, she found it was too heavy for her, but the lid opened easily and she removed the contents, metal goblets, probably used to accommodate extra guests at the many banquets given at the Governor's Hall. She dumped the last of the vessels onto the floor. They poured out onto the flat stones with a loud rattle. She held her breath, thinking better of what she had done. She didn't want to call attention to her movements.

Waiting, listening for approaching footsteps, she heard none. She let out her breath and lifted the now empty box on to the larger one. Then she carefully climbed up the tower she had fashioned. She could just reach the opening, which looked like it was made when a stone in the wall's construction had fallen out. She pressed her cheek against the wall to look through the hole. The stones felt cool against her skin. In the dim light of what she realized must be early morning, she could just make out a small, hunched form. Cate sat on a small stool, rocking her infant son and crying. The scene tore at Lydia's heart.

CATE HAD BEEN awake before dawn. She had fed Andrew and then sat, staring across the room without seeing. Her misery allowed her to do nothing but sit and cry. Her tears fell on the wrapping that swaddled her son, but she didn't seem to notice.

Sam had come to check on her hours before, bringing her something to eat. "To keep your strength up," he had told her. "So you can feed the child." His look of concern did not escape her.

When she pressed him about what was happening, he wouldn't look her in the eye as he murmured that no decision had yet been made about "anything." When she pressed him further, he finally told her that the Dark Monk wanted the fire prepared by morning. He looked lost, piteous, as he told her that there was nothing to be done. They had tried to slow the preparations, but the monk had caught on to them and they were forced to move more quickly now or risk their own lives. He had apologized over and over until she had told him not to worry, that she didn't hold the men of Willowglen responsible for what was happening.

After Sam left, she found all she could do was cry. What else was there? She and her son had been abandoned. It was obvious that no one could exert enough influence over the priests to gain her release. Soon, she and her son would burn. She looked down at the tiny child in her arms and felt a deep sadness at the thought that his life would be over so soon after it had begun. That's when the tears started to flow in earnest.

Earlier, in the dark, she had slept fitfully on some old blankets stashed in the corner of the room, but she had awakened before first light. The thoughts that had flooded her every waking moment since then were not comforting. She wondered how hot the fire would be and how long it took to die by such means. She had heard somewhere that if your judges were merciful, they strangled you before they lit the fire so that you felt not the pain of it. She shivered. That meant that the fire would be excruciating. Looking down at Andrew, tears started to flow again. She had been sobbing for a long time when she finally heard a voice calling her name–a woman's familiar voice.

Sniffling, trying to stop herself from heaving so that she could listen, she finally heard it again.

"Cate. Cate, up here, look up high on the wall opposite you."

Cate looked around. She still couldn't tell where the voice came from, but she recognized it now.

"Aunt Lydia?"

"Yes. It's me. Look up."

Cate looked up and realized that there was an opening in the wall. She stood up and walked halfway across the room.

Lydia said, "Now you've got it. I'm up here."

Looking wide-eyed at the opening, Cate cried, "Oh, Aunt Lydia, I'm so frightened. What shall we do?"

"I don't know," came the response through the opening. "But I think we must remain calm and alert. I am sure that Catherine is organizing some plan as we speak. There has to be a way for us to escape the awful fate that those two madmen have bestowed on us."

Cate's thoughts turned to the commotion that she had heard the night that Isadore confronted Lydia. "What happened in there the other night? I heard screaming. Did they harm you?"

Lydia hesitated. "No. Do not trouble yourself about me. The screams you heard came from Isadore."

"Isadore? Who's Isadore?"

"The Dark Monk. He's someone...someone I knew a long time ago. Apparently, this is what all of the trouble is really all about. You and Andrew are no more than pawns in his designs to get to me. I'm sorry Cate. I wish that it would never have happened, that you would never have been involved."

"Why would this man, this Isadore, want to get to you?"

In Lydia's mind, Cate Pritchard was still a child to be protected from the ways of the world. How could she tell her that Isadore had desired her from childhood? How could she explain his now obvious and unreasonable desire for her? But Cate was no longer an innocent, Lydia reminded herself. She was a grown woman with a child of her own. She, too, had been a part of a man's manipulations. She would probably understand.

"He wanted to lay with me. He has wanted it for a long time. He thought he finally had me. He didn't count on the swift kick between his legs that I gave him."

"Oh, my!" Cate's hand flew to her mouth.

"Cate, listen to me, I don't know how we're going to get out of this, but you have to be ready. Catherine — and Fiona — will come to our rescue, I feel certain of it."

Cate shook her head, "No, you're wrong. They've abandoned us."

"How do you know that?"

"Sam told me that neither of them have been seen in town ever since that priest told them to get out or be condemned with us. I'm afraid they've gone, Lydia. We have to face the truth. They will not save us." As she spoke, tears started to fall again.

"No, you mustn't think it," Lydia shouted. "Please, Cate, do not despair. Something will happen. You'll see. We must be ready. We must watch for them. We may have to act quickly when the opportunity comes. We should be glad that, at least, they haven't tormented us. They have not harmed you, have they?"

Cate shook her head back and forth.

"Good. I've heard that such things happen. They do all manner of terrible things to try to get people to confess sins that they haven't even committed. We've been lucky so far. They haven't done this to us. We still have our strength and we have our wits about us. Just do as I ask, Cate. Stay alert and be ready. We *are* going to be rescued. Do you hear?"

Reluctantly, Cate nodded. She had little hope that anything they could do would gain their freedom. Thoughts of fire came to mind again and she shivered. She couldn't help it. Even though she tried to push the thought away, it flooded her mind. She looked down at the sleeping baby in her arms. Tears overflowed her lower lids again and slowly made their way down her cheeks. She tried to stifle them for Lydia's sake, but she could not. What she didn't know was that, Lydia, too, was crying softly as she peered through the opening in the wall at Cate and her son, so deep was her sadness at the sight of them and Cate's suffering. Still, she had that feeling...that deep knowing...Catherine would come.

Chapter
Twenty-nine

CATHERINE AND FIONA each took two men and headed
down separate paths behind the shops on Market Street and Potters
Row. Hubert sent Roger on ahead as he and the two men that
remained with him crept in and out of alleyways, threading their
way down Market Street, trying to keep out of sight.

The houses and shops of Willowglen were shut up tight. Not
even a dog barked. Occasionally, the soft rustle of mail could be
heard, but it was no more than a whisper in the ears of the group
from Briarcrest as they made their way to the Market Square.

FIONA TOOK UP a place in the shadows of a doorway in one
of the ancillary buildings of the Church of St. Stephen. Her
accompanying men from Briarcrest hid nearby waiting for her
signal. From her position, Fiona had a clear view of what was
happening in the town square. Although she couldn't see
Catherine, she knew that she was positioned at the end of Potter's
Row with some of Hubert's men. They, too, would have similar
views of the square. Hubert stationed himself along Market Street
with his remaining men.

The three hidden groups watched as a few of the constable's
men busied themselves in the square. No one gave any indication
that they were aware of the presence of those from Briarcrest.

Fiona fought against the anger, her eyes slits, her fleshy lids
straining to contain the look of revulsion that would betray her
feelings at witnessing the scene unfolding before her. Several of the
constable's men piled branches and kindling around a large pole
that had been erected in the middle of the square. They formed the
pile into a pyre methodically, standing the longer branches up so
that the thinner ends leaned against the pole at the top. The thick
bases rested on the kindling and small logs on the ground inside
the base. Sam Cooper was among the men. Fiona sniffed to think
that they thought him a friend. On the other hand, she supposed he

was helpless to do anything now that Cate and Andrew's fate had been sealed. He probably thought he should act in a way so as not to make his own life more difficult at the hands of these lunatic priests. She concluded that she couldn't blame him.

As these thoughts tumbled through Fiona's head, she saw Cooper look around surreptitiously. Everyone in the square was occupied elsewhere, most with their backs toward the constable. Quickly, he removed one small underlying branch and dropped it without a sound as soon as it cleared the pile. He jumped back several strides and turned away from the structure just as the entire edifice came crashing to the cobbled surface. Fiona saw his face as he turned back. The look of shock and wonder revealed a hidden mummer's talent. All eyes turned to see the entire construction clatter in an ineffectual heap around the center pole. The men stood looking at the pile of rubble, their confusion evident.

With a growl, Sam said, "I told you that you needed to interweave the wood more. Now we'll have to start again. You, there." He pointed to a group of his men standing with disbelieving looks on their faces. "Clear this all way. We'll have to build it right from the start. This time, let's try to do it the proper way."

As the men scrambled to pull the fallen pieces of branches, logs and twigs away from the pole, Cooper turned to another of his men. "You," he barked, "go tell the priests there will be something of a delay."

The man grimaced as he nodded in obedience to Cooper. Then he turned away and plodded toward the Governor's Hall with slumped shoulders.

Fiona's mouth turned up at the corners in a wry smiled. So, Cooper was still one of them. Reassuring warmth permeated her body. Perhaps they would succeed after all.

THE SUN ROSE higher in the sky as the reconstruction progressed slowly, Cooper's men trying to do a better job of it this time. When they were about halfway done reassembling the structure, the tall priest appeared with the Dark Monk by his side. Fiona wrinkled her nose at the sight of the men. Her hand twitched on the hilt of her sword, but she didn't move from her vantage point. The two Churchmen exchanged words with Cooper. At one point, Sam raised his voice, but his words were unintelligible. He sounded defensive as he gestured violently while speaking to the two priests. The only words Fiona finally heard were "we can do it quickly or we can do it so that it will not fall again." At that, the Churchmen left abruptly heading back toward Governor's Lane.

The reassembly work continued. As the morning wore on,

people gathered in the square. The curious came, and those looking for the perverse pleasure of witnessing another human being killed. Fiona studied their faces as they arrived. Some had looks of utter terror. Others looked as though they would rub their hands in delight at the event that was about to take place. The happiest ones tried to hide their enjoyment, but Fiona could see it, could feel it, even from her hiding place.

She wanted to beat them back into their houses and make them all stay away, but she knew she could not. She took a deep, steadying breath and touched her sword handle for comfort. As the crowd swelled, a soft buzz arose. The excited tone made Fiona's stomach heave.

She spied movement from the corner of her eye. When she turned her head, she found Roger standing at her elbow with a grin on his face. "I've just overheard the constabulary. They are still not for this at all, but they are at a loss about what to do. Once they realize what's happening, I don't think we'll get any trouble from them."

Fiona nodded. Then she whispered, "Do the others know?"

"You were on my way. Lady Catherine next, and Hubert after her."

"Good," she said as she continued to watch the movement in the square. When she turned to offer Roger her thanks, he had disappeared.

THE LAST OF the branches were again fixed against the center pole. Sam left the square and Catherine steeled her gaze, staring in the direction that Sam had gone, toward the Governor's Lane. Lydia and Cate would come from that direction. A few minutes later, a group appeared at the mouth of the Lane.

The tall priest came first, his eyes hooded, his lips moving in mumbled prayer. Cate walked behind him flanked by two of the constable's men. Her upper arms were bound with a thick rope that allowed her to still hold her son. Catherine felt a stabbing pain in her chest when she saw the fear in Cate's eyes.

As the group moved forward and shifted, Catherine caught a glimpse of Lydia behind Cate. A single guard walked with her. Both her arms and hands were bound. Catherine saw that Lydia's eyes blazed with anger as she walked with her shoulders back and her head high. The gray-green eyes, filled more with fire than their cool, natural color, told Catherine that Lydia was not about to give up. Tears welled up in Catherine's eyes, but she knew that she must not give in to them. She felt the sting in her throat as she tried to swallow the emotions she felt. She had to be strong. She had to save

Lydia. In order to do that, she needed to be alert. She couldn't let her feelings get the best of her, not until this was over.

The Dark Monk came next, almost unseen because of those who walked in front of him. Sam Cooper brought up the rear, looking grave and cheerless. Several other men walked behind Sam, their somber expressions matching his. As soon as the procession reached the square, the crowd went quiet. Catherine felt as if a great weight rested on her chest, preventing her from taking a breath.

THE DARK MONK stole a look at the stacked branches and smiled to himself. He wanted to wring his hands with pleasure, but he knew he could not. He could not risk anyone knowing just how much satisfaction he would derive from this experience. Watching the women burn would be exciting, rewarding. But he wouldn't stay long. He would disappear before Gaspar got any inkling of his plan to escape.

He had already arranged for a wagon. Once he heard the women's screams, he knew that they would soon perish, and he would be on his way. They would be dead by the time he reached the Old Roman Road. He savored the anticipation of the lifting of his burden. When the woman died, when Lydia was no more, he would be free. To ensure that he remained so, he had to get away from Gaspar. Thus, his arranged flight.

THE MEN ON either side of Cate guided her up onto the woodpile and bound her to the center pole including Andrew in their lashing to keep her from throwing the baby out of the fire. The baby, sensing either his mother's fear or having some awareness of his own impending doom, started to wail. Cate appeared to Catherine as if she were numb and exhausted. The young mother did not seem to notice her son's howling.

When the men finished with Cate, they repeated the process with Lydia. Catherine's heart ached. She wanted to run to Lydia and Cate, cut off their ropes, and carry the women away. She could not. She knew she would have no chance alone. Although it seemed that some of Sam's men were on their side, there were too many others in the square who were certain to be angry if this grisly affair did not take place. They had been promised a witch burning and they would have one. They were wrong, however, very wrong, for there would be no witch burning today. Catherine took a deep breath and prepared for what she knew would be their next move according to the plans they had made with Hubert before they entered Willowglen.

AS FIONA TRIED to block the surge of emotion she felt watching Cate and Andrew being tied to the pyre, someone—a woman—broke free of the crowd and ran to the priests and threw herself at the tall one's feet, sobbing and pleading for Cate and Andrew's life. Fiona recognized Sarah and again felt as though her heart would break in two. Still, she did nothing.

Finally, Will trudged over and dragged his wife away. Even from a distance, Fiona could see how distraught he, too, was.

Fire flared up from two torches in the hands of Cooper's men, but before they approached the pyre, the Dark Monk stepped forward and held up his hand. A murmur ran though the group, but it quieted quickly.

Father Gaspar walked to the monk's side and, in a thin, nasally voice, said, "My brother monk and I have prayed about these women and the child and have found it to be God's holy punishment that they should die in this holy pyre, thereby purifying their souls." A single shriek came from the crowd. It was Sarah reacting to this final pronouncement. "The woman called Catherine Lydia Pritchard has been found to have lain with the devil, producing a child of evil."

From her position of hiding, Fiona cringed at the words and tried to quell her anger as she willed herself to stay put and not to run out to the pompous priest and run him through on the spot with her sword.

CATHERINE STOOD HIDING behind a large oak tree at the end of Potter's Row. From her vantage point, she saw Lydia being escorted to the pyre. Her nostrils flared as the men secured Lydia to one of the beams, and Catherine's breath quickened as her anger rose still more. She balled her hands into fists to help push away the vision of what she would like to do to these arrogant Churchmen. She needed to keep her wits about her and to be ready to move with her companions hiding in the shadows around the square. Without her full attention, she might miss a chance to react, endangering the lives of all involved. She narrowed her eyes and watched the proceedings, trying not to allow herself to be affected by the priest's haughty words as Gaspar continued.

"This woman," Gaspar gestured toward Lydia, "dared to endeavor to present an obstacle to our righteous pronouncement. From this, we must conclude that she needs to be taught her place and, so that all may know that no one must hinder the work of God and the Holy Office, which we represent. Therefore, this woman called Lady Lydia Wellington of Briarcrest must also die by fire."

The air hung heavy and silent. No one moved. No dogs barked.

No birds could be heard in song. Finally, the monk nodded to the constable's men and Sam Cooper flinched in response. For one fleeting moment, it seemed he might call his men back, but he did not. The torchbearers walked toward the pyre. Black smoke billowed from their torches as they walked, filling the center of the square. The two men made eye contact and both brought their flames to wood at the same moment. As they did, chaos broke out in the square.

Fiona jumped out from the doorway. As she did, her companions rushed to join her, swords drawn, ready for battle. Across the way, from Market Street, several more men emerged led by Sir Hubert of Middleton, armed and shielded. At the same moment, another group of knights, fit for battle, ran into the square from Potter's Row. It took Sam and his men some time to recover from their surprise and muster together from the fringes of the square. The men with the torches turned from their task and thrust the flaming weapons at their attackers. Easily knocked away, the torches clattered to the cobbles where they went out. Swords flashed in the bright sunlight. Onlookers grabbed what weapons they could from around them and joined the fray. A scream rang out. In spite of the advantage that the men of Briarcrest had, their opponents, especially the townspeople, fought hard. Several of Hubert's men staggered away after being cudgeled. It was anybody's fight. That is, until the Smiths entered the brawl.

FIONA SAW HER brothers and father running for the square from Bookbinders Row, swords raised, just as she reached Cate and Andrew. A broad smile appeared across her face briefly, and she turned to Cate and said, "Hold still" and cut the bindings from her arms releasing Andrew as well. She then freed Cate from the rest of the ties. Cate slumped into Fiona's arms in relief, still grasping her son. As Fiona turned, she met the flash of a rod from an attacker. But as she brought her sword up to meet it just in time, he lowered his weapon and stumbled back. Not realizing that the man had decided not to fight Fiona, one of their party came up behind him and hit him so hard between the shoulder blades with the hilt of his sword that the man fell, gasping for breath. Then, the knight jumped into the still smoldering flames and cut Lydia loose, pulling her out of the fire. The fanning of her skirt as she jumped from the pyre caused the fire to flare up, catching more branches. A small flame flashed up from the hem of Lydia's dress. The knight batted at it until it became no more than a puff of gray smoke.

From the helmet of the victor, Fiona heard a familiar voice. "Get them out of here," Catherine said and she turned to face off with the Dark Monk, who grabbed at Lydia's dress, trying to wrench her from Catherine's arms.

Catherine grasped the monk by his cowl and twisted him around until he lost his grip on Lydia. As Sir Hubert caught Lydia in his arms, Catherine continued to spin the monk around while he struggled to escape, screeching as if he were being ripped apart. Catherine threw down her sword and grasped his hood with both hands. Pulling the cowl from his head, she met his eyes for an instant. A flash of recognition, images of a Hallows Eve night long ago, crashed through Catherine's memory. She knew immediately that she had seen those eyes before.

As Hubert steered Lydia away from the fray, she called over her shoulder, confirming what Catherine already knew. "Be careful, Catherine! It's Isadore."

The monk pulled and tugged as the fire behind him raged higher and higher, the frightening force of it building to a conflagration. Catherine held on, trying to make sense of the images from the past as they bombarded her. Finally, the monk gave one last tug and pulled away from Catherine with all his might. She staggered back as he bolted toward a cart that waited at the edge of the square.

"Stop him," Catherine shouted. Several of Cooper's men ran toward the cart as Isadore mounted. The wagon started to move off slowly, the horse straining to overcome the weight of the cart. Before the men could reach the wagon, a form rose up from the rear of the wagon. Throwing off a thick burlap covering, the man grasped the monk by his robes and pushed him from the cart. Catherine recognized the assailant. "Roger," she whispered with a smile on her lips.

The monk landed with a thud. Gaspar ran up to him, screaming, "Where are you going, Iago? You were going to leave me, weren't you? Why? Why would you want to do that?"

The monk staggered to his feet, ignoring a trickle of blood that oozed down his temple. He turned and tried to clamber back into the cart, but under Roger's orders, the cart driver continued to urge his horse on. Isadore ran after it, trying to keep his unsure feet from slipping out from under him. Gaspar chased after the monk. With a lunge worthy of a younger man, Gaspar reached out and grabbed Isadore by the robe and dragged him back into the square, railing at him with a piercing cry, his eyes blazing with rage.

Isadore shrank back from the priest, afraid of his rantings, realizing that he had slipped over the edge now, into total madness, but Gaspar only pounced on him again. The two men fell toward the raging fire. As they struggled, Isadore's robe caught a spark and the hem of his garment ignited. In his panic, he thrust

Gaspar away from him.

The priest stumbled backward toward the pyre and hit the structure with such force that it collapsed on him, the flames igniting him instantly. As men rushed to pull Gaspar free, Isadore ran screaming from the square, his robes now fully ablaze.

The fighting had all but stopped. A rescue attempt to remove Gaspar from the flames proved impossible. The fire was just too hot for anyone to get close enough to pull him out. Gaspar did not scream. Instead, he lay among the long white-hot tongues that licked at him in earnest, large beams crossed atop his body.

In the distance, flames still raged all around Isadore as he ran. When he collapsed on Bookbinders Row, his cries finally ceased.

A heavy silence hung over the crowd. Hubert moved toward Sam Cooper and his gathering men. Everyone sheathed their swords and dropped their weapons. Cooper and Middleton spoke in hushed tones. Duncan and his sons found each other and clustered together, waiting to see what would happen next.

FIONA WASTED NO time. Sheathing her sword, she picked Cate up in her strong arms and cradled her the same way that Cate continued to cradle Andrew. Fiona strode quickly toward Potter's Row. As they slipped between two houses into an alley, they heard the horrendous screams coming from the square. Fiona set Cate down. Cate looked up at her and smiled weakly, a bewildered expression on her face.

Fiona gazed into the gold-flecked eyes of the woman she loved. She put a thumb to Cate's cheek and wiped away a sooty smudge. "It's going to be all right, Cate. You're safe. You and Andrew are safe. I won't let anyone hurt you."

Cate smiled up into the blazing, deep blue eyes. "Thank you," she whispered. She looked down at the baby in her arms and added, "From both of us." She moved toward Fiona and rested her head against her shoulder. Fiona put her arm around Cate and beamed.

Someone ran past the alley where Fiona and Cate hid. Fiona only caught a glimpse of the person, but she thought that the man was carrying a large bundle. The sound of the footsteps receded and Fiona let out a relieved sigh. Then, the footsteps sounded as if the runner had reversed direction and was coming closer again. Fiona let go of Cate and Andrew and stepped in front of them. She drew her sword and waited.

The sound of the footsteps stopped when Hubert appeared at the opening of the alleyway. Relief washed over Fiona when she recognized him. Then she realized what his bundle was. A bedraggled Lydia smiled at them from Hubert's arms.

As Hubert stepped further into the dim alley, Lydia said, "Put me down, Hubert, I am unharmed. I am perfectly capable of standing."

Hubert set Lydia down gently. She looked up at him and said, "Now, please, go back and get Catherine out of there before she gets into any more trouble. She'll need rescuing herself by now."

"Are you sure you're all right?" Fiona asked.

"Yes, I'm fine." She turned to Hubert and demanded, "Go, Hubert. I'll be fine here with Fiona."

"Right you are." Hubert started back toward Potter's Row. As he ran he called over his shoulder. "Take them to Briarcrest, Fiona. We'll follow as soon as I get Catherine out of here. If need be, I'll stay behind and clear up the misunderstanding here."

Fiona nodded.

"Take the horses. I'll make sure that Catherine has an escort." He stopped at the mouth of the alley and smiled at the women. "Good luck."

"Thank you," Fiona said. "We may still need some measure of luck to get out of town. You will need it, too — to straighten out this mess. So, good luck to you, Sir Hubert."

Hubert turned and dashed down Potter's Row. Before he reached the square again, the three women were making their way across the deserted green toward Market Gate and the horses that would take them back to Briarcrest.

REACHING BRIARCREST WELL after sundown, Lydia and her companions entered Briarcrest Hall. Lydia made sure that her guests received something to eat and were able to clean themselves up. She had one of the household staff relieve Cate of caring for Andrew, insisting that she needed to rest after the ordeal that they had just been through. Cate reluctantly gave up the baby to the care of the kindly old woman named Elspeth, who toddled off whispering cooing words to the baby and patting him under his little chin. The three women sat by the fire in the Great Hall without speaking for a long time. Each wondered how the others had faired back in Willowglen Township.

Fiona watched Lydia as she sat staring into the fire, wringing her hands. "She'll be fine. I'm sure they're on their way here already." She hoped it was true, for Lydia's sake.

Lydia turned to Fiona. Her eyes clouded with concern. "You don't know Catherine. She sometimes doesn't know when to keep her opinions to herself."

One corner of Fiona's mouth turned up as she tried to suppress a smile. "Of course, I don't know you so well either, Lady Lydia, but you seem to have a bit of the same problem yourself. I have a feeling that we would only have had to rescue Cate and Andrew if you hadn't been so bold at the Governor's Hall."

"No, Fiona, you're mistaken. Cate and Andrew were but pawns in Isadore's fiendish plot. I was the one he really wanted. Once he had me, he didn't care about Cate or Andrew, but Gaspar had already condemned them, so Isadore was willing to allow them to die along with me. Of course, he only wanted me to die after I rejected him...again. This time with a finality that he understood at last."

Fiona raised an eyebrow, questioning Lydia's last remark.

Lydia responded, "I kicked him where it hurt most."

"In his manhood?" Fiona asked.

"In his pride."

Now all three women laughed, helping to lift some of the tension they felt.

"Who is this Isadore?" Cate asked. "How do you know him?"

"The people of Willowglen gave him the name 'Dark Monk' because he kept himself hidden in his cowl, which I see now was purposely made large. His real name is Isadore. He was my childhood tutor at Greencastle, where he lived with my father and me and my nurse, Marian.

"When I was a child, he used to constantly badger Marian to leave me alone with him so that he could school me, but she wouldn't let me out of her sight when I was with Father Isadore. She had not one bit of trust in the man, and rightly so."

Fiona's eyebrows disappeared under the black hair on her forehead. "He had designs on you even as a child? The man is a louse!"

"Yes, I'm afraid he is, and he has tried to harm me before because I would not do his bidding."

"He has?"

"It was a long time ago. I acted foolishly and put myself at risk. It was at a time when I was so distraught that I didn't care what happened to me. Marian had just died. My father wanted me to go to France to further his own prospects, and Catherine...Catherine and I...well, I never thought I would see her again."

Lydia looked down at her hands and started to wring them again. The other women sat in silence for a while watching the flames dance in the fireplace. Finally, Cate said, "My mother told me once that you had been badly hurt at the hand of a terrible man. She said that you almost died."

"Yes," Lydia answered, not taking her own gaze from the fire.

"Was it him? Was it this Isadore?"

"Yes."

Cate whispered, "Why?"

"Because he wanted me. And he could not have me."

Fiona offered, "So he has harbored this twisted desire for you all these years, finally making his way with this priest, Gaspar, to get his revenge."

"I think his intention was not revenge at first. While I was held, he came to me and told me he had plans to take me away with him after Cate and Andrew..." She shivered at the thought of what had almost happened to this mother and child because of her. "After the...b-burning."

"He would let two innocents die and all the while he had no intention of letting you go to the flames with them?" Fiona asked.

Lydia whispered, the word sticking in her throat as she thought about Cate dying for her. "Indeed." As she looked into Fiona's eyes, her own blazed with indignation, and added, "But everything changed when I hurt him."

"How did you manage that?" Fiona asked.

"He came to me in the night—alone. I still didn't know who he was, for I had never seen his face or heard him speak. It was strange, though, because even then I had the feeling that I should know him. When I did finally hear his voice, the feeling became even stronger. Then I realized who he was—a man who had once tried to take my life from me. We had heard nothing of him for years. I had thought he was long dead.

"He started after me in that little storage room where I was held. I had nowhere to flee. I was desperate. He flung himself at me, but I managed to push him away. On his second attempt, I jammed my knee between his legs and gave him a good blow. The guards heard his cries and came to his rescue, taking him away from me."

Fiona's face brightened. A vision of the slightly built Lydia getting the best of the lustful old man put a wry smile on her face. Fiona clapped her hands together and roared, "Hoo, that must have been a sight! I wish I had been there."

"No," Cate cried. The two women looked at her in disbelief at her outcry.

She lowered her voice and then repeated shyly, "No, you don't wish you had been there. It was awful, not knowing if we would live or die...or when our end would come. No, I didn't want you there. I couldn't bear knowing that something might have happened to you."

Fiona gazed into Cate's eyes and felt her heart bursting with love and pride at her expression of care and concern. Lydia watched both women intently while an unspoken exchange took place between them. When the two women continued their eye contact, Lydia began to feel as if she were intruding on them. She cleared her throat and offered, "I'm very tired. I think I'll go to bed. At this point, I don't think I could keep my eyes open even in my concern for Catherine."

Cate pulled away from Fiona's gaze. "Yes, I should think we are all very tired. It's been quite an ordeal."

"Shall I show you two to your rooms, then?" Lydia asked.

Cate looked back at Fiona and studied her face as she said, "We shall only be needing one room, Aunt Lydia."

Much to Lydia's relief, she managed to suppress her surprise at Cate's bold statement. She looked at Fiona in order to see if she agreed. The smile on Fiona's face was incredible.

Trying to sound more nonchalant than she felt, Lydia said, "Well, then follow me, ladies." Turning to Cate, she asked, "Would you like me to have Elspeth take care of Andrew through the night, Cate?"

"No, I need to feed him. My breasts are already aching — perhaps if we could have a basket for him, though, I'll put him to sleep in it after he's fed."

"Wait here," Lydia told her companions. "I'll talk to Elspeth and see what she can find. It's been a long time since Briarcrest Hall saw such a tiny child." A twinkle appeared in Lydia's gray-green eyes as she added, "Indeed, perhaps I was the last."

Chapter
Thirty

CATHERINE PACED BEFORE the large dais in the Governor's Hall, where Gaspar, only days before, had condemned to death some of the people that she cared about most. Now, Benjamin Godling sat there, looking pained from the tongue lashing that Catherine had just given him. Hubert stood quietly watching her from a few feet away, his hands folded calmly in front of him.

Godling had already apologized several times. Now he said, "I can't say it enough, Catherine. I'm sorry. I thought I was taking the best action for Willowglen. These priests came out of nowhere and took their authority from God-knows-who. They had the local priest under their thumb. The man fairly cowered whenever they came near him. When they wouldn't leave the Pritchards alone, I knew we were in for it. That Father Gaspar started acting like a madman. Once I realized that, I thought I'd better get help. I had hoped that the sheriff would be able to be of assistance, but he was hesitant to send men to Willowglen for what he termed a minor dispute when there is so much trouble abroad with all the robberies happening on the road from London. I never thought that things would worsen in such a dreadful manner here."

Catherine stopped and stared at him. Her face reddened again and she said, "Will Pritchard, a pillar of this town, almost lost his daughter and her innocent child. The Lady Lydia of Briarcrest, who has been a great friend to Willowglen, also came under the wicked influence of these men. They almost died, Benjamin. You abandoned Willowglen. You abandoned all of them."

"I've explained all of that, Catherine. As I said, I went for help."

"Which never came."

Godling turned and looked out the window into the waning light. A thin column of smoke still rose from the smoldering pyre in the town square. The chief constable turned back and admitted, "Which never came. But how was I to know that the sheriff would refuse my request? I left my most capable man in charge."

"Yes, thank goodness for that," she said loudly. "If it wasn't for Sam Cooper, things might have been worse. Sam saw that Andrew was cared for and that Cate wasn't mistreated. He also tried to slow down the wretched events that almost took place here by asking the men to work slowly in their preparations for the burning, but if he had not..." Catherine didn't want to think about what would have happened if Sam had not had the presence of mind to hinder the preparations, if his men had not been willing to do his bidding, if she had not been able to arrive from Briarcrest with help in time. Her voice caught in her throat as she said, "Innocent people almost died, Ben."

He looked down at the table in front of him. "I'm sorry. I don't know what else to say, except that I'm glad that you were able to bring help and save Cate and her son—and Lady Lydia—from coming to any harm."

Catherine stopped pacing and sighed deeply. "I know you did what you thought best, Ben. It's just that it was so frightening. That mad priest and his companion should never have been allowed to go so far. You should have stopped them as soon as the trouble started."

"They invoked papal authority. My hands were tied. I felt that my only hope might be from the sheriff since he is close to the king." Ben sighed before adding, "At least everything turned out for the best. Cate, her son, and Lady Lydia were rescued, thanks to you and your people. And, it seems, God has seen fit to deal with his Churchmen so that we don't have to decide their fates."

Catherine looked out the window behind Ben and saw the thin plume of smoke rising in the distance. The events that followed the rescue flashed through her mind as she still tried to make sense of it all.

For some reason, the Dark Monk had been prepared to leave Willowglen quickly. A cart and driver awaited him at the edge of the square. When they interviewed the man, he had told them that the monk had approached him and offered him a tidy sum to take him to London. He had been instructed to move into position once the women were brought into the square. As soon as the Dark Monk climbed into the wagon, he was to move off quickly up the Governor's Lane toward the Old Roman Road and on to the city. What the Dark Monk didn't know was that the driver's horse was known to one and all in Willowglen as being notoriously slow. He was strong and steady, but he never moved any faster than the horse himself decided.

Roger Malmsbury, true to his crafty inclinations, had managed to find out the purpose for the cart in the square and had hidden in it, waiting for the Dark Monk to make his escape. When the monk fled Catherine's grip, she had no idea that he was about to leave Willowglen. However, Gaspar, mad as he was, sensed Isadore's intention to abandon him as soon as he made for the wagon.

When the scuffle ensued between the two Churchmen, Catherine felt helpless to do anything. At that point, all the other fighting in the square had stopped and everyone stared at the monk when, in an attempt to get away from Gaspar, he threw the tall priest into the fire. When Gaspar's body hit the center pole, the pyre, now burning fiercely, collapsed onto Gaspar immediately, engulfing him in its inferno. By then, the Dark Monk was running down Bookbinders Row, screaming as the fire seared the skin beneath his own burning robes.

A few men tried to pull Gaspar from the fire, but they were buffeted by the heat and had to back away. Meanwhile, halfway down Bookbinders Row, the Dark Monk had collapsed. His lifeless body, now a blackened lump, lay in the cobbled street, still too hot to touch. Catherine shook off the horror of the scene and turned her attention back to Ben Godling.

"Yes. You're right, of course. Even though we are in disagreement as to how this should have been handled, at least it's over. Those who tried to wreak so much havoc on Willowglen will no longer trouble this town's inhabitants."

Godling picked up one of three silver goblets on the table and poured dark, red wine into it from a large ewer. He held the cup out to Catherine. "Please, come sit beside me and drink some wine. You look exhausted. This will revive you a little." He glanced over at Hubert and pointed to another goblet, inquiring with a look if Hubert would join them. Hubert waited until Catherine walked around the table and sat beside Godling before nodding and joining them.

Sir Hubert took the cup the chief constable offered him. "Perhaps we could presume upon your hospitality tonight. As you have noted, Mistress Catherine is very tired. It has been a very difficult few days for her. She needs to rest before we make our way back to Briarcrest." Hubert held Godling's gaze.

Godling tore himself from the accusing look Hubert gave him and turned to Catherine. "Of course. Please stay. Avail yourself of any of the benefits that this grand Hall has to offer." He turned to Hubert again and added, "Both of you."

"Thank you, Constable. We will," Catherine responded with a sigh.

Godling lifted his vessel toward Catherine and said, "To good fortune, in the end, and a peaceful future for us all."

Hubert joined them in raising his goblet.

"For the good," Catherine said. She took a long drink, then, with great effort that reflected her weariness, she wiped her mouth with the back of her soot-smudged hand.

Ben spoke again. "I asked the sheriff if he knew who these Churchmen might be, if they came at the behest of the king. He said he had never heard of them. That's another reason he was hesitant to send help. He felt that it was a local affair, something we should be able to take care of ourselves. I couldn't seem to make him understand how dangerous these men were. So they have gone to their grave without our knowing anything more than that which they have told us about themselves. I'm not so sure that I believe they came at the behest of the Pope."

"We were able to gather a little information," Catherine said. "The one people called the Dark Monk was someone well known to Briarcrest."

Benjamin Godling's interest was piqued and he leaned toward Catherine to hear what she had to say.

"The Dark Monk was a priest called Isadore. Although not associated with Briarcrest, he served at Lady Lydia's former home at Greencastle. He has long had — shall we say — an interest in Lady Lydia. A long time ago, Isadore inflicted great bodily harm on Lydia. We almost lost her." Catherine trembled at the memory before continuing. "Isadore fled after that. Briarcrest's men looked for him long and hard, but he had disappeared. At first we worried that he might show himself again and bring Lydia more trouble, but when years passed and we heard nothing of him, we thought he was long gone or perhaps even dead. No matter what, we didn't think him a threat any longer. From what we could determine, he fled to Spain and took up with Gaspar. From my own experience, I think that Gaspar was, shall we say, quite taken with Isadore." Godling raised an eyebrow at the remark as Catherine continued. "About Gaspar we know little other than what he has told you and the whole town. He was a priest of the Dominicans, although he did their founder a great dishonor with his actions here. It became clear to us from the events that we witnessed that Isadore was the one who was in control. Indeed, Gaspar couldn't seem to function without him. We think Isadore chose to keep himself covered with his monk's cowl to avoid being recognized in the town. I even suspect that he and I have had an altercation. That, too, was a long time ago on a Hallows Eve night. He tried to seize Lydia then, as well. He was unsuccessful that time, too, thankfully."

"This Isadore was not a good priest," said Godling, more to himself than to his companions.

"Mercifully, he can no longer do anyone any harm," Hubert added.

"To be sure," Godling responded. "My men will bury the

priests tomorrow. Father Lawrence has decided that their actions have made them unfit to be commended to God with the Church's blessing. We will dig a hole outside of town and bury them there. I can only hope that burying them will put a final end to their deeds as well as to their bodies. Perhaps the people of Willowglen will no longer dwell on these events once this is done."

Catherine nodded. "I assume that the Pritchards will no longer have to endure any torment over their daughter's indiscretion?" She wanted to make sure that no lasting trouble would result for her friends, the Pritchards, because of the Pewsey daughters. "And Cate's son will not have to suffer any more accusations for a few hairs of a different color on his small head?"

"I think not," said Benjamin. "The Pritchards have all suffered quite enough. When I spoke to Will Pritchard upon my return, he didn't look at all well. This has been very hard on him. I hope he will recover now that this terrible tragedy is behind us."

"And the Pewseys?" Catherine pressed.

"I will speak to Oliver. He will be required to do something about his daughters. It is clear that both of them mean trouble to our town. I think Winifred especially will benefit from having a match made for her, from what I've heard. I plan to advise him to do so with haste and that a man from another town to which Winifred would move once they are mated would be best for everyone. Perhaps, then, if he just kept a close eye on Isobel, it would all work out for good. Be assured that I will insist that Isobel have nothing more to do with the Pritchards."

"Thank you," Catherine said. "I agree with your judgment and am happy to hear that this, too, will be put to an end."

"I have heard that Mistress Cate and her son were taken to Briarcrest. Is this true?" Godling inquired.

"Yes. I've already talked to Will and Sarah about it. They have agreed that she can stay with us until she is ready to return to Willowglen. However, I have also told them that, should she not want to return, she is welcome to stay with us permanently. We would be glad of her company."

Benjamin nodded. "The Ladies of Briarcrest have always been known for their generosity and hospitality."

"Thank you, Benjamin, I appreciate your sentiments." Catherine stifled a yawn.

Noting her weariness, Hubert placed his cup on the table in front of him and said, "I think we must avail ourselves of your offer of beds for the night, Chief Constable. My Lady is quite fatigued from the day's events."

As if on cue, one of the men entered the hall through a side door. "Ah," Godling said, "Martin, would you please show Sir

Hubert and Lady Catherine each to a room in the east wing. They are both tired and would like to rest before returning home. Perhaps you could bring them a meal in the morning and some warm water to refresh themselves." He looked at Catherine and continued, "Unless you would rather bathe tonight."

"I know I must look a mess," Catherine said," but I feel that I cannot even lift this goblet to my lips another time. I will sleep first, and then get cleaned up for my journey back to Briarcrest in the morning. Thank you for your hospitality."

Benjamin rose from his seat and Catherine pushed herself up from her chair to make her way out of the Hall. After offering his thanks to Benjamin Godling, Sir Hubert started to follow Catherine, but he was intercepted by a small figure of a man who appeared in the doorway.

ROGER MALMSBURY CONFIRMED that the two Churchmen were, indeed, dead and that their bodies had been moved outside of town where they would be buried the next day. "Covered 'em with sacks and rocks to keep the scavengers from 'em. More 'en they deserve."

Hubert nodded and said, "I have one more task for you tonight, Roger, if you're up to it."

A wide grin appeared across Roger's face. "Always ready to do your bidding, Sir."

"Good. I'd like you to go back to Briarcrest and tell Lady Lydia that we will stay the night and be along sometime late on the morrow. I know that she will be concerned for the welfare of Mistress Catherine and would appreciate word of our course." Hubert grasped Roger's shoulder in a firm hand. "Are you able to make the journey?"

Although Hubert couldn't have imagined Roger's wide grin getting any wider, it did. "Be there before sunrise, Sir Hubert."

Before Hubert could utter his thanks, Roger disappeared into the shadows of the Hall and was gone.

Chapter
Thirty-one

CATE SAT ON the edge of the large tapestry-draped bed feeding Andrew. She caressed his soft, warm legs while her eyes were fixed on Fiona. The tall Scot sat at a small table by the window overlooking Briar Wood with pen in hand.

Fiona moved the quill across the paper with large, sweeping movements, writing of the events of the past few days. At the bottom of the page, she scratched an outline of the Dark Monk, his face nothing but a pool of black ink, and wrote about her feelings regarding the malevolent priest. She wondered if she would ever truly understand what prompted him to act as he had done. Surely he could not have had the same kind of feelings for Lydia that she had for Cate. What would she have done if Cate had rejected her the way that Lydia had said she had rebuffed the monk? She had to admit that even when she rescued Cate, she had no idea whether or not they would ever be together. But her love for Cate left her no alternative but to pull her from that burning pyre, even if it meant she would never see Cate Pritchard again once it was over.

Much to her surprise, Cate did want to see her again, in a very intimate way. When they were alone in the bedchamber that Lydia had shown them, Cate quickly lunged for Fiona and gave her a more passionate kiss than Fiona had ever experienced. Fiona hadn't been sure that she would ever be able to catch her breath again, but it didn't matter. She melted in Cate's embrace and both women pulled away only when someone knocked on the door bringing Andrew and a large basket filled with fabric-covered straw on which the baby could sleep.

This time, as Cate fed the child, Fiona didn't turn away. Once Andrew was settled into his basket, he promptly fell asleep and the two women quickly stripped off their clothes and fell into each other's arms in the large bed.

They made love most of the night—over and over again. In between, they dozed. In the early morning hours, Fiona thought she heard voices in the hall outside her door. She wanted to get up and check on the activity outside, but Cate had awakened and fanned the flames of her passion once again, leaving her with little care for what was happening outside their door. Cate felt so wonderful in Fiona's arms that she thought she was dreaming at times. She could hardly believe that she had made love to this woman with whom she had been enamored and had come so close to losing. Once more, she pulled the sleeping Cate closer to her.

Cate snuggled against Fiona and opened her eyes. As Fiona gazed into them in the dimly lit room, she saw that they were immediately filled with desire. Cate reached out tentatively and caressed Fiona's breast. Fiona responded with a moan and her nipple pebbled under Cate's palm. As Fiona surrendered to Cate's touches, the loneliness and longing that had long been Fiona's constant companion, dissipated.

Their lovemaking was both intense and sweet. The two women had finally drifted off to sleep a little before dawn. Just before Cate succumbed to a peaceful, sated sleep, the two women promised that they would spend the next day planning what the future might hold for them. As Cate slept in Fiona's arms, Fiona drifted in and out of slumber, unwilling to give in to her weariness completely, wanting to revel in this moment of happiness a little while longer.

Now, as she started to write of her feelings after a night of lovemaking with Cate, her thoughts strayed back to the last thing she remembered as she drifted off to sleep, the voices in the hallway. As she recalled them, the tones didn't seem to convey any danger or urgency. Brushing the thought aside, she decided that she would have to ask Lydia about it when they went downstairs. She went back to her scribbling, pouring out her thoughts of Cate and her love for this beautiful woman.

She looked up at Cate through tear-filled eyes. How had they come to this day? She had no idea how she had come to such good fortune, but it didn't matter. They were here, together, and today they would discuss how they could be together always. She knew there was no question. They would be together. They just had to decide where and how it would all work out. Cate, busy with Andrew, didn't see Fiona looking at her. Fiona quickly wiped a tear that overflowed her eyelid onto her cheek. Glancing down at the sheet in front of her, she decided that she had written enough for today. She grasped the stack of rough papers in both hands and straightened them. Then she slipped them into the leather folder and tied the ties that held it closed. She put the stopper in the ink bottle and wiped her pen on a small fragment of cloth before putting everything into a larger leather satchel.

When Fiona looked up, golden gray eyes beamed back at her and her breath caught. When she recovered, she asked, "Shall we go down to the Hall?"

"Yes, I'm very hungry. I need to eat something." Cate looked down at the sleeping child in the basket at her feet. "Will you help me carry Andrew down in the basket?"

Fiona pushed herself up from her seat and walked over to Cate. Gathering her lover in her strong arms, she kissed her fully on the lips. Cate's chest heaved with the passionate feeling that quickly ignited within her and she pulled away, saying, "If you kiss me like that, we shall never get anything to eat."

A wide grin broke out across Fiona's face as she handed her bag to Cate. Cate raised her eyebrows in question but took the bag anyway. Then Fiona bent down, scooped up Andrew in his basket and strode toward the door. She turned back to Cate and asked, "Coming?"

Cate blinked, sighed deeply and said, "I did say I was starved, didn't I?" Cate shifted the strap of Fiona's bag onto her shoulder and motioned for Fiona to lead the way. The two women laughed as they headed toward the stairway that led to Briarcrest Hall.

"THANK YOU, ROGER," Lydia said. The small man exited the large Hall quietly as Cate and Fiona made their way from the stairs to Lydia's side.

"Is everything all right?" Fiona inquired as she watched Roger go.

"Oh, Fiona, yes. Everything is fine. Roger just came to report on the state of our horses. I wanted to make sure that they were properly cared for after our journey yesterday. We were all so tired and distracted, that I neglected to check on them last night."

"I heard voices in the hall early this morning, too."

"Ah, I'm sorry if we disturbed you. That, too, was Roger. Hubert sent him from Willowglen to ease my concern about Catherine. They stayed the night so that Catherine could rest. Apparently, Ben Godling, Willowglen's constable, returned just as the battle ended and they had spent some time clearing up any misunderstandings and exchanging information about the terrible events that went on during his absence.

"Since Catherine was tired, Hubert suggested that they not make their way back here until they had rested. He knew I would be worried if he didn't send word, so he asked Roger to come and let me know what their plan was. He was right. I was worried about Catherine. As tired as I was, I still only slept fitfully. Once Roger brought me word, I was able to nod off peacefully for a while and get some rest."

"It is good to hear that all is well, then."

"Indeed. So," Lydia looked from Cate to Fiona and continued, "what do you two plan to do today?"

"We just thought we'd let Cate and Andrew recover from their ordeal a little. We'll discuss our plans for the future today and see if we can come to some resolution." Fiona gazed down into Cate's eyes. Lydia noted the look they gave one another and recognized that a great deal of emotion passed between them. She smiled and nodded at the younger women.

As Lydia looked from one to the other of them, she said, "Briarcrest is at your disposal. Please rest as much as you can. If you'd like Elspeth to take care of Andrew for a while, please let her know. It will be good for you to be able to spend some time with Fiona without having to worry about him."

Cate's cheeks turned a bright rose color as she thanked Lydia. "He's really no trouble, Aunt Lydia. He's a very good boy." She saw Fiona watching her, "But perhaps a little while to ourselves to talk about the future is what we need. Thank you. I'll ask Elspeth to care for him until I need to feed him again."

LYDIA FOUND IT difficult to concentrate on anything after the noon meal, wondering when Catherine would return. For a while, she tried to sort through some papers that needed her attention regarding Briarcrest's estate, but found herself staring out the window more than once, not knowing how much time had passed.

Finally, she went to a large cupboard and unlocked it with one of the keys that hung at her waist. Opening the heavy door, she removed the annals of Briarcrest, the record of all major events for the house and its inhabitants. The events of days past in Willowglen were important and needed to be noted in the tome. As she looked for the end of the entries so that she could add her own to it, she glanced at the handwriting and recognized her aunt's bold entry. She smiled at the thought of her Aunt Beatrice. Love and gratitude filled her heart for the warm, loving women who had meant so much to Lydia. She ran her fingers across the faded script and felt close to Beatrice for a moment. Tears welled up and spilled onto her cheeks. She blotted them with a small cloth that she kept tucked in her sleeve and quickly turned the pages again to find the one on which she would make her own entry in her delicate hand.

April 28,1482 — Within the Octave of Philip, the Apostle
Cate Pritchard, daughter of Will and Sarah Pritchard of Willowglen and friend of Briarcrest, and her son Andrew, were condemned to death by fire unjustly and without reason.

Because the accusations were unfounded, I, Lady Lydia Wellington, would not allow this mockery to be made in the name of a Church that claims to be a vehicle of God's infinite mercy, so I protested, and came to be condemned to the same fire as Cate and her son...

An hour later, when she put the pen down, Lydia felt cleansed of the iniquity that had followed her from her moment of condemnation in Willowglen until now. She took a deep breath, the odor of early summer flowers wafting into her nostrils. *Finally,* she thought, *I can no longer smell the awful burning stench that threatened Cate and Andrew and me.*

She stretched her arms out before her, closed the book and returned it to the cabinet, locking the door again. As she got to her feet and turned toward the door, she let out a tiny mewing sound, surprised to see Catherine standing there. Recovering from her shock, she ran toward Catherine and fell into her open arms. Both women stood in silence for a long time.

Pulling Lydia in closer, Catherine, her voice catching in her throat, whispered, "I thought I would lose you. You gave me such a fright."

Lydia looked up at her, her eyes green pools of shimmering light. "I know. When I was in that dark hole, all I could think of was that I would never see you again. The pain in my heart at such a thought was unbearable."

"Do not think on it now." Catherine pulled her close again. "It's over. We won't have to worry about those two evil men ever again."

Lydia pushed away from Catherine enough to look at her face again. "How do you know that?"

"Dead," Catherine pronounced,

"Dead?"

"Yes, dead. Both of them. They'll not trouble us — or anyone else for that matter. In the end, they created their own undoing. They died by the fire in which they had hoped to see you three burn."

Lydia raised her eyebrows and winced at the thought of anyone, even those who would have killed them, dying in such a manner. "A fitting end, I suppose."

"Let us not speak of them. It is finished." Catherine brightened. "How are Cate and Andrew?"

"They are recovering, I think." Lydia's countenance changed. The smile that appeared on her face betrayed the secret that she harbored.

Catherine cocked her head and matched her smile with a

raised eyebrow, questioning Lydia.

"Wait until you hear. When I offered to show Cate and Fiona to their rooms last night, quick as could be, Cate fairly shouted that they would only need the one bedchamber."

"Oh, my."

"Indeed! And this morning, when they came into the Hall, they both had that glow of contentment that said that they had acted on their feelings for one another."

"Oh, my."

Lydia laughed at Catherine's apparent surprise.

"And where are they now?"

"They've spent the better part of the day in the garden, save for when Cate needed to feed Andrew. Elspeth has been taking care of the baby most of the day. I thought it would give them more time together unencumbered, so that they would be free to talk about the future without distraction."

"That sounds wise. Have they said anything to you about their plans?"

"Nothing. They came in for the noon meal, but they only spoke of pleasantries like the beauty of the garden and their appreciation for the hospitality of this house. I didn't feel that I should press them. They'll come to their decisions on their own."

"Do you think we should put forth the suggestion that they stay here?"

Lydia thought for a moment before replying. "I had not thought of it. But now that you mention it, it would be a lovely idea. Just think how it would be to have a little one growing up here, Catherine."

Catherine could tell that the prospect of having Andrew around excited Lydia. "I'd better go and speak with them. I have news, especially for Fiona. Her family has left Willowglen. I talked them into stopping here on their way, even though it is a departure from their return course. They were taking their leave of Edward and John and following right behind us. I expect that they will be here by early evening. We should make sure that we have all the rooms ready for them. We shall fill Briarcrest Hall for a few days."

"It's only a few days until the May Feast. Do you think we could tempt them to stay?"

Catherine smiled at Lydia. She knew that Lydia would love to fill the house with even more revelers than usual for the celebration. "I'm not sure if they would agree, but we can certainly ask them."

Lydia's mouth turned up in a broad smile. "Yes, let's ask," she said breathlessly.

Catherine bent down and kissed Lydia on the forehead. "I

should go and talk to Fiona and Cate," she said with some reluctance.

"Yes. Then go and get cleaned up, and I'll have some food brought up to our chambers."

"Thank you, love. That sounds wonderful." Catherine turned and made her way down the hall toward the garden in search of Fiona and Cate.

CATHERINE SAT ON one of the garden benches surrounded by the fragrance of sweet blooms. The little pool in the middle of the garden rippled as a pair of robins drank and splashed at the water's edge.

Cate and Fiona had just finished telling her that they had decided that they wanted to stay together and make a life with one another. With a blush, Cate told her of her love for Fiona, and how the feelings she had for the Scottish woman were so much deeper than anything she had felt for Andrew's father. It was at that point that Catherine put forth the suggestion to the two women that they remain at Briarcrest. Realizing how Beatrice must have felt when she proposed the same thing to Catherine and Lydia years before, Catherine encouraged the two women to consider the offer. They promised that they would think seriously about it.

"Ah, there is one more thing," Catherine said. Looking at Fiona, she added, "Your family is on their way to Briarcrest."

"They are?" Fiona looked incredulous.

"Yes, I invited them to take a small diversion on their way home. No doubt they consented because they thought that you might accompany them back to your home. I suppose that is still a possibility if you and Cate decide that is where you'd like to go."

"We hadn't gotten that far in our plans," Fiona said. "We only spoke of wanting to be together always. Now, I guess it's time to decide where we will stay together."

Cate nodded in agreement.

"I'll leave you two alone, then, to continue your discussions. I need to get cleaned up anyway. And Lydia has promised to meet me in our rooms with some refreshment." Catherine wiggled her eyebrows and the younger women flushed at her meaning. Catherine leaned over and patted both women's hands and rose to leave.

"When will my family be here, Catherine?"

"Any time now, I think. They had only to make their farewells to your grandfather and uncle and they were ready to leave. I'm hoping that they will be here before nightfall."

Fiona took one of Cate's hands in hers. "Then we'd better talk about our future some more before they get here."

Cate's eyes sparkled as she gazed into Fiona's. "Let's do," she said, breathlessly.

AS THE SKY turned red and purple with the setting sun reflecting off puffy white clouds, the din in Briarcrest Hall became almost unbearable, and yet Lydia beamed. The Smiths had arrived in full force and the reuniting was a happy, noisy one.

The children ran in circles around the great table that spanned the length of Briarcrest's main hall. Catherine and Lydia walked among their guests, inviting them to take their places so that the evening meal could be served. At last, the guests sat and managed to bring the children to a halt at their games. When everyone was seated, the conversation quieted a little.

Lydia took her place at one end of the table and Catherine sat at the opposite end. The meal was served from great wooden platters and everyone ate heartily. As they all sat back, enjoying conversation, their stomachs full, Fiona cleared her throat and everyone turned in her direction.

"Father, I know that you are expecting me to return to my little house on our land with you and the rest of the family. However, Cate and I have decided to make a life of our own." Almost everyone in the Smith family raised an eyebrow at Fiona's statement. She cleared her throat again and continued. "Lady Lydia and Catherine have offered their hospitality to us, and we have discussed it, and think we would like to stay, at least for a while. Cate would like to be able to have her parents enjoy Andrew's childhood, but she has no desire to live in Willowglen, for it holds too many unpleasant memories for her now. At least if we stay here, Master Will and Mistress Sarah can visit us and they will be able to see a little of their grandson as he grows up."

The Smiths sat staring, saying nothing.

Lydia spoke up. "Of course, we aren't really offering Cate and Fiona hospitality. That would imply that they were guests in our home, but that is not our intention. We would like them to be a part of our household. We would like them to consider staying permanently. That decision may follow later, but we wanted it understood that we shall need someone to take over Briarcrest after we are gone. We can think of no better people."

"Aunt Lydia, you are too generous," Cate said softly.

"It was your Aunt Catherine's suggestion. I merely agreed. Of course, I did so wholeheartedly." Lydia looked at Duncan and Adianna and said, "We promise to take good care of your daughter. She will be like a daughter to us, as Cate is already. And Andrew will be the heir to Briarcrest eventually."

It was Duncan's time to clear his throat. As he spoke, his voice trembled. "I cannot say that I will be happy to have my Fiona so far from home. Her mother and I will miss her terribly. I'm sure the rest of the family will, too." Fiona's brothers and sisters-in-law all nodded enthusiastically. "But all we want for Fiona — for any of our children — is to be well and to find happiness. If Fiona finds her happiness here, then we shall be content." He looked lovingly at his wife and asked, "Isn't that so, mama?"

Adianna nodded in agreement. A tear spilled over her lower lid and streamed down her cheek. She quickly wiped it away with her hand.

"Thank you, Father," Fiona said, her own voice hoarse with emotion.

After a moment, Catherine spoke. "Well, your home to the north is not so far away. Perhaps Fiona and Cate can travel there upon occasion. We can certainly supply them with an escort and assistance on their journey. And the Smith family is welcome here any time you care to make the trip."

Adianna smiled. "Thank you both. We might just do that. True Duncan?"

He smiled back at his wife. "True, Adianna."

Adianna turned to Cate, who sat next to her holding Andrew in her arms, and held out her hands to take the baby. As she cradled him to her ample bosom, she crooned, "Well, little man, not only might you become the Lord of this great Briarcrest, but you are now part of the Smith tribe. Welcome to the family." The Smiths clamored their noisy approval. Then she turned to Cate and said, "Welcome to the Smith family, too, dear," and she kissed Cate on the cheek, causing her eyes to well up as well. A loud huzzah echoed through the hall.

TO LYDIA'S DISAPPOINTMENT, the Smiths decided to push on toward home and not linger to celebrate the May Feast at Briarcrest. The evening meal on the day that the Smiths left was quiet, almost somber. In order to liven up the remaining group of four, Catherine said, "I think I should tell you the story of how Lydia and I met."

Fiona brightened and nodded. "Yes, please. I'd love to hear it."

Catherine began by telling of how she opened the door to her herb and spice shop on Market Street one morning to find Lydia staring at her from across the street. The four women lingered long over their evening meal that night as Catherine and Lydia finished the tale.

Fiona gently asked of the two older women, "Would you mind if I wrote this down? It's a wonderful story and someday, we might even be able to tell it to others."

Lydia's face turned a light shade of cherry as she waved Fiona's suggestion away. "Who would be interested in such a tale?"

"Well, we would for two," said Fiona looking at Cate who shook her head in agreement. Cate added, "I know so little of your lives before I was old enough to remember you. I'd love to hear it all."

Lydia looked at Catherine and shrugged. With a sigh, she said, "I'm not sure what purpose it will really serve, but if you desire it, we shall tell you of all of our days together—and of a few apart—for Fiona to write on those sheaves of paper that she carries around with her. It may take a while, though."

Cate looked down at Andrew, lying in her arms, then looked back at Lydia. "Well, Aunt Lydia, we seem to have ample time and no plans to go anywhere, so your story will be told and recorded, I think. Don't you, Fiona?"

Fiona nodded and smiled. "I shall start this evening by writing down what you have just told us."

"And we shall go straight through until the events that have just passed in Willowglen," Catherine said. "They, too, must be told so that this kind of wrong is never allowed to happen again."

"And there will be more," Cate said. "There will be the happier days ahead to add to the story."

"Yes," Catherine and Lydia both said together. Then Catherine raised her goblet in a toast. "There will be many happy tales to tell of future days at Briarcrest."

Fiona's eyes blazed as she looked at Cate and broke into a broad grin.

Also available from
Yellow Rose Books

The Heart's Desire

Book One of the Briarcrest Chronicles

Travel back in time to the early Renaissance world of Willow-glen Township. Catherine Hawkins, a spice merchant and healer, is preparing for the autumn faire when she is captivated by a woman with the most beautiful eyes. Join Catherine as she first struggles to come to grips with her feelings for a mysterious noblewoman and then against those who mean to keep the two women from their "heart's desire."

Find out how they overcome the many obstacles standing in their way in this first look at the women of Briarcrest.

ISBN 978-1-932300-32-1
1-932300-32-5

FORTHCOMING TITLES

Family Affairs
by Vicki Stevenson

Assigned to work undercover in a small-town nursing home, insurance investigator Stacey Gardner sets out to find fraudulent medical claims. When she meets local resident Liz Schroeder, romance begins to bloom. But then she discovers widespread elder abuse of which the entire nursing home staff is aware, and she fears that the whole town may be participating in a cover up.

Liz persuades Stacey to trust her to accept help from her LGBT family in exposing the abuse. The family discovers an elaborate scheme that seems to defy exposure. Many of the nursing home staff members are dedicated to stopping Stacey at any cost, and the rest are too intimidated to reveal any information.

The family presses on, determined to bring justice to the perpetrators and relief to the suffering patients. While the bond of love between Stacey and Liz grows ever stronger, they face the agonizing reailty that success will spell the end of the chance at happiness that both women desperately crave.

Second Verse
by Jane Vollbrecht

Gail Larsen lives in the Tennessee woods and edits lesbian fiction for Outrageous Press. Good thing her professional life is satisfying, because she has not had much luck with her love life. Her first lover left her to pursue a different path; her next died in an accident. It has been two years since Gail has dated, and she is seeing a therapist, hoping to put her life back on track.

A special editing assignment throws Gail together with Connie Martin, one of the leading ladies of lesbian fiction. Gail is at first amused by Connie's Pit-bull personality in a Pekinese body, but amusement turns to attraction, and attraction to heart-wrenching anxiety that leaves Gail anguished and unsettled.

After an intense month working with Connie on her book, Gail's life-long friend Penny invites Gail back to Plainfield, Minnesota. Gail has always harbored an unanswered longing for Penny. Many old ghosts re-emerge, and they are forced to confront them. To Gail's annoyance and amazement, Connie tracks her down while she is in Plainfield, and now she fears she is trapped between two women, one she will never have and one she does not want. All she has ever wanted is a lifemate she could dance with for the rest of her life. Can she find someone who will last through the second verse?

Available January 2008

OTHER YELLOW ROSE TITLES
You may also enjoy:

Family Values
by Vicki Stevenson

Devastated by the collapse of her long-term relationship, Alice Cruz decides to begin life anew. She moves to a small town, rents an apartment, and establishes a career in real estate. But when she tries to liquidate some of her investments for a down payment on a house, she discovers that she has been victimized by a con artist.

Local resident Tyler Sorensen has a track record of countless affairs without any emotional involvement. Known for her sexy good looks, easygoing kindness, and unique approach to problems, Tyler is asked by a mutual friend to figure out how Alice can recover her money.

While Tyler's elaborate plan progresses and members of her LGBT family work toward the solution, they discover that the con game involves more people and far higher stakes than they had imagined. As the family encounters unexpected obstacles, Tyler and Alice struggle with a growing emotional connection deeper than either woman has ever experienced.

ISBN 978-1-932300-89-5

Download
by J. Y. Morgan

Cory Williams's settled and predictable life as a young, successful teacher in a small town in the middle of England is upended when she discovers the Internet and the joy of emailing friends all over the world. Her comfortable existence is thrown into total turmoil when she begins exchanging emails with an on-line American friend, Dylan Matthews, a computer technician who's having problems with her partner, Sarah.

The intensity of her friendship with Dylan forces Cory to examine choices she's made and secrets she's chosen to hide. The relationship between Cory and Dylan escalates, and both women realize that despite enormous obstacles impeding their hopes to be together, their feelings for one another are too powerful to deny.

Ultimately, Cory must choose between her true love and what she believes is her duty to her job, her country, and her family and friends. Cory's journey of self-discovery is complicated by the re-emergence of all her inner demons, the death of her beloved grandfather, and the pressures exerted on her by well-intentioned associates.

What course will Cory choose? What will be the upshot of that message from Dylan she opted to *Download*?

ISBN 978-1-932300-88-8

OTHER YELLOW ROSE PUBLICATIONS

About the Author

Anna Furtado is a California transplant from Massachusetts. She lives with her partner of 20+ years in the San Francisco Bay area. They have two fur-kids of Scottish Terrier descent, Randolph Scott and Molly Brown, who entertain them with their antics. Anna's day job is as an internal auditor for a medical device company; the creative writing process is a welcome change from the compliance requirements of Quality Assurance.

The Briarcrest Chronicles series follows the lives of the strong, brave women who all have ties to Briarcrest. It is Anna's first full-length novel series. *Book One, The Heart's Desire,* was a Golden Crown Literary Society Award finalist. Anna is also a featured columnist at the Just About Write Web site, a resource for lesbian writers and readers. You can read her book reviews on that same site as well as at the L-Word fan site in the literature section. Anna is a member of the Golden Crown Literary Society and has participated on conference panels on various writing and book promotion topics. Stop by Anna's Web site at www.annafurtado.com.

VISIT US ONLINE AT

www.regalcrest.biz

At the Regal Crest Website You'll Find

- The latest news about forthcoming titles and new releases

- Our complete backlist of romance, mystery, thriller and adventure titles

- Information about your favorite authors

- Current bestsellers

Regal Crest titles are available from all progressive booksellers and online at StarCrossed Productions, (www.scp-inc.biz) and also at www.amazon.com, www.bamm.com, www.barnesandnoble.com, and many others.

Printed in the United States
93175LV00003B/94-153/A